PASSING HEIGHTS

PASSING HEIGHTS

A story

Leighton Mark

To order additional copies of this book, contact:
Xlibris Corporation
1-888-795-4274
www.Xlibris.com
Orders@Xlibris.com
25260

CONTENTS

*In loving memory of my mother, Sue Y. Mark,
and father, Wing S. Mark.*

This book would not be possible without the love of
my wife, Karen, and my children, Lauren and Ian.
This project also allows me to share my love for
my brother, Clifton, and sister, Cynthia.

1994

Physician conventions may be predictably tiresome, but I frequently feel both entertained and overwhelmed by the menagerie of interactions among the attendees. As I walk through the cavernous passageways of this enormous hotel/and convention center complex in Nashville, Tennessee, I can see the strategic groupings of people scattered about the hallways. A practiced, skillful voice on my left resonates with self-importance as the distinguished-appearing individual holds audience for a small attentive group who can barely disguise their desire to bask in the speaker's reflected glory. The hushed tones on my right reveal a group of younger society members who have yet to mark their professional boundaries but secretly plot to someday be recognized as a political or an academic alpha male. I soon find myself weaving my way across the richly smooth dark brown carpet, passing many randomly clumped groups of people with slightly bored affectations. They are sipping coffee and mingling before the major presentations that they hope will be at least marginally educational and perhaps even provide some practical information for use in their daily practices. Within the background murmuring and clanking of silverware on coffee cups, I can detect a scatter of whispered though just audible voices of a few cynical attendees, who impolitely bemoan that most of the speakers seem motivated by a different type of agenda that is only thinly disguised by a nearly transparent veneer of educational altruism. They suggest that the main, if not only, priority of many of the speakers seems directed at presenting themselves in an impressive light within a national forum while the education of the audience is treated as a mere incidental or ornamental byproduct of their self-aggrandizement.

This particular convention is the annual meeting for a highly subspecialized and select group of physicians from many countries though the registrants are mostly Americans. The academic, scientific, and political stature of the meeting usually demand months of preparation from the organizers as well as the presenters. In other words, the stakes are high, and many individuals try to use this occasion to advance their academic careers.

I find myself balancing a mixture of feelings as I slowly walk to the edge of the stage in the large main meeting room filled with several thousand people. I had been invited as a lecturer to provide a presentation on brain anatomy, but the anxiety that I feel does not come from this topic that I feel so comfortable with or the size of the audience, which I am less comfortable with. Some members of the crowd might see me as just another Asian dotting this enormous conference hall full of neuroradiologists. My accent-free English reveals my nonimmigrant status to some of the other Asian physicians in the room. Some of my colleagues only think of me as a quiet Ivy League—trained academic radiologist. Would they be surprised to know that I can sometimes still smell the urine-tinged stairwells of the Alfred E. Smith projects of my childhood on Manhattan's Lower East Side?

The moderator introduces me as the next guest speaker, and I start to climb the steps toward the podium during the brief polite applause. I am momentarily blinded by the intense spotlights that not only highlight my role on the stage but also provide the ability for a simultaneous televised broadcast. It is an eerie sensation to be moving and seeing corresponding movements of a large televised image of myself directly behind me over my head. During the moments that I am adjusting the microphone and futilely trying to scan the audience that is rendered invisible by the blazing spotlights, I begin to wish that my mother was here. No, this is not the wish for maternal protection from paralyzing stage fright. My immigrant mother had died several years earlier. Her extraordinary life did not allow for an extension into old age by modern standards. That same life enabled my current stance at the podium. With some regret, perhaps slight sadness, and much warmth, I wished my mother was here . . .

World War II

Suit Ying could barely restrain her happiness while thinking about the cakes under her bed. Those cakes were part of the weekly treats sent to her school by her grandmother. Everyone at the school knew that the Chin family was the wealthiest in Guangdong Province in China, so it was only natural that their eldest child would receive the best pastries made. Suit Ying knew that her friends were all waiting for her to open the carefully wrapped red packages and share the mouth-watering booties. Just to prolong the suspense for her close friends, she deliberately picked up a book and ignored the boxes.

"*Ay yah*, you are a rascal!" Suit Ying's good friend Mai said. "You know that we have been waiting all week for that pastry; besides, I have been starving myself all morning so that I could gorge on the sweet red-bean-rolled cakes with the glazed almonds on top."

Suit Ying was giggling as she reached down and pulled out the boxes. She teased her friends by slowly removing the wrapping in a meticulous fashion.

Mai had reached her limits and bellowed, "If you don't hurry up with those packages, I will eat that gold bar that you keep in your suitcase!"

The other girls in the room started laughing with the mention of the gold bar because it was considered a foolishly extravagant item to keep in the dormitory of the nursing student's residence. Many of the nursing students kept jewelry in their drawers, but all of them felt the gold bar was only functioning as a doorstop. That gold bar was given to Suit Ying by her grandfather, who believed in being prepared for unexpected emergencies, but even Suit Ying thought the gold bar was going too far and perhaps a bit paranoid.

Suit Ying finally finished unwrapping the boxes with a graceful but exaggerated flair, placed the open boxes on the table, and then presented the contents to her friends with an inviting wave of her hands. A dozen girls proceeded to compete for their favorite pastries. There had to have been at least two dozen varieties of sweet, gourmet-quality baked and fried delicacies. Suit Ying called out to the other girls on the second floor to invite them to the sweet feast in her room. A young servant girl watched Suit Ying as she quietly stepped back without taking any food. The young girl was a bit offended that the other students did not even notice that her mistress had given all the treats to her friends while taking none for herself. That resentment, however, melted to love and warmth as she saw her mistress's contented smile as she stood by the window to observe the joy and laughter of her companions.

The other girls were initially baffled by Suit Ying when she first arrived at this elite nursing school. They were all from well-to-do families, but the delivery of this attractive young girl by an American limousine far exceeded anything they had ever experienced. Everyone knew that the girl's grandfather created the great Chin family fortune in America during the early twentieth

century. The fortune was so vast that the loss of millions of dollars
during the great stock market crash of 1929 hardly dented the
family's finances. Many of the businesses and buildings in the
huge metropolis of Canton were known to be owned by the Chin
family. This young girl also arrived with her own servant girl to
tend to her daily mundane needs. She was the only student with
her own servant. The nursing school didn't even have to provide an
extra bed as the servant insisted on sleeping on the floor beside her
mistress's bed. The other students slowly understood the servant's
devotion as they found themselves drawn to Suit Ying's
unpretentious ways, caring heart, and sincerity. Initial jealousies
gave way to the esprit de corps that Suit Ying created among the
girls. Suit Ying did not have to use stirring speeches or self-
promotion. The students were inspired by her daily conduct and
her consistent attention to the welfare of her colleagues before seeing
to her own needs.

The doctors at the nearby hospital were also taken by this
attractive, hardworking nursing student. Her keen intelligence had
distinguished Suit Ying from the other nursing students, who were
already chosen from the very best students in the entire province
with a population that exceeds the East Coast of the United States.
Suit Ying's exceptional skills, deep understanding, and manual
dexterity led to the obstetrical ward's reliance on this young lady
to daringly perform the extraordinarily dangerous procedure of
manually rotating unborn babies away from the breech position
during childbirth. Doctors were impressed by this young nursing
student's dedication, and she seemed to possess an inner standard
of excellence that was almost palpable to those that worked with
her. Her inner and outward grace was an intoxicating combination
that very few of the doctors could resist. In fact, Suit Ying would
receive a marriage proposal from a prominent physician during
her years at the hospital, but only she would know that her heart
was meant for another.

The servant girl approached Suit Ying by the window and
placed something in her hand. "Here you go, mistress. I managed

to save one of these delicious fried sesame buns for you before all those selfish cows can get to it."

Suit Ying looked lovingly at the servant and said, "You are my cherished companion and so dear to my heart. You are always looking out for me. I noticed that you haven't yet eaten, so I insist that you eat the bun."

The servant looked sternly at her mistress but with tears welling in her eyes. She placed the bun on the table and yelled out, "This bun is for my mistress! Anyone who touches it will feel the odorous sting of my farts!"

The other girls burst out laughing at the quaint though coarse language of the servant girl, whom they frequently dismissed as an uneducated country peasant. Very few of those privileged girls, however, could match this servant girl's perceptiveness and humane values. Fewer still possess the love and selflessness that will enable this servant girl to make the extreme sacrifice that will occur in the days ahead.

Mai approached Suit Ying, who was staring out the open window and basking in the warm humid air and bright sunshine. She was soaking in the dense countryside vista and staring toward the northern horizon.

Mai asked, "What are you thinking about, dear sister?" She used the word "sister" as a term of endearment.

Suit Ying said, "The Japanese have already taken over northern China. I was just wondering how much time we have before they sweep down to the south and destroy our comfortable lives."

Mai gasped, "How can you think about such things during this happy period of our lives! Those Japanese barbarians will never be able to disrupt us all the way here in the south; besides, even if some horrendously spiteful gesture by our ancestors would allow the Japanese to make it here, you will be protected and whisked away to safety by your family's vast fortune."

Suit Ying glanced at Mai with a graceful turn of her head and said through warm but sad eyes, "Whatever happens, my dearest sister, we should remember to stick together." The tone of her voice, however, gleamed with the same strength and drive that she radiates in the hospital.

1999

My thoughts tend to wander with highway driving that is longer than fifteen minutes. One of my esteemed colleagues politely described my mental driving state as meditative. He proposed a better use of my time in the automobile by dictating letters during my daily thirty-to-forty-minute commute to work. I mentioned that any type of dictation would be a distraction and potentially dangerous while driving, but I concealed my need to spend my quiet moments with the emotional gifts from my extraordinary parents. At this particular time, I am driving to the airport to pick up my father, who will be spending the Christmas holidays with my family as he does every year. My father is a gregarious man who is completely unselfconscious and openly engaging. He never fails to entertain with his amusing anecdotes and instructive insights. He is also the best card player that I have ever seen, particularly at Chinese poker played with thirteen cards per player. His seventy-seven years of life have not diminished his uncanny ability to memorize the entire deck of cards as they are dealt and played. My two children love him dearly, and my wife knows in her heart that she has gained another father I usually find it difficult to conceal my moist eyes when I see him approach me from the airport gate.

This particular Christmas is especially poignant because it has been ten years since my mother's funeral. As my thoughts wandered back to that heartrending day ten years ago, my lips and hands were trembling while I tried to maintain my grip on the steering wheel. I especially remembered the unexpected interruption of my thoughts by four elderly women who had been standing in the back of the funeral parlor for hours. They had apologized for not introducing themselves earlier, but they were not familiar with most of the people and did not want to intrude; besides, they were embarrassed for having arrived late after a long drive to New York City from Canada, where they had been living for the past forty years. They had only received notice of my mother's death the day before from indirect sources and knew that no matter what else they would do in their lives, they must first attend my mother's funeral.

I did not quite understand their connection with my mother. I had known that my father had relatives who lived in Canada, but I was unaware of any relatives on my mother's side who lived north of the border.

Sensing my puzzled expression, the older lady on my right grasped my hand and said, "Please excuse my presumptuousness, but I would very much like the honor of touching your hand." She slowly raised my hand to the level of her chest and then proceeded to gently stroke the back of my hand with her other hand.

I was taken aback by this intimate gesture because it was exactly what my mother had always done to me as an act of affection.

This strikingly dignified lady then raised her eyes and said through a tear-stained voice, "I am your Auntie Mai. I have to tell you a story about your mother."

World War II, Canton Province

T wo days before the typically expected delivery of pastries to the nursing dormitory, a distant rumbling echoed through the valley.

Suit Ying heard the rumbling and said to Mai, "Little sister, why don't you close the windows before the rain arrives."

Mai defiantly replied, "You are not the only one who is studying for next week's exam. You are doing better in the course than I am, so it is only right that you pull your nose from the book and close the windows so that I can spend a few more seconds reading what you already know."

Suit Ying sighed with mock exasperation and walked over to the window. She looked down and saw her servant hand washing her laundry. She noticed that she had also washed Mai's soiled shirts though she would tell Mai that she washed it only to spare her mistress from having to tolerate the odors ingrained in her clothes from her hairy, sticky armpits. Everyone by now was used to the servant's grumpy style that could not hide her love for her mistress's friends.

Suit Ying looked up and was surprised by the clear blue skies that stretched from one horizon to the other. Coldness infiltrated her heart as she slowly turned toward Mai and calmly said, "Dearest sister, I think it is time to pack a very small bundle of clothes that you can carry."

Mai looked up tiredly from her book and said, "No time for fun. I still need to read five chapters."

Mai's voice grew quiet, however, as she saw the pale look on Suit Ying's face. She intuitively realized that the growing thunder was from the killing storm of the targeted marching of artillery shells impacting on the earth. The Japanese had arrived.

1989

Auntie Mai explained, "I haven't seen your mother for decades because I did not know where she lived after she left China in 1948. I, like the other three ladies here, were schoolmates of your mother. No, no, that is not quite accurate. We were all sisters of the heart."

Auntie Mai continued to tell me about the events during the shelling of the school. All the girls were looking out the windows in horror as the massive explosions marched down the valley following a long line of frantically running villagers. Hundreds of wounded were streaming into the hospital next door, screaming with agony. The girls gasped in shock as the artillery continued to follow a deadly impersonal exploding line that culminated at the hospital itself. The devastation was beyond their darkest nightmares.

Suit Ying's servant realized that the dormitory was aligned along the path of the explosions. She immediately sprinted into the dormitory and threw herself with the wet basket of laundry at her mistress. Mai and Suit Ying were knocked down to the ground as the servant covered their bodies with her own. The servant sobbed, "The heavens and my ancestors must protect these girls. Please save my mistress!"

The next shell exploded in the room, throwing the two young girls out the door. They were cushioned from the flying chunks of glass, wood, and concrete by the heavy load of wet laundry that covered them. Suit Ying staggered to her feet and noticed that she had lost her equilibrium and had gone deaf. Still, she managed to wade back into the burning, shattered dormitory to find the splintered body parts of her dead servant. Suit Ying cried out with a grief that she would have thought unimaginable and unbearable in her young life.

The Run

Mai's voice was trembling with the memory of the events that occurred half a century ago. Her kind eyes assumed a withdrawn posture punctuated by a single tear meandering slowly down her creased cheek. The next words were bathed in love and affection when Mai looked warmly at me and said, "What happened after the shelling is what your mother called 'the run,' which we would be forced to endure for two years."

Suit Ying emerged from the dormitory rubble in stunned silence, bleeding from numerous cuts on her arms and legs. Her clouded mind slowly cleared with the growing concern for her friends. She found Mai sitting on a tipped concrete slab. Her stony expression broke with relief as Mai saw Suit Ying and ran crying into her arms. It was then that Suit Ying realized that her deafness had dissipated, which created a tiny sense of hope in a desperate situation.

"Dearest little sister," cried Suit Ying, "my dear, dear sister," she repeated.

Mai was still sobbing hysterically when Suit Ying slowly raised her face to make direct eye contact. Suit Ying then told Mai that they must look for other survivors. The hospital no longer exists, and the Japanese soldiers will soon be in the town. It was a common description from refugees fleeing from the north that the artillery destroyed everything before the Japanese troops moved into the devastated area.

Of the eighty girls in the nursing dormitory, Suit Ying and Mai could only find ten other survivors who were fit enough to walk. Only Suit Ying and Mai were able to salvage some clothes from the rubble as their laundry had been propelled out the door with them. The two girls proceeded to distribute all their wet laundry to the other ten girls. Suit Ying, however, hung on to one oddly knotted shirt, which she stuffed under her clothes while glancing at the sky and muttered tears of thanks to her dead servant.

This small band of surviving girls joined a long line of people fleeing the town just ahead of the advancing Japanese troops. As the girls climbed halfway up the slope of a hill overlooking the town, Suit Ying witnessed an act of malice that would haunt her memories for decades. She saw two Japanese officers drive into town before all the people could leave. A young woman, who was heavy with pregnancy, was not nimble enough to move completely out of the path of the honking jeep. The jeep brushed the side of the woman, knocking her down. The officers in the jeep suddenly stopped the vehicle, but they did not do so out of concern for the swiped woman. Instead, the officer in the passenger seat instructed the driver to back up the vehicle to ensure that the tires would deliberately run directly over the downed woman's swollen abdomen. The other nearby stragglers, who stood there gaping at this stunning act of brutality, were summarily decapitated by the sword-wielding officer who had stepped out of the passenger seat of the jeep. Suit Ying would revisit this horror when she would describe the events of this day to her youngest son twenty-five years later.

The girls found out that they were cut off from the roads that led home. They, like the entire line of refugees, were forced along a single path of least resistance, moving away from the areas of bombing, artillery fire, and advancing troops. This group of young girls was taxed beyond imagination with a constant mixture of running and walking, very few hours of sleep per day, lack of food and water, and nonexistent sanitation. The girls had no idea that this nightmarish flight from death would continue for the next two years.

"How did you all survive?" I asked. I knew that my mother led a pampered life of the wealthy elite. She must have been ill-prepared for the devastation of war, particularly since the normal resources for life were already sparse in a poor country like China.

Auntie Mai answered, "Only five of the original twelve girls survived. It was a miracle that even five of us lived. We owe our lives to your mother." The trickle of tears had now become a uniform sheen covering all of her cheeks. "Please excuse this sentimental old woman," she continued. "You must also understand that these are not tears of sorrow but of affection and gratitude for your mother."

Mai continued to explain that survival was extremely difficult on a daily basis. They ran from town to town, just always ahead of the Japanese artillery and troops. The war had driven all the routine activities of life into the black market. Nothing was available for business. All the stores, shops, restaurants, and inns were destroyed or boarded up. A drink of clean water, which used to be free, could only be obtained for a certain price. Tea was a luxury that only the wealthy could afford. Those in the open road counted themselves lucky if they could find free space under some dense foliage for a night's shelter. With this kind of environment, the girls grew desperate within a week. Only Suit Ying's constant encouragement kept the younger girls from sobbing and giving up. She helped the others maintain a positive spirit and consistently insisted that everyone search for solutions to their daily obstacles rather than fixate on the hopelessness of their predicament. Her warm affections for the girls were virtually palpable and vitally sustaining because it was mixed with her steely determination that their actions and correct decisions would control their outcome. In the face of unavoidable disaster, she refused to despair and prevented the entire group of students from succumbing to that tempting state of mind.

When it was clear that dehydration and starvation were draining their bodies, Suit Ying reached under her blouse and unraveled her knotted shirt to reveal her gold bar. She proceeded to shave small bits of the bar for each of the girls. They used these small samples of precious metal to buy handfuls of rice and water from the black-market sellers in rat-infested alleyways. This was how they survived, but Suit Ying was always afraid of running out of gold before this ordeal would end. It was hard to understand how that bar of gold lasted for two years, but it provided just enough sustenance for survival. Fever and dysentery still claimed the lives of seven of the girls. Suit Ying herself suffered from bouts of fevered jaundice, which were at times completely debilitating. She suspected that she had contracted hepatitis, but she was unable to foresee the toll this disease would extract from her later in life.

When these five surviving girls finally found a safe passage back to their homes, they had each lost about one-third of their body weight. Their families had thought the girls were all killed and had given up hope. Many initially feared that the girls were ghosts, who had come back from the dead, as their emaciated forms bore only faint resemblance of their vibrant appearances before the run. All of the families, and especially the great Chin family, celebrated for days with much incense burning to honor and give thanks to their ancestors for preserving the lives of their daughters and returning them to their warm embrace.

Daughters are commonly held in less esteem than sons in many traditional Chinese families, but these specific girls were the offspring of progressive and loving families. The Chin family, in particular, valued a more worldly perspective with less emphasis on gender. Suit Ying's grandfather had traveled over much of the world and consistently dealt with westerners for commerce in the bustling cosmopolitan city that was Canton. While the white man's style appeared coarse compared to Chinese ways, the grandfather was also perceptive enough to recognize the good virtues in all people.

He learned to judge all people by more intangible standards such as ethics, morality, compassion, insight, education, and respect. His attitude reinforced the wisdom and universality of the Confucian ideas of right actions and words flowing from right mindedness. His family was Chinese, but his friends were not defined by skin tone or culture. Grandfather lived his life by these values and insisted that his bright and energetic granddaughter also be exposed to the best of values and cultures; besides, the grandfather rapidly identified with this young granddaughter, who was so precocious in her character, intelligence, and inquisitiveness. Suit Ying easily became the grandfather's favorite in this vast household of children, grandchildren, and servants. The other well-to-do families in the province had their own traditions and family dynamics, but they frequently looked up to the Chin family as a moral compass.

After our conversation, these four women slowly reapproached my mother's casket. They bowed three times in unison. They then extended their respect by kneeling down and repeating another three bows. They struggled back to the standing position and still bowed for another three times. This was an extraordinary gesture of profound honor by the four distinguished elderly women.

Hospital Room, Summer 1989

My grief always seemed unbearable every time I approached my mother's room at the hospital. She had been drifting in and out of consciousness because her liver cancer could no longer adequately clear her blood of the daily accumulation of toxins. I usually took comfort in the feel of the tiny hand of my very young son holding my right hand while my slightly older daughter transmitted her mixture of love and worry at the sight of my ill mother through my left hand. My wife, Karen, was the first to reach the room as usual. Her first thoughts and actions were immediately directed toward any perceptible needs of my mother. I really should say "her mother" because they developed a relationship that was knitted from the strands of mother-to-daughter love.

This particular visit was slightly different because I saw my father in the room. My mother, with lidded eyes, was unsuccessfully attempting to sit at the edge of the cold institutional hospital bed. My gray-haired father was bent over, his slumping form giving her a warm embrace. He was crying. I had only seen my father cry twice in my life. The first time was when I was very young and living in the projects on the Lower East Side of Manhattan. I was thought to have polio and an ambulance had arrived to take me to the hospital. I was lying on my parents' bed when my father walked over to me, laid his head on my chest, and wept. This second time in my mother's hospital room occurred after a lifetime of shared memories that started halfway around the world.

South Pacific during World War II

My childhood memories of my father frequently run in my mind like an old moviola showing a man who exudes robust health, athleticism, and movie-star looks. These 1950s images, however, show only the body, which had already recovered from the physical wasting endured during the grueling South Pacific military campaigns during World War II. Just a few years after Suit Ying's flight before the Japanese onslaught, Wing S. Mark was huddled in a foxhole, enduring endless shelling by Japanese artillery. He had joined the American Army at the outbreak of World War II to fight for the principles of a country that he loved. The promise of gaining American citizenship for signing up, however, could also be interpreted as highly significant secondary gain. The U.S. Army, in its infinite wisdom, chose to send this Chinese (now American) private to the South Pacific where his physical resemblance to the enemy put him at risk for being shot by both sides in the conflict. His engaging personality, leadership, and bravery on the battlefield, however, not only earned the respect of all his fellow American soldiers but also gained Wing a medal and promotion to sergeant. He was involved in almost every major military invasion in the South Pacific battle theatre. At one point, he was among the twenty thousand American troops who waded in to shore on an island filled with heavily entrenched Japanese troops. Wing was also one of the only nine hundred of the original twenty thousand troops who was able to walk away from that island. He frequently spent weeks to months hugging the dirt of his foxhole, enduring shelling by night after fighting all day. His foxhole became his bedroom, toilet, shower (rain), and dining table. The boy who could swim a mile against the ocean tide at Coney Island beach before the war was only an emaciated shadow of his physical self after the war, having lost about one-third of this body weight during the years of constant battle. The man who emerged from this trial, however, gained the admiration of many who witnessed his actions and character up close. The soldiers who suffered and shed their blood with him during this brutal period would forever remember Wing's valor and leadership under fire and count themselves as his brother. These intense feelings of love and loyalty would be reignited with moving tributes of honor some sixty years later.

Hong Kong, 1960

I remember walking into a dark musty room that was filled with equally dark teak furniture. The high ceilings provided no relief from the humid Hong Kong summer heat. My mother had brought me to this strange, dimly lit apartment to meet an important relative though the significance was opaque to my third-grade mind. A gnarled, gray-haired, balding old woman dressed in a black shirt and black pants shuffled into the room through a circular doorway. She was cackling when she caught sight of me and took her seat at a thronelike teak chair with inlaid pearly stones. My mother whispered deep respects to this lady and introduced me as her youngest son. The lady knowingly nodded and smiled again to reveal a single tooth just behind her bottom lip. She waved me over and introduced herself as my great-grandmother on my father's side. She said she was overjoyed to meet my father's son and spoke glowingly of my father. Being one hundred years old did not dissuade her from smoking her cigarette and drinking Chinese whiskey while trying to engage this shy, insignificant small boy in conversation.

Her smiling wrinkled eyes gazed at my face. "You have your father's lucky spirit," she intoned in the familiar Toisanese dialect, "but I can also sense your mother's reserve and depth of character." She was beaming when she continued, "What great fortune for the family line to be blessed with such an heir that exudes goodness and gentleness!" I had no idea what she was talking about, but the little boy in me was mildly uncomfortable as I glanced at my mother to reassure that she had not abandoned me. My great-grandmother's words were interpreted in my mind as complimentary, but my heart felt as if she had dropped a great burden in my life. Her tone implied expectations that I felt unqualified to meet. I was acutely aware of my own faults. How could anyone see high-minded, esoteric qualities in me when I have difficulty following through with everyday concrete issues such as keeping my shoes shined for school and drinking (without vomiting) that awful milk and raw egg mixture that my mother forced on me every morning?

My great-grandmother's joy signaled a need for momentary celebration, which she expressed by indulging in another deep puff of the cigarette followed by a tiny sip from the small cup filled with the dark-colored but strong-tasting Chinese whiskey. This was all capped by a soothing drink of warm oolong tea that was simmering in a nearby ornate teapot decorated with pictures of golden dragons.

As she reached out to touch my face with her gnarled fingers that were topped by tobacco-stained fingernails, she said, "I see that you are a polite little boy for humoring a very foolish old woman from the countryside. You have no idea what I am talking about because you are American and have not lived the life of your parents and ancestors. Other Chinese will call me just a peasant and you, just an empty bamboo [*juk sing*], but those terms are meant to be hurtful and will not change the great rising spirit that runs in your family line. Your mother can tell you about her grand family history that you are also inheriting. I would like to share with you a short story about your father's unquenchable spirit that I see is so abundant in your essence."

My great-grandmother's eyes turned slightly misty as she looked inward toward her memories. Her voice vibrated with the warm yellowish red mist of the early-morning southern Chinese countryside. I could almost feel the soft ground and the caressing breeze of the farmland that my father grew up on. She told me that my father, Wing, had lived in a small one-room house with walls constructed from a combination of old bricks and mud. The beds were mere ledges that jutted out from each wall, and there was only room for one table and several chairs on the bare dirt floor. This rudimentary house was situated on a fairly large tract of barren land that had long been overfarmed. Wing, however, never felt deprived or impoverished. Since his birth, he had exhibited an infectious happiness that was never dampened by despair. He was also lucky enough to be the firstborn son, which entitled him to gratuitous emotional support. My aunt was a teenager when he was born, and he did not have too many years to play with her before she left the house for marriage. Wing, however, would forever remember his sister's strong personality, loud voice, and maternal-like bonding with him. His younger brother had a loving nature and adored Wing, but his temperament was far more placid and less adventuresome. My grandmother was a kind woman who raised some animals and delighted in the simple events of life, which included the evening-time relaxation with a cup of strong Chinese whiskey and some cigarettes. Wing had barely gotten to know his father, who had left home to search for other means of supporting the rest of the family. This search led him halfway across the world to Manitoba, Canada, where he opened a small shacklike Chinese restaurant in the frozen Canadian tundra, barely making a living by Canadian standards. The meager but steady monthly sums of money that he sent back to China, however, were enough for his family to survive and to enable the children to attend school.

Wing spent much of his early childhood years under the supervision of a slightly older first cousin, who seemed to him like the most beautiful and affectionate girl in the world. He could consistently convince his cousin (my dear *bale goo ma*) to take him to every small restaurant in the area that employed a cook that created specialty dishes. She always looked at Wing with humor and warmth as this little boy would smile at her through grease-stained lips, knowing that his cousin would always pay for the tasty meal. This delight in the culinary arts would be a trademark throughout Wing's life, and the taste for good food from a variety of cultures would also be instilled in his children and grandchildren.

Wing's infectious personality was also magnified by a quick intellect mixed with compassionate insight. His preference for fun and play did not diminish his academic performance, which gained Wing acceptance into a prestigious boarding school on the island of Macao. He flourished at the school and made new friends from all over southern China. In addition, the school provided a venue to express his natural athleticism. He excelled in basketball, volleyball, and swimming. The combination of his outgoing personality, quick intellect, and obvious physical gifts allowed him to glow like the traditional yellow Chinese evening lamps and become the center of attention in an otherwise starkly dark environment. Wing liked everyone and always assumed that everyone would like him, a trait that would gain him friends all over the world later in life. A vague uneasiness and yearning, however, burned within him, seeking definition. This need for exploration and actualization of his personal potential would lead Wing to board a boat and head for the United States of America by himself at the age of thirteen.

Pacific Ocean, 1930s

The Pacific Ocean leaves a variety of impressions depending on the individual's perspective. The ocean was a beautiful backdrop for dramatic sunsets and promising mornings when my father was attending the island school in Macao. He saw the ocean as a vast avenue of opportunity when he peered at the hundreds of boats in Hong Kong harbor unloading their array of goods to be brought back and forth to market. Standing on the deck of a rolling freighter in the middle of the ocean left him feeling small and vulnerable in the face of overwhelming vastness. Even the waves generated by modest storms dwarfed the initial large impressions of the ship under his feet.

Ocean travel was not for the faint of heart during this time period of the twentieth century. I am not referring to the wealthy Americans who danced the night away on ocean liners. I am referring to the vast majority of Chinese immigrants who attempted this perilous journey crammed into available spaces on cargo ships. The people who traveled this way were generally poor, but they differed in their official status. Some were hired by companies as cheap labor, many were illegal aliens hoping to disappear in the California population long enough to work and send some money back to China, and still others were "paper sons" who carried legal papers generated from illegal qualifications.

This type of travel was also dangerous from sources other than the ocean. The weeks of close confinement of many different people would inevitably generate conflict and unsavory activities. Silent threats whispered during the darkest hour of the night would result in transfer of ownership of the most valuable morsels in the meager possessions of already poor people. A few women exchanged sexual favors, which carried the appeal of toilet activity, for the hollow promise of jobs when they arrived at the golden mountain, a term used to refer to America. Gambling, however, was by far the most common and favored activity among these Chinese travelers. Wing was fascinated by the strategy and rapid rise or fall of the gamblers. He never participated because he had nothing to wager with, but his quick mind allowed him to anticipate moves and results. He was convinced that he could have won most of the games that he observed.

The other young teenage boys on the ship were accompanied by either their families or emotionless keepers employed by ruthless businesses, who will indenture the boys. Wing was among the very few boys who traveled alone. Most of the other boys gravitated toward Wing as the center of attention. One particular teenager chose to indulge in gambling with the seedier elements of the ship. He quickly accumulated a debt that he obviously could not repay, and his anticipated death was a foregone conclusion. Everyone else avoided eye contact with this doomed teen, but Wing befriended him. He recognized a fellow adventurer who had fallen victim to his own natural human failings and naiveté. Wing approached the angry older gamblers during the night and managed to talk them into sparing the other youth's life. His quick arguments and analysis of the gambler's mindset defused their anger and replaced it with a sense of camaraderie and compassion. The young teenage gambler was hugely grateful to Wing for saving his life, and the two quickly formed an unusual bond. This early but significant bond was the unguessed motivation for Wing's intervention to again salvage this fellow traveler's life some fifty years later when the then young gambler would later evolve into one of New York City's largest heroin dealers.

Manitoba, Canada, 1930s

Wing was exhausted from the nonstop traveling since his arrival in San Francisco. His papers were processed on a small island off the coast, and he didn't understanding a word of what was said to him. The city itself was a fascinating amalgamation of races and cultures from all over the world. The signs and activities were incomprehensible to him. He could not, however, stop indulging his fascination with this new world, and he continued to travel with the handful of dollars and short instructions from his father in his pocket.

After weeks of surviving by his wits and rapidly learning the rudimentary elements of American and Canadian street culture and language, Wing struggled out of the numbing coldness of Manitoba to a shack that advertised itself as a Chinese restaurant. He had never experienced such coldness and was ill-prepared for it, especially since his clothing was more suited for a tropical climate. He quietly walked past the handful of tables, which stood empty, forming small puddles on the floor from the snow melting from his shoulders and hair.

As he stood at the uneven wooden counter, he meekly whispered, "Baba?"

A face peered through the small window on a swinging door, which opened into a tiny kitchen, and two worn yellowed eyes inspected the shivering young teenager. The door swung open, and a bent man with prematurely graying hair shuffled up to the counter while trying to straighten his once strong body now beaten down by loneliness and stress.

"Come in, come into the warmth in the kitchen," he said through a voice that was chronically hoarse and smelled of cigarettes.

As Wing edged into the kitchen with his small suitcase, his father appeared much older than he remembered. He wanted to rush into his father's arms and embrace him but, instead, just reached out to touch his father's hand. Even this small gesture made the older Mark somewhat uncomfortable because he was unaccustomed to overt physical expressions of emotions and intimacy.

"Let me make you something to eat. You must be hungry and tired."

Despite the bare-boned condition of the tiny kitchen, Wing's father quickly conjured tasty dishes of noodles and rice with just the right amount of flavor imparted by the hot wok. This was simply culinary artistry, skill, and judgment because the equipment was lacking.

As Wing sat on a small footstool and proceeded to devour the delicious dishes, his father stared at him with near vacant eyes and, in a monotone voice, said, "My life is over. There is only drudgery for me as I continue working and await the day of my death. Hopefully, I will continue to send money home for as long as our ancestors allow me to stay on earth. You, on the other hand, need not walk down my path. You are still quite young, and life has yet to unfold for you. I can see that the sparkle of adventures, challenges, and happiness shines in your eyes. You must leave right now after you are done eating and go to New York City. I will give you enough money to make the trip by train. When you get there, go to this address. I have an old friend who may be able to find a place for you to live if he is still alive."

Wing's father reached above him to pull out an old cigar box filled with coins and dollar bills. He counted out some money and pressed the folded bills into Wing's hand.

When Wing had finished eating, his father grabbed him and his suitcase and proceeded to push him out the back door of the kitchen into the blowing snow and cold. He said, "Go and fulfill your destiny. Much awaits you in life. Remember to care for your family, but you do not have to remember me as I am now."

Just as Wing turned to leave, he felt his father's hand on his hand, and he turned briefly to also notice a single tear dripping down his cheek.

After the Communists took over China in the late 1940s following the end of World War II, Wing's father would discover that all the money that he had been sending back home over the decades to support his family had been confiscated. He was overwhelmed by grief, and shortly thereafter, he died in Canada with his heart broken.

Wednesday, 7:30 a.m., 1990

The conference room near the hospital cafeteria was barely large enough to hold the entire contingent of faculty, residents, and medical students from three clinical services for the neuroscience conference every Wednesday morning. Problematic cases are usually presented to obtain input from the various members of the departments of neurosurgery, neurology, and neuroradiology. I was not particularly attentive during the discussion of a difficult case of a patient with severe neurological symptoms and confusing test results. I was instead concentrating on the fine points of the case, whose films were on my lap, that I would be presenting later in the conference; besides, the imaging findings of the current case under discussion were being managed by one of my esteemed colleagues. In fact, he is my professional mentor. I became vaguely aware of a fairly busy discussion with many questions raised but very little agreement. My colleague's smooth, reasoned voice soothed some of the apparent disagreements, but there was still an air of dissatisfaction in the room. After a rather pregnant pause of silence, I glanced up and was alarmed when I saw that all eyes in the room were directed at me. Were they really expecting an erudite opinion from me when the various experts in the other fields could not reach a consensus? Did they know that I didn't even hear the question? If my opinion would differ from my mentor, how do I avoid the risk of offending him in front of an audience?

I slowly stood up and walked over to the overhead projector, examined the magnetic resonance images [MRI] of the patient, and embarrassingly worked for more time by inquiring about the patient's most critical symptoms and findings. I chose to concentrate on what the exams can do and can show rather than the issues that were beyond the capabilities of the technology. In order to salvage something from the moment, I thought to turn this predicament into an opportunity to educate the trainees in the room at the same time. As I discussed the case findings, I punctuated my monologue with basic and esoteric anatomic points. Interjections of self-effacing humor and open admission of my lack of readiness seemed to deflect any initial impressions of oratorical incompetence. After about ten minutes of analysis, basic review, strategic organization, and humor-laced anatomical tutorial, the audience was smiling and seemed satisfied with an effective plan for the patient's difficult care. I returned to my seat wondering to myself. How did I learn to work an audience? My normal inclinations not only tend toward the passive side, but I find my not-so-subtle performance to be mildly offensive and perhaps too overt or, dare I say, American. It would be too obvious to superficially interpret this inner contradiction as the result of the abrasive interface between my Chinese and American background. I, however, just inwardly smile because there is no conflict at all. My Chinese and American backgrounds are well integrated, and I have always felt the unanticipated benefits of both combinations to create a unique union that is greater than the sum of the parts. My mixed feelings about myself during and after the conference are, instead, more a reflection of the different contributions from my mother and my father.

Staten Island, New York, 1967

I was probably one of the few students in my high school who did not look forward to the weekends during the school year. In fact, I felt the same even during the summers. I had been spending every weekend helping out in my father's restaurant since my junior high years. It would have mortified me if I was clairvoyant and was able to see that I would continue to work this way every weekend through college. The work itself was not completely unpleasant, and I never complained. It was just that the restaurant's success had created a volume of business that frightened me. During the height of the dinner hours on Friday and Saturday nights, it was not uncommon for the line of patrons waiting to be seated to be stretched out the door and extend partway down the street. It almost looked like the lines that formed outside of theatres during big movie premieres in Manhattan. Instead, this was occurring on the then quiet and almost forgotten borough of the five that make up New York City. The constant barrage of people who needed to be served pushed my tolerance to its limits, and I often felt unable to keep pace with the business. The work was not just demanding but also relentless and tedious. In addition, the speed and expertise of all the other workers, including my warm older first cousin who also helped quite often in the restaurant, added to my feelings of inadequacy. Just walking into any restaurant, even though my role is now as a customer, can still occasionally generate a vague sense of uneasiness within me.

My father, however, was quite within his elements during those torturously busy weekend evenings. He had a way of handling the customers that bordered on magical. I can still hear his voice from the past as he greeted each customer with a cry of "*cugino!*" which was meant to be an Italian word for cousin but was heavily accented by his unique blend of Lower East Side Chinese American English. He brought such cheer to the customers that they didn't mind or had forgotten about the long wait for an empty table. Many waiting customers were offered free drinks at the bar as well. The noise, the laughter, the cigarette smoke, and the clinking glasses mixed with the aroma of sizzling meats on hot oil and crispy appetizers popping on small flames at various tables created a kind of maelstrom that my father organized and reveled in. He loved the joy that people felt when they came to his restaurant. He had a way of welcoming everyone that fed the pride of the celebrities, respected the desire for anonymity of the powerful, and spread familial warmth to the everyday individual. No one left dissatisfied, and everyone felt like the center of attention. The two large dining rooms were the orchestra, and my father was the conductor. The only music played were happy tunes. I slowly came to the realization that my father *was* the restaurant.

My mother would be beaming during those busy, hectic years. I remember her standing at the bar while many married men spoke flirtatiously with her. She easily disarmed them and dismissed their remarks with good humor and self-effacement. This not only entertained the men but also cultivated a sense of admiration for my mother from their wives. My mother accomplished this while simultaneously mixing a long list of orders for drinks and keeping an eye on the cash register and my performance as I moved constantly between the kitchen and dining room. While my father commanded attention in the room, my mother would prefer to remain silent and monitor the details of the business. One longtime customer would, in the later years of the restaurant, refer to my mother as "the general."

No customer was beyond the reach of my father's generosity. I can recall one embarrassed customer, who had been recently released by his company, was unable to pay for his meal. My father not only dismissed the bill but also clandestinely gave the man enough cash to travel home and pay for another week's worth of meals.

I had asked my father, "Baba, why were you so generous to that man? After all, he must have known that he could not pay for the meal before he even came into the restaurant. We should have called the police. He probably thought we were fools."

My father answered, "*Dai dai ah* [little brother], he may have come in because he wanted to maintain his pride even though he had no money. Even if his intentions were dishonorable, a man with even the slightest hint of humanity within him would feel embarrassed by an act of kindness in the face of his own duplicity. Either way, we will have gained a friend rather than an opportunist, who would try harder to deceive us next time. We will have done a good deed, forged goodwill, and hopefully created a slightly better image of the Chinese in America at least in one person's mind, which may have some benefit for the next Chinese person that he meets."

Some of my father's acts of generosity, however, were more mystifying for me. One evening, a wealthy customer who had owned a large waste-removal company had admired my father's jade ring. That ring contained a very high-quality large jade bought years ago and was meant to be a family heirloom. My father matter-of-factly removed the ring from his finger and insisted that the customer keep it. I looked on in shock, but I could see that my mother's face expressed even greater outrage. She told me that she could understand helping the needy but giving riches to the rich was to forget the vivid years of struggle and poverty that my parents endured when they first came to this country.

I asked, "*Mahmee ah*, are you talking about our years living in the projects?"

She laughed and said, "Dai dai ah, you are such a knucklehead. I'm talking about the time before you were born. When we lived in the projects, your father had steady jobs—first as a waiter and then as a bartender while I worked in the sweatshops on the Lower East Side and was able to string beads [ten cents a string] at night."

I had often wondered about those early years and how two seemingly very different people like my parents managed to meet and marry.

China, Post-World War II, Pre-Communist Revolution

W ing Mark couldn't help the introspective mood that preoccupied his mind as he stood next to the railing on the upper deck of the passenger ship that was approaching Hong Kong harbor. He was returning to China a very different person compared to when he initially left his home years ago. The memories of his brief meeting with his father in the frozen tundra of Canada still carried the potency to chill him even though the warm humid breezes of Southeast Asia now caressed his hair. He remembered the long train ride from Manitoba to New York City, tiring his then thirteen-year-old body while his young mind crackled with the prospects of a new life full of adventures in America. The thirteen dollars in his pocket at that time lasted just long enough for him to find a small room with a half dozen other young Chinese immigrant boys and a back-breaking job carrying barrels of cooking oil from the delivery truck to the restaurant kitchens in New York's Chinatown. The U.S. Army would later give him the opportunity to serve and become a citizen of this country that he rapidly grew to love. Wing now stood on the deck of the boat as a fully grown man looking especially handsome in his sharply creased army uniform that was filled out by a trim and muscular body. His smooth tanned skin and ready smile created an air of easy approachability that drew the admiring glances of many of the Chinese and Caucasian female passengers. He left China as a boy but was returning as a man, a veteran, and, most proudly, an American.

The trip from Hong Kong to his village in Toisan was relatively short, but Wing was surprised to enter the empty mud-and-brick house that used to be his home. He went to a neighboring house to inquire about his family's whereabouts when he was shocked to learn that his mother had been ill for several weeks and was now hospitalized. Sick with worry, he ran back to his house and picked up his rusty old bicycle to travel to the local hospital that was miles away.

The winding packed dirt roads from his house to the hospital revealed a continuous path of destruction left by the Japanese troops during their invasion into southern China. Wing was troubled by the world's need for ladling an additional helping of misery to an already poor country. The years of war had damaged his body but never managed to touch his spirit until now. His legs grew more weary with each passing mile of devastation. He passed many families living in the shadows of the half-blasted remains of walls that used to support shops and restaurants. Many of the war's survivors appeared skeletal and dirty, which accentuated the severity of their suffering given their cultural pride in personal cleanliness and hygiene. The destruction also demonstrated a tornado-like arbitrariness with a completely intact and still-operating restaurant sandwiched between ruined buildings that appeared to be flattened with deliberate malignancy.

When Wing arrived at the hospital, he noticed that the building had that incongruous look that resembled a half-destroyed structure that was hastily repaired only to the point of functionality without regard to aesthetics. The nurse at the front desk was mildly shocked to see a handsome young Chinese man wearing an American military uniform walking toward her. After the man signed in and indicated the patient that he would be visiting, the nurse was again surprised to see that he had not come to visit one of the wealthy or important patients on the wards.

As he approached the bed assigned to his mother in the large ward filled with at least fifty patients, Wing noticed that a beautiful young nurse was giving his mother a soothing sponge bath with a knowingly soft yet disciplined hand. She was murmuring gentle comments of kindness and affection while cleaning the face, neck, and feet of his mother.

"Ah Ma, how are you feeling?" asked Wing.

His mother cried out, "Ay yah! My son! My loving son has come back! I thank the heavens for bringing my most cherished son back to me!" Then she sobbed continuously for twenty minutes while Wing held his mother's hand and stroked her face.

"I'm home now, Ma. I'll take care of everything."

Suit Ying stood back to give this patient some time for her warm reunion with her son. She tried not to stare at the son from the background, but it was difficult not to notice this strikingly handsome young man with the American military uniform. Her heart simultaneously went out to the emotional catharsis between mother and dearly loved son separated during these years of world devastation.

The patient then looked up and made the introductions. "Son, this is my wonderful nurse who had been taking such good care of me since I've been here. Isn't she lovely? Her name is Suit Ying. She is the eldest child of the Chin family. Imagine that? Your simple mother being cared for like royalty by a member of the great and wealthy Chin clan!"

The slow initial eye contact between Wing Soon and Suit Ying felt like the soothing caress of a summer's sunset in their hearts.

That silent moment slowly stirred the whispers of their unspoken hopes and dreams, but rather than generating a feeling of urgency, they both sensed the sweet promises of fulfillment, contentment, and understanding.

Wing intuitively felt that any loud speech or pretentious bravado would violate the moment. He smiled inwardly and softly said, "Thank you for caring for my mother. I'm sure that your affections for her are as much of a comfort as the medicines that you give her. I am her eldest son, Wing Soon."

Suit Ying was beaming inside and averted her eyes slightly when she said, "I am honored to be caring for your mother. She has rare warmth and compassionate nature. It is so refreshing to see such humanity in your mother during these difficult times."

In the coming months, Wing would be regularly calling on Suit Ying at her home.

Six Months Later

As Wing was trudging up the slight incline toward Suit Ying's palatial home, he was spied upon from the second-floor window by the husband of Suit Ying's younger sister. He had always looked with disdain upon Wing despite his shiny uniform and American citizenship. Wing had represented nothing more than an undereducated country peasant hoping to hit the lottery by marrying into the great Chin fortune. Of course, he was only projecting his own motivations onto Wing. After all, if his own motivations were opportunistic, then everyone must also be made from the same cloth.

While Wing was also carrying boxes of cakes hanging from the ends of a wooden pole on his shoulder, Suit Ying's brother-in-law derisively barked with undisguised sarcasm, "Suit Ying, a beggar is coming up the path. Don't let him into the house. Be sure to kick him back down the path toward the dirt hovel that he came from. Definitely do not encourage him by giving him food, or he will come back like our dogs."

Suit Ying's very elderly grandfather, the grand patriarch of the family, who is now mostly bedridden, has always disapproved of his youngest granddaughter's husband. He realized, however, that his shy granddaughter would not attract many prospects other than the blatantly mercenary ones like her current husband. The grandfather had always despised that man's ruthless comments and lack of class. That disdain grew even stronger now that his hateful comments are directed toward a man that the grand patriarch not only liked but admired. This young Chinese American was more than twice the man of the in-law. He beamed with character and always conducted himself with pride and respect despite having virtually nonexistent financial resources, especially compared to the Chin family. Grandfather was proud of Suit Ying. She was able to recognize the person that was her harmonious completion when the heavens allowed the two to meet. Grandfather intuitively sensed that this young man, Wing Soon, would not only do great things in a measurable way but he would, more importantly, contribute to the world in real and meaningful ways that were immeasurable. His sarcastic in-law, on the other hand, seemed doomed to the life of a mushroom, feeding on the dead when it suits him.

This assessment from the insightful, strong-willed patriarch would prove prophetic in the years to come after his rapidly approaching death. Wing would later save the surviving members of the Chin family years after the grandfather's death. One of those lives would also include Mr. Sarcasm because Wing would time and again prove to be the man of great character as predicted by the grandfather. True to his jealous nature, Mr. Sarcasm would later repay Wing by betraying Wing and his family and creating an unsealed rift in the remaining Chin family.

1948

Nineteen forty-eight would prove to be a bittersweet, historical turning point in the grand history of China. The Communist takeover united a fractious and fractured political landscape that was already reeling from one hundred years of foreign intrigue and exploitation. Unfortunately, the ruthless application of another foreign concept (Communism) by yet another ambitious Chinese tyrant would forever change the essence of China. Several generations have now passed under the new face of China, creating a population that resembles the history and culture of the Chinese only by their physical appearance. The brutalities that forced this massive change continue to generate many written accounts of the horrors by its survivors. Very few people are still alive to represent the rich history of Chinese life and values before the country's self-inflicted cultural destruction.

The onset of this tumultuous period had just begun to trickle into Guangdong Province when Wing asked Suit Ying to marry him and leave for America.

Going to America, 1948

Suit Ying's decision to leave the comfortable life of the financial elite of China would seem to be completely irrational especially when compared to the nearly destitute status of her fiancé. In addition to very little immediate tangible resources, Wing could only offer promises for the future. Suit Ying's sister and brother-in-law warned her that this is nothing more than the work of a flimflam artist. The grand patriarch of the Chin family, however, silenced all this talk as nonsense. He demanded that these accusations come to a complete stop because they are unworthy of this great family. The assumptions are not only flawed but reflect underdeveloped character and intelligence.

"Is everyone here a complete idiot? Don't you all think that if Wing were to try to take advantage of the family, he would have stayed with us in China where the fortune is based? He never expected or asked for money or any other type of support. He came with no money and left with no money. He even refused my offer of financial support until he could support his family by himself. Wing has demonstrated a greater depth of principle and morals than some who currently live under my roof. Some of you may even think that Wing is a high-minded fool for not taking anything. In truth, he is the wisest person of all because he left with the greatest prize of all—my dear sweet Suit Ying, who is a more worthy person than all of you combined!"

Suit Ying was leaving a palatial three-story house (or more accurately described as a complex) that would survive the Communist revolution and ultimately be turned into a school some forty years later. The multitude of rooms housed a large support staff, servants, and of course, all of the immediate and extended members of the Chin families. The grounds were large and houses were even built for the comfort of the dozens of dogs that were favorite pets of Suit Ying's father. Those canine houses could qualify as luxurious dwelling for most of the countryside's poorer population. In fact, the dogs' caretakers and their families lived quite comfortably with the pets in their housing.

There was an element of adventure and idealism when Wing described life in a new land to Suit Ying. America was a vast land with people from all over the world. No one needs to abandon their cultural heritage to be called an American. In fact, it is that very cultural diversity that defines the American character. Opportunities are everywhere, and all that is needed to succeed is motivation and willingness to work hard. Wing then naturally began to speak about the feelings that were closest to his heart about America. These feelings motivated him to go to war and risk his life for a land that he wasn't even born into. He whispered that America is more than just the land, people, businesses, and opportunities. More important and definitely more powerful than the physical existence of America is the idea of America. The great power of this type of idealism provides motivation in a person's life and is worth dying for. "It is worth far more than money. That is why I didn't take your family's money. Money is only money, and I am confident that I will make enough for us to survive. What we need, what everyone needs, is a life in a 'country' that cannot be touched but only felt in your heart. I am proud of my Chinese cultural heritage, but I am an American."

Suit Ying watched Wing as he spoke. His eyes danced and his face beamed. Their hearts were inflamed not just from the thought of traveling to America but also from the love between them. She left behind a vast fortune and an excessively materialistic lifestyle for love. She would have followed Wing anywhere on the earth for this idea that, like the essence of America, cannot be seen or heard but only felt with her innermost heart.

Pacific Ocean, 1948

It has been several weeks since Suit Ying left her cramped quarters on the passenger ship. She was suffering from prolonged seasickness that was exacerbated by the storms during the voyage. Several of the women in the room with her were kind enough to bring small amounts of food and water to her every day from the galley. Wing could not see her because the men and women were segregated on the lower decks of this ship, where the immigrants with little money were treated like animals being transported for slaughter. It did not help that Suit Ying was already about a month pregnant. She could not determine if her nausea was related to the rolling seas or her pregnancy.

Suit Ying thought of the past several months as she lay on the floor with her eyes closed. Her wedding in Hong Kong was not what she would have anticipated when she was younger. The ceremony was treated like an afterthought because the main reason for being in Hong Kong was to catch a boat to the United States. She had no family members at her wedding, which was virtually a civil ceremony. This was clearly not what her father and grandfather would have wanted for the marriage of a Chin daughter. All this, however, was of no consequence for her because she only wanted to be with Wing and go to America with him.

Welcome to America, 1948

Suit Ying never appreciated the spectacular sight of the American shoreline as the boat approached the harbor. She was physically weak and mentally foggy from the endless weeks of nonstop nausea. If it wasn't for the kindness of a group of women who were her fellow travelers, she did not believe that she would have survived the journey. The ship's crew was absolutely of no help. In fact, they viewed the lower deck passengers with unconcealed disdain.

As Suit Ying was debarking and struggling with her luggage, she noticed that she was on an island just off the mainland. Many people jostled her on the overcrowded dock, and every sign was completely incomprehensible. The men and women were still segregated while they were being herded for official processing. The wealthy Caucasian tourists returning from their "exotic" Asian adventure vacation were quickly ushered along their separately cordoned-off aisles, past the congregating masses of packed Chinese immigrants on the other side of the barriers, and were rapidly returned to the ship after a cursory review of their paperwork. The color of their skin easily distinguished them from the noncitizens. The ship would then leave the island for its official dock on the mainland after having discharged their profitable though undesirable human flotsam with minimal disturbance of their regular passengers.

Suit Ying just followed the crowd of Chinese women in front of her. After hours of waiting, she was feeling faint from her continued nausea. In addition, she was quite uncomfortable because her pregnancy had caused her to have nearly continuous feelings of urinary urgency. She tried to ask the guards for directions to the women's toilet but had no effective means to communicate with them; besides, the guards seemed unconcerned with her discomfort and just kept pushing her back in line.

When Suit Ying finally reached the head of the line, two men were seated at the other side of a long wooden desk in this drafty building that reeked of stale seawater and green grime. One of the men spoke brusquely to her, but she had no idea of what he was saying. His speech sounded like a barking dog to her. Worst than that, his mannerism was clearly rude, condescending, and completely disrespectful. This was quite a foreign experience for Suit Ying, who was treated with the utmost respect during her entire young life. After several more minutes of the official's barking speech, which was interrupted only by brief intervals of silence that was punctuated by his staring at her, Suit Ying was alarmed when the man signaled to a guard. This guard then roughly manhandled Suit Ying and dragged her into the bowels of the drafty building. Suit Ying was highly offended by their treatment of her but had no means of expressing it. She was also completely baffled by this whole experience. She would soon learn her fate as she was escorted down many corridors and then pushed into a dark moldy cell. The door slammed shut and locked behind her. She realized that she was in jail.

West Bend, Wisconsin, 2003

My wife and I stood at attention with the other parents in the stands beside the large indoor pool. We were there to watch my son compete in a high-school swimming meet. The air was warm and heavy with the scent of chlorine. The sticky indoor humidity was in marked contrast to the dry, frigid outside air so typical of the middle of a Wisconsin winter. I stood with everyone else to face the flag and recited the pledge of allegiance just prior to the beginning of the competition. I couldn't help but think of the slimy moist air that infested my mother's nostrils when she was thrown in jail after she first set foot on American soil. This is the same America whose flag I was now pledging allegiance to in a comfortable expensive facility that was built for privileged families to provide their children with the best advantages and opportunities in life. Just like my father, I said the words of the pledge from my heart. It was a poignant moment for me to stand there in that environment, which my parents, who suffered through so much in their lives, would never be able to share with me. It was also poignant because my parents would never see their grandson perform in a manner that would have undoubtedly generated an unbridled sense of joy and pride within them.

My son was standing on top of the starting block just prior to his heat in the fifty-yard freestyle, which is his specialty. He stood tall while slowly shaking his hands and shoulders for relaxation. My father, who also enjoyed the challenges of swimming, would have been astounded at my son's sleek and toned body that oozed with athleticism. At the referee's whistle, my son coiled his body and sprang loose at the starting buzzer. He cut through the water like a dolphin, creating a wake behind him while easily outdistancing his opponents. My heart was laden with the regret that my parents could never witness this.

These memories of my parents also brought to mind a specific, unusual circumstance in 1988 during one of their visits to Wisconsin to spend the holidays with my family. My cousin had earlier informed my mother that he had just returned from a vacation to China where he encountered a fellow tourist who claimed to have arrived at the United States at precisely the same time and on the same boat as my mother. That lady, coincidentally, owned and operated a Chinese restaurant in the Milwaukee area. This sparked my mother's interest to meet this woman. We decided to make a family trip to investigate this opportunity to renew a relationship that had been paused for forty years. As we drove up to the modestly appearing restaurant at the southern edge of the city, my mother fidgeted with both excitement and anxiety. Upon entering the establishment, my mother immediately encountered the proprietress, who gasped in surprise and said my mother is still easily recognizable after forty years. My mother hesitated a bit to stare at the woman when joy and recognition finally washed over her. This was the same woman who shared the jail cell with my mother when she first arrived in America.

The proprietress introduced herself to me as Mrs. Moy as she hurriedly prepared a table for my family and parents. She could not believe that she would again set eyes on her former cellmate after nearly a lifetime. During a belt-straining luncheon of Midwestern-influenced Chinese food, Mrs. Moy recounted my mother's endurance of six months in a musty damp jail cell. The toilets were repulsive, which tended to discourage the elimination of bodily wastes. Personal hygiene could barely be maintained when stained water in a rusty basin and oil-tainted rags were the only supplied resources for washing. The food was barely edible, which exacerbated the nausea that Suit Ying felt during her entire six months in the cell. Even sleep was difficult because the scratching noises from the rats in the dark corners of the room sparked nightlong fear and vigilance. It had taken six months for my father to clear the paperwork for my mother to enable her release from jail. There was no explanation or apology for the detention. People behaved as if it never happened.

Rats, 1948

Wing Soon and Suit Ying, now officially recognized as Mr. and Mrs. Mark, settled into a tiny two-room apartment in a tenement building on Baxter Street in New York's Chinatown. The building felt, smelled, and looked like it was at least one hundred years old when it was, in fact, more than 150 years old. Wing was proud of having his own place of residence and a steady job waiting tables at a local Chinese restaurant. Suit Ying was silently horrified at the apartment because her father's dogs lived in better housing than her. She was, nonetheless, happy because Wing was happy, they were young, and their lives was full of promise.

Wing felt mildly appalled at his new wife's lack of domestic skills, which was not surprising because she had lived her whole life with an entire staff to handle those chores. He was, however, disappointed that Suit Ying literally did not know how to boil water. This was an egregious burden for a man who had loved to eat well his whole life. Still, Suit Ying was a willing student and observer. She soon learned to create meals that delighted Wing and put a spring in his step every night as he walked home.

Not long after moving into the apartment on Baxter Street, Suit Ying felt the unfamiliar urgings that signaled the onset of labor. She had no help or guidance because all of her family was left behind in the wake of the boat that brought her to America. Wing took Suit Ying to a Manhattan hospital. Labor and delivery were less traumatic than Suit Ying feared because general anesthesia was in common use for a woman during delivery in the United States. This practice was most unusual for China where Suit Ying participated in numerous childbirths.

Suit Ying gave birth to a beautiful baby boy whom she named Mak Gick Yee, which was a noble name. She and Wing, however, realized that their precious child's life in America would be considerably smoother with an American name; besides, the proper American name would mark their son as a true American. Both were at a loss, however, to create a correct name as Wing's English was rudimentary and Suit Ying's was nonexistent. A local tabloid in the hospital room provided their only source for research, but after several hours of deliberation, they managed to settle on the American name of Clifton to supplement his Chinese name. So that is how my big brother Clif came into the world. He would grow up to be someone that I adored and loved even during the occasional times when he would inflict some brotherly torment upon me. My heart would hurt when he was disappointed, and my heart would sing when he was happy.

Mr. and Mrs. Mark carried their first newborn son up the stairs of the dingy tenement into their little apartment. It was sparsely decorated, but it did contain a small crib that was given to them by friends. The "couch" consisted of several stacks of *Life* magazine that were discarded by others. These stacks were then covered by a restaurant tablecloth that conveniently found its way to the apartment. Life seemed wonderful.

Suit Ying expected her new baby to cry but was unprepared for the voracious screaming that occurred that first night back on Baxter Street. She was mortified when she turned on the overhead light in the kitchen-living room-dining room-baby room. There were four to five large dark rats crawling and scurrying over little baby Clifton. Suit Ying frantically lifted my brother out of the crib, which caused the rats to jump up after the baby. Wing began swatting at the rats, causing them to retreat back into the dark grungy recesses of the apartment. The next morning, the apartment floor was littered with rat traps and baby Clifton's crib was moved into the bedroom.

Slightly more than a year later, Suit Ying gave birth to a delicate baby girl. Using the additional advice of cousins who had also come to America, the Marks gave their new daughter the elegant name of Cynthia to supplement her equally elegant Chinese name of Mak Guark Chew. Suit Ying did not feel the need for more children beyond the perfectly balanced boy-and-girl combination that she now had. Wing was, at the same time, doing exceptionally well in the restaurant where he consistently demonstrated an unlimited aptitude and enthusiasm for every facet of the business. He soon became invaluable to the owner and functioned as the de facto manager. During this time period, he was spending most of his time behind the bar making drinks, minding the cash register, and entertaining the customers. His character was beyond reproach, and the owners trusted Wing like a family member. The work behind the bar proved educational for Wing in subtle ways that would provide essential skills for his later success. The interaction with people from all walks of life ranging from the local Chinese store owners, to Caucasian federal court judges, to Puerto Rican delivery men stimulated the development of social skills that would endear Wing to everyone and anyone. The only pressing need in their lives was to improve their living conditions or, at the very least, stall the dangerously cagey rats in the apartment as they were so numerous that their defeat seemed impossible.

Staten Island, 1960s

My brother and sister were both away at college, and I would get up early every morning to be greeted by my mother, who waited for me in the basement with a bowl of flavorful noodles laden with meat and vegetables seeped in a steaming hot rich broth. She performed this daily ritual despite having just gone to bed at three o'clock in the morning. It was her habit to wait for my father to come home after closing the restaurant sometime between midnight and two in the morning. She would greet my father with a small meal and do most of her unfinished household chores before retiring. My mother loved this early-morning time with me because she would unburden her heart to me while I ate. She would take my hand and slowly stroke the back of it while she spoke of her hopes and dreams for me. These talks would stay with me my whole life though it did not carry much emotional impact for my teenage-addled mind at that time. Before leaving the table, I always had to force down my mandatory glass of milk under my mother's sternly watchful eye. I used to think that my overly distended stomach during school was related to all the meat that I ate for breakfast. Years later, I would learn that the name for my condition was called lactose intolerance.

Staten Island had become a heavenly refuge for me, having come from the projects in Lower Manhattan. During one of my early-morning sessions with my mother, I was informed that everything is relative because the projects were a savior for the Mark family from their Baxter Street apartment.

My mother said, "There was no affordable apartment for us to move in to if we had left Baxter Street even though the conditions were unacceptable. Remember that your brother and sister were both very young. I had to find a way to make more money, so I learned to sew from the other women in Chinatown. This simple skill enabled me to find work in the sweatshops in Chinatown."

"But Mahmee ah, why didn't you move to the projects earlier?"

"You are still the knucklehead that you were as a baby. There were no projects there in the beginning. When they were being built, your father immediately applied for an apartment and was given first preference because he was a veteran. We were overjoyed to move into the government housing that had cockroaches but no rats. Best of all, the rent was quite affordable and the rooms were clean."

I can remember going to the payment office with my father to give the monthly amount of thirty dollars to a lady who sat behind a window covered with metal bars. It seemed like a great deal of money to me, but my father would usually tell me that it was a great financial deal. This bargain carried the additional benefit of enabling him to send extra money back to China to support both his and my mother's family. At the time, I was too young to recognize the significance of what he said because it should have been staggering to the point of nearly complete disbelief that the great Chin family would need financial help from a bartender and sweatshop seamstress in New York's Chinatown. The entire vast Chin fortune was smashed and confiscated during the Communist takeover of China. In fact, most of the surviving members of each clan were now refugees in Hong Kong.

My own memories of the projects were colored by the Italian teenagers, with carefully coiffed and greased hair, harmonizing on the benches outside the buildings during the hot summer months; large black teenagers constantly punching, fighting, and bleeding on each other; Puerto Rican thugs who instigated conflict if none could be found spontaneously; and drunks, with the world's worst personal hygiene, sleeping in the stairwells during the winter.

My mother viewed our years in the Alfred E. Smith (first Catholic governor of New York State) projects in a very different light. During the years of our early-morning talks before school, she would reveal disjointed tidbits to me about how our family life in the projects was a hopeful period. I would frequently respond with disbelief that anyone could view the projects as anything other than a gray, depressing, violent, and despairing experience. There were, however, interspersed moments of color and sunshine as many of the residents were also new immigrants to this country with strong, rich cultural traditions and hopeful attitudes. My mother would describe how the projects represented a new and good beginning for her and our family. She was no longer carrying on the traditions of the Chin family because she was now married; besides, she was pretty much on her own now with no more Chin resources to draw from. She would start her own family traditions though her Chin roots will never be forgotten. Those same roots may influence the direction of her own family, but they will not limit or define the growth of her new family line. Far from despairing from the loss of family and fortune, she shared her husband's sense of adventure while forging a new beginning with unlimited potential. The projects were not a problem but a launching pad. Her two perfect children also symbolized this new beginning. Material poverty seemed like just another obstacle that will be dealt with rather than allowing it to loom over life as a defeated state of existence.

Alfred E. Smith Projects, 1950s

During our time in the projects, my father would work twelve-hour days in the restaurant in New York's Chinatown, but I would always look forward to his days off, which frequently fell on a Tuesday. It did not only signify an opportunity to spend more time with him, but he would frequently cook dinner for that night. That was a special treat because he was a spectacular cook who infected all of us with his love for eating well. The meals with Baba were not limited to Chinese cuisine because he also loved Italian food as well as just about any other type of cuisine with aromatic flavors. His idea of Italian, however, included the heavier elements of crown rack of lamb, thick huge hot sausages, and savory stuffed steaks. Meats were the first three choices of every multicourse meal not only because of the flavor but also because meat was a symbol of the good life to my father, no matter how little money we had. Those days were clearly before the age of cholesterol, HDL-to-LDL ratios (high-density lipoprotein-to-low-density lipoprotein), and heart attacks.

My mother would work ten-hour days in the sweatshops, earning just a few coins per dress, but she quickly learned to be quite fast and efficient. After dinner, she would frequently sit in the living room and string beads to create necklaces until I went to bed. She would be paid a few pennies per finished necklace, but over the course of a month, the coins added up to significant money to send back and support her displaced Chin family members. She was starting a new life in America, but she never forgot about her family in China. Working herself to the bone and abandoning any ideas for small luxuries were inconsequential. The sacrifices she made could not quench the love and devotion she felt toward her surviving siblings. She frequently choked with the guilt generated by the dilemma of sending meager resources to China while her own children needed those same resources for everyday life.

My mother beamed, however, when she spoke of her children.

"Dai dai [little brother, which was a term of endearment used to refer to me. Unfortunately, it was so frequently used by my parents that everyone in the community used that term as my only name, even when they were not related to me], those early days were filled with joy by your brother and sister. In fact, I felt so blessed with having one child of each sex that I did not plan on having any more children. Your brother was a marvelous baby who was even more handsome than his father. Those big round eyes, sunny disposition, and precocious intellect made everyone fall in love with him. In fact, I had entered him in a local Most Beautiful Child Contest, and he won!"

She looked a little sullen when she continued, "My fear, at that time, was that we would not be able to provide enough stimulation or educational resources to allow his very strong intellect and spirit to develop properly. In addition, the environment of the projects was somewhat harsh, and your brother was precocious and perceptive enough to see the realities around him. My hope was that his hope and idealism would not be suppressed or changed by the lack of a positively nurturing life outside our apartment door. Still, Clifton was my firstborn, my son, and my heart's sunshine. The room just glowed wherever he went. The dynamic Chin and Mark's spiritual legacies were clearly rising within him.

"Your sister, on the other hand, was delicate while your brother was rambunctious. She was sensitive, quiet, and contemplative. Your brother's intellect was a raging energy source whereas your sister's intellect was more focused and tempered though just as intense. In addition, it was wonderful to have a girl so that she could be everything that I had always wanted to be. She could be dainty yet strong, feminine yet assertive, and beautiful yet not reliant on it. Your sister was a lovely baby who was very comfortable curling up in my arms, basking in the warmth of my embrace. My love for her is a special bond that exists only between mother and daughter.

"And you, you knucklehead, were just an accident. You also had the audacity to come into the world on the precise day of your brother's birthday, which completely disrupted the grand party that we had planned for him."

Edison Theatre, St. Louis, 2002

I was sitting in the audience with my wife, Karen, watching the curtain rise from the stage, and a cone of light illuminated a curled dancer on the darkened stage. As the music started, the dancer uncoiled and proceeded to spin, glide, and move transitionally from one graceful movement to another, perfectly timed to the music while physically expressing the mood of the music. She never left the boundaries created by the cone of light but made that illuminated small area seem like a whole world of experience. The entire performance was aptly titled, "The Body Poetic." The dancer was my daughter, and I watched her create magic on the stage that night. I noticed that the rest of the audience was also transfixed by that same magic. It was the type of magic that my mother tried to describe to me but would never get the chance to see her granddaughter exhibit. My mother held such high hopes and wishes for my daughter when she was born. Her heart was visibly beaming when she held her newborn granddaughter, her first grandchild, but even she may never have predicted the extent of my daughter's future development. I knew, however, that my mother always held that unspoken hope in her heart without creating the burden that comes from expectation. As I watched the end of the performance, I imagined the joy that my mother would have felt that night, and my eyes moistened at the thought. I tried to recall the numerous fragments of conversations about personal development that my mother murmured to me over the years, as I tried to discreetly wipe away the tear that began to roll down my cheek.

One of those conversations occurred during my early high-school years. I had been struggling mightily with the routine coursework and just wasn't doing well. My feelings of defeat were accentuated by the easy academic successes of my older brother and sister. Their high-school experience was handled with the type of casual effortlessness that was enabled by their extraordinary, innate intelligence. I would struggle for hours every night and consistently fail to "get it." After several months, I not only began to despair, but I also lost any appreciation for studying dead authors and their works that I couldn't understand, the history of another continent that I could care even less about, and obtuse scientific points that I was convinced would have no practical value in my future life or afterlife. Why couldn't I just play ball, watch TV, and live with my parents for the rest of my life?

My mother had returned home early from the restaurant because she was bone tired. She had gone to bed at 3:00 a.m. and left the house at 9:00 a.m. after making my breakfast at 7:00 a.m. It was 9:30 p.m. when I greeted her at the door. She seemed more tired than usual, but I always thought that my mother didn't need much sleep. My adolescent mind did not realize that my mother had and continued to work with severe chronic fatigue out of need rather than choice. Life was unkind to her. To the rest of the world, my mother enjoyed the blessings of material success at this stage of her life, but she never measured her life by material standards. If that were the case, she would never have left China.

My mother greeted me with a smile and routinely asked, "Have you finished your homework?"

"I don't know. What difference does it make?" I answered in a sullen voice.

My mother then poured herself a customary cup of plain boiling water and asked me to sit with her in the basement. "Come sit with me and let your tired mother look at your face."

I felt another lecture coming on, but I sat down on the curved cold bright orange plastic chair that resembled a refugee from the GM Pavilion at the New York World's Fair.

"You think I only care about you if you do well in school?" she asked.

I gave her my usual reply, "Mahmee ah, you just don't understand."

She took my hand in her left hand and proceeded to gently stroke the back of my hand with her other hand. "I'm not as smart as my American-born son, who has all the advantages of being born here, but I can see your heart. I know you."

She paused and gently re-emphasized, "I know you. Your heart is my heart.

"Don't compare yourself with your brother and sister," she continued after a few seconds. "Each of you is different and will meet life's challenges in your own way. Life will also unfold uniquely for each person, often with unpredictable consequences. How you deal with your current problems and the decisions you make will shape the person that you will become. The important goal is your personal development and not getting the highest grade compared to others even though a high grade would allow me to brag to our insufferable relatives.

"I know it is hard for you especially at your first quality high school. You have no friends, everyone seems so smart, and your grammar-school preparation was not very competitive. You must think of yourself as inadequate because your brother and sister had the same preparation, and they did so much better, but you cannot predict how their lives will turn out just because they are so smart.

"The grade is not the goal. No matter what your relatives say, the number or letter of the grade has no real value. The process that you go through to master your studies is the real goal no matter what the result. That process, not the grade, is the secret and goal of education. The attempt is its own reward, and that struggle will change you. The decisions that you make when you encounter difficulties during the struggle to learn will shape you, the *you* that is in your heart and mind. The real you, not the physical *you* that you see in the mirror.

"I'm not sending you to school so that you could train for a job. I am sending you to school to get an education so that you will emerge at the end as a very different person from the boy who started in the beginning. You may look the same at the end, but you will be a completely different individual.

"If you allow the process of education to be fully engaged within yourself, you will begin to develop your potential, and a new world, which will offer possibilities that were previously unimaginable, will open in your mind. I'm not talking about job opportunities. I'm referring to the more important world of mental awareness, sensitivity, and maturity. The simple experiences of life such as breathing the air, feeling the sunshine, and listening to the music will be different and more vibrant to you. Only then will you start to fulfill what life has destined for you.

"This is why you should study dead poets, foreign languages, and early European history. It doesn't matter to me what your exact grade is—provided it isn't too low. What matters is that you decide to continue to try when it is difficult. Do it for your own sake and not to please me. What matters is the exercise and effort of studying those various subjects.

"Now why don't you go upstairs and do some more work before it gets too late."

My mahmee then walked behind me and put her face close to the top of my head and inhaled. It wasn't to check to see if I needed to wash my hair. It was an act of affection that she had performed since I was a baby.

I actually did go up to study more that night. I also watched less TV. My grades eventually (very slowly) improved, and my enthusiasm for school increased (even if slower). Every day, however, my mother continued to trudge back to the restaurant with her back more stooped, joints more fatigued, and increasing pain in her flank.

Lower East Side Manhattan, 1950s

S taten Island presented a whole new unaccustomed way of life for me that was as different from the Lower East Side of Manhattan as the clean, salty ocean breeze at South Beach differs from the clouds of diesel fumes that belch from the back of the green First Avenue bus. Life on the Lower East Side, however, possessed a cultural uniqueness that the weedy rural solitude of Staten Island could not match.

The projects bordered right on the edge of New York's Chinatown, which at that time was an unusual environment. It seemed like the hand of God had reached down and scooped up a part of pre-Communist China and placed it right in the middle of Lower Manhattan. Most of Chinatown's inhabitants were from the region surrounding Canton, and virtually, all spoke either Cantonese or Toisanese. This is in marked contrast to the current Chinatown that should more appropriately be called Asiatown. The population is much more diverse now with every dialect of Chinese spoken including various iterations of Vietnamese, Thai, Korean, etc. Mandarin, which sounded like Greek to me as a child, is now commonly spoken in most of Chinatown's restaurants. Everyone in modern Chinatown speaks English with the ease of a native-born American, but Chinatown used to be a place where a person could live out their entire life carrying out all the usual activities such as school, health care, shopping, working, and funeral arrangements without ever having to speak a word of English.

I used to walk through Mott Street as a child and be able to recognize most of the shop owners and grocery workers, who frequently waved at me as I passed while shouting my "name" (dai dai ah). After a while, even the other children called me "little brother." I would frequently go into a particularly small Chinese laundry run by a family that lived in a small area behind the machines. They would watch over me after school until my mother could pick me up after work. I remember that I frequently intruded on them just before their dinner hour, which filled the shop with delicious aromas that made my young mouth water and my stomach churn. They, however, never offered me any food, and I never dared to ask. After all, they were doing the favor by allowing me to stay and wait for my mother.

I used to walk just east of Chinatown with my mother to buy fruit. Those area streets were still formed by cobblestones at that time. The large fruit-laden wooden carts that lined the street were pulled by shaggy large horses with great uneven patches of hair. I used to be fascinated by the enormous size of the coiled stool that the horses produced. Those large steamy brown mounds astonished my seven-year-old imagination and promoted the development of mental math as I ruminated about rectal capacity and anal elasticity. During the summers, the flies would constantly flit between the horse manure and the nearby fruits, which spurred a better appreciation for Del Monte's canned fruit cocktail. I would also go into the nearby basement of a beige-colored corner building to buy chicken. This sawdust-covered, fowl-smelling, dimly lit room did not contain the rows of the sterile-appearing, neatly wrapped choice chicken pieces found in the modern supermarket. These were live clucking chickens all packed into cages that were stacked up on top of each other against the walls of one grimy room in the building. My mahmee would typically ask for a five-pound chicken, and the man with the blood-stained, foul-smelling apron would reach into a cage and pick out an appropriately sized chicken, which he would weigh under my mother's watchful eye. The man would then decapitate the chicken and hang it upside down while he ripped off the feathers. When the naked bird stopped moving (and bleeding), he packed it all into an old paper bag and handed the bag to my mother just before we headed home for dinner. My mother would frequently pick up the head to include for the dinner. If the man, with the odd European accent, was rude or insulting my mother, she would ask that the chicken be reweighed again at the end so that she would only pay for the chicken that she walked home with and not the feathers and blood, which stayed on the floor. I had learned never to pay the initial asking price for chicken. My mahmee taught me that, on the Lower East Side, prices were artificial and always negotiable. I also learned that chickens were nasty-looking, nasty-smelling, and nasty-tempered creatures. I could never fathom how my sister developed a taste for the chicken's mean skulking head while my great big brother preferred the chicken's filthy ass. But then, they never came chicken shopping with me.

Mulberry Street, which ran north from Chinatown into Little Italy, was also a fascinating place that captured my senses. Gray-haired Italian ladies stared out the windows of most of the buildings that I walked past. Most of the young Italians teenagers exuded their Sicilian heritage and turned T-shirts and Brylcream into cultural icons. To this day, I can still taste the pleasure of sweet, freshly made, cool lemon ice that had just been shaved and then scooped into a paper cone during the hot New York summers. The fall also brings warm memories of hot doughy zeppoles covered in fine powdery confectionery sugar bought from street vendors during the Feast of San Gennaro. I probably best remember the Italian restaurant Giambone's, which was situated more in Chinatown rather than Little Italy. My father would frequently take me there so that he could conduct business while the owner or bartender would treat me to a dish of spumoni or sometimes even a plate of mouth-watering linguine with white clam sauce. I could never understand my father's "business" in that restaurant because it just seemed like socializing to me. I would later understand that the restaurant was a favorite meeting place for federal judges, senators, congressmen, lawyers, and police commissioners. My father's engaging personality created a web of extensive connections into the power infrastructure of government and society.

Norna's butcher shop near Giambone's would also hold fond memories for me. The old Italian owner and his son would warmly greet my father, and both never failed to recognize my insignificant presence. Moreover, their carving skills seemed like an artistic performance on every slab of meat. They frequently custom carved a variety of meats for my father and included gratuitous samples of other meats for my father to take home and enjoy. I felt a sense of community and connection with so many people of diverse cultural backgrounds that I would acutely recognize its absence later in adult life. Even the streetlights, which consisted of large dingy yellow hanging globes, exuded more character than the bright and modern stainless steel halogen security lights of today.

I usually go to work every day, carrying my generic, ballistic cloth bag that can hold a laptop computer, papers, pens, books, and business cards. This surrender to convention differs from my childhood when my mother would take me a few blocks north of the projects to a whole neighborhood of Orthodox Jews with their multitude of shops, including one that was packed with a variety of top-quality leather luggage. My mahmee would pick out a sturdy leather schoolbag for me and had the owner engrave my name onto the bag. The portly shop owner, with the incredibly long sideburns that hung down to his chest, would proudly present me with the substantial bag with my name on the side accompanied by a warm smile and a pat on my head. The rich smell of leather would last for months before my ritualistic abuse of the bag, including spilling milk and squashing sandwiches in its inner compartments, would sap the bag in its innate vitality. I just think of all the sensations that the children of today miss as I drive past them, waiting on the corners for the school bus while sitting on their generic nylon backpacks. I just glance at my own black bag and realize that I have become just a grownup version of them.

Utilizing that leather schoolbag was also a different experience from my children's suburban grammar school. My school's building was over 150 years old at the time of my attendance. As usual, I struggled with an inability to match the performance of my two older siblings who preceded me (a recurring theme during my entire childhood). Each class consisted of at least fifty students with one teacher, who taught every single subject. This was possible because the teachers were not only very special but were probably not even human. They were nuns. They were covered from head to toe with a black robe and a black knit headpiece with white collar, which covers their neck up to their forehead. Skin was only visible on their face and hands. Perhaps they had no bodies under all that black cloth, and the face and hands existed only to enable them to interact with normal human beings. I have no memory of any nun ever sweating even during the hottest day of the year. They were truly supernatural human beings not subject to the laws of man or nature. My überimage of the nuns was reinforced by the immediate obedience to their commands by the meanest, orneriest, strongest, and toughest kid in my class. He was the toughest of the toughest Puerto Ricans in school who was already fifteen years old when the rest of us had yet to reach double digits. I heard that he had been left back quite a few times. (That was before schools discovered sports teams, and everyone had to prove their academic competency before advancing a grade.) He was a man among children. One Friday morning, he had forgotten to genuflect before entering the pew as the entire school was filing into church for mass. My teacher simply reached into the pew and lifted the tough guy up by the belt and collar into the air and threw him into the aisle so that he could show his respect to God with a proper genuflect. That one act of supernatural strength was seared into all of our infantile brains housed in our small bodies that were covered by conventional Catholic school uniforms. Discipline was never an issue in my class for the rest of the year. Being sent to the principal could generate thoughts of suicide. If our teacher-nun possessed supernatural powers, then it was only logical to assume that facing the mother superior was a fate worse than death.

When I grocery shop with my wife, we always check that the charged price of our items match the prices of the actual items. This is just a good and safe shopping habit that does not reflect any suspicion of underhanded intentions on the part of the grocery store. Modern computerized checkout procedures maximize convenience but also make it difficult to spot the sporadic system errors. This type of suburban checkout experience contrasts my memories of being sent to the grocery store when my mahmee was unable to go or was working. I was very young with no concept of money and a total inability to recognize the various coins. I remember pulling the two-wheeled tilting shopping cart behind me, walking past elderly people who sat on the wooden benches that lined the walkways of the projects. They frequently smiled at me and murmured something in Italian or some eastern European dialect, which I obviously could not understand. I used to think that they were ridiculing me because the shopping cart was taller than I was, but their comments were probably kind. Filling the cart with groceries was a monumental logistical challenge for me that would have been a hopeless endeavor if not for the help of the checkout girls. I would then reach into my pocket and just hand over to the girl whatever money that my mother gave me, and the girl would always give me back the correct change (so my mother told me). During my struggle to roll the cart back to the apartment, I frequently passed the same elderly people who would sit on those benches until the sunlight gave out.

The Lower East Side was a friendly small town in the midst of one of the world's largest and most modern cities. My childhood experiences there felt like being in a little village with people from every major corner of the earth pursuing and defining the American dream. At that particular time of my life, however, I would have been happy just to make it back home without breaking the eggs.

It was against this backdrop of a provincial-like community within a major metropolitan setting that two relationships formed, which would ultimately bring one bad and one good outcome for my parents. The first concerns my mother's younger sister and her family. My parents had managed to sponsor them to come to America. My mother had managed to bring to fruition all those years of saving coins and stringing beads to save her family. My aunt (*ah yee*) and her family provided good company for my mother. Every weekend was spent watching Chinese movies at the three movie houses in Chinatown. These were all within walking distance from each other, making it quite convenient for two adults and their horde of children. My brother showed a lack of interest in these types of movies and usually did not participate in these weekly nighttime outings. My cousins and I were usually busy playing at the back of the theatre while our parents watch those horribly boring and campy movies that were made in Hong Kong. It was not uncommon for my cousins and I to crawl along the filthy theatre floor to reach beneath seats for empty soda bottles. Returning those bottles to the concession stand would allow us to trade those bottles for penny candy treats. Candy never tasted better. I later stopped this behavior when I encountered a hairy large rat going for the same sticky Coke bottle that I was reaching for.

The reuniting of family and bonding of the surviving Chin family members and their children, however, meant the world to my mother. The years of tacky weekend movies, cherished dinners, loud birthday parties, and hot summer activities were times that will never be forgotten. Those very close moments, however, only added to the deep scoring pain from a breaking of those extended family bonds years later.

The second relationship concerns my father and one of New York's more notorious characters.

Fulton Fish Market

M y father's engaging personality, easy approachability, accepting attitudes, and honorable demeanor endeared him to many people from all walks of life during his time working in Chinatown. He was not only recruited to work in several different restaurants but was also asked to work undercover for the police, command the local American legion post, and counsel the local Chinese "associations." His sense of loyalty committed him to work primarily for one establishment. My father also never delegated his expanding duties when he felt that he could perform the job better himself. This included walking to the Fulton Fish Market in the early morning hours to choose the best fish for the week's menu.

The Fulton Fish Market is a fascinating place with most of its activities occurring before sunrise when the numerous fishing boats return to shore to unload their night's catch for New York City. Its central function as the sole source and gatekeeper for a single commodity for the country's most important metropolitan area made the fish market a focal point of political and social intrigue. Whoever controls the Fulton Fish Market would wield great power, money, and advantage. The various permutations for direct and indirect financial gain were limited only by the imagination's capacity for duplicity. Of course, the attraction of the Fulton Fish Market for organized crime was irresistible since its beginning.

Wing's keen intelligence and street savvy quickly alerted him to the undertones of hidden power during his first few visits to the fish market. It was his honorable behavior and refusal to engage in cunning activity to cheat his unsuspecting employer, however, that would lead to his being befriended by "Joe." Joe was a stocky, muscular middle-aged man of Italian descent who, to the superficial eye, blended in with all the other workers in the market. He wore a blood-stained apron and rubber boots like all the other workers. He, however, never lifted a crate or filleted a fish. Workers cleared a path wherever he walked, and his instructions were also immediately followed and never questioned. Joe followed the pattern of other successful heads of organized crime families by affecting the demeanor and appearance of the common working man while leading with the personality of a loving grandfather and the strategic calculations of a grand champion chess player. Machiavelli, himself, would have been eaten for breakfast at the Fulton Fish Market.

Wing was initially unnoticed by Joe because of the large size of the usual Asian and Caucasian representatives of the city's large, small, upscale, and run-down restaurants. There was the predictable daily bickering over price, quality, and delivery times. Joe had learned that all the different cultures and personalities of the world shared the common thread of money and greed. Everyone tried to extract small or large personal profits at every point in the process of buying and selling at the fish market. Wing, however, slowly began to stand out from the rest of the crowds because he always bargained only for the benefit of the restaurant that he represented. He even resisted the minimally higher price for the restaurant in exchange for personal profits in money and goods that would go unnoticed by anyone else. In addition, Wing bargained with a complexity of cunning and strategy that even drew the admiration of those who were succumbing to the power of his arguments. Part of that admiration was related to Wing's smooth and friendly personality. Wing was never adversarial or confrontational. He always worked on the assumption of a cordial relationship that would be mutually beneficial. Wing would even accept the short end of a negotiation if he sensed that he held such an overwhelming advantage that the bargaining may cause the other person to risk losing face. Wing's reputation on the waterfront grew, and Joe began to take notice. Joe walked up to Wing one day and introduced himself. Despite their physical differences, each recognized in the other a formidable person and a deep sense of honor. The friendship was immediate and would be long lasting. Joe admired Wing even more when Wing never showed any inclination to work for any advantages at the fish market through their growing friendship. Wing never discussed business directly with Joe though the mere association with him allowed Wing to buy from a greater-than-usual selection at the best prices. Wing was even astonished at the vast array of different types of seafood that were made available to him though they were never on display or noted on any list. Joe found Wing to be a good confidante. He gradually explained the inner workings of the Fulton Fish Market to Wing, and Wing listened to his pieces of advice and strategies. Being an outsider, Wing was able to provide a fresh, unprejudiced perspective that Joe frequently found refreshing, insightful, and extremely clever. Wing learned from his experiences at the waterfront but never used that knowledge for manipulation, power, or personal gain. Honor and friendship always held the highest priority in his mind. Joe greatly respected this.

After about ten years of friendship and business, Joe raised an unusual topic with Wing over drinks one evening.

Joe said, "Wing, I gotta go away for a while. I don't quite know how long yet, but I want you to do a favor for me."

Wing looked at him silently, knowing what Joe did for a living and that Joe had never directly involved him in any illegal activity.

Joe continued, "I want you to hold on to this envelope for me, but you gotta promise me that you never open it. Just hold on to it for me until I get back. I know that I can trust you and nobody else."

Wing just simply said, "OK."

Joe disappeared the next day. He did not resurface until four years later. When Wing next visited the Fulton Fish Market after his return, Wing thought that Joe had aged.

Wing said, "*Cugino*! Good to see you again. Where did you go for so long?"

Joe quietly mumbled, "I was in jail. The feds have been after me for a long time, and they finally got me on some garbage charges just before the last time I spoke with you. Meet me tonight at Giambone's and bring that envelope that I asked you to hold on to for me."

After work, Wing stopped home at the apartment and fetched the wrinkled envelope. As he entered Giambone's restaurant, Joe was already there, sitting in the back along the wall just in front of the door to the kitchen. Wing sat opposite Joe, who had already ordered a scotch for Wing. Wing took a quick sip and discreetly handed Joe the old envelope under the table.

Joe noticed that the aging envelope was still unopened when he said, "Wing, this envelope contains my emergency plans. I didn't know how the fish market was going to be when I got back. As you know, there are a lot of guys out there that would like to take over. It turns out that everything's OK. I'm back and nothing's changed. For your friendship, loyalty, and being an honorable man by not opening the envelope, I'd like you to have this." This time, Joe pulled out his hand with the envelope from under the table and handed over to Wing the same envelope that was just given to him. Wing quickly and calmly returned the envelope to his inner jacket pocket but not before the bartender, two waiters, and several of the regular patrons (including a federal judge) witnessed the transaction. Eyebrows were raised throughout the restaurant.

Joe said, "Get outta here right now and don't open that envelope 'til you get home." He raised his scotch and said, "Salut!"

As Wing walked through the length of the restaurant, his already solid reputation within the community was silently raised to an unprecedented height. An uncommon event just happened. A Chinese American was silently saluted by a room full of New York's powerbrokers.

When Wing arrived back to the apartment, he was noisily greeted by his three children. He sat down to a satisfying dinner of steamed sea bass and soy sauce chicken. His eldest son could eat at Wing's own prodigious rate while his daughter picked at her food. The youngest son was still a culinary retard preferring to eat plain white rice mixed with a fried egg drenched in oyster sauce.

After the children were put to bed and Suit Ying returned to stringing beads, Wing sat down on his bed and pulled out the envelope from his jacket pocket. As he opened the envelope, his eyes widened as he gasped, "Ay yah!"

There was fifty thousand dollars in cash in the envelope.

Sweatshops, Early 1960s

The first dozen years after Wing's arrival back to the United States with his new bride consisted of nonstop restaurant work and management. Wing never minded his situation. In fact, the exposure to a very wide cross section of society very much appealed to Wing's natural extroverted tendencies, zest for discovery, and keen analytic abilities to understand the many games of intrigue that washed through everyday life. He was in his element but had been giving more thought to his wife's suggestion that he open his own restaurant. The idea was very attractive even though he never felt singularly compelled toward that goal. Wing always held the attitude that life was good and exciting. He was even positive about life on Baxter Street and in the Alfred E. Smith projects. Suit Ying, however, was acutely aware of and desperately wished for greater life-fulfilling opportunities for her children that their current economic status could not provide. Toward that dream of owning his own restaurant, Wing and Suit Ying had been saving pennies and dollars over the years. Wing knew, however, that he was missing several enabling factors. Their rate of savings would never be fast enough unless they lived to be one thousand years old. He would never be able to obtain a loan because he had no collateral. No bank would be so cavalier to risk a great deal of money merely on the word of someone with no track record. Borrowing from relatives and friends would not even account for 5 percent of the money that would be required for such an enterprise. The monetary gift from Joe, however, changed everything.

Even after Suit Ying had recovered from the shock of discovering the contents of the envelope that Joe had given to her husband, she continued to dutifully return to work at the sweatshop every morning. She knew that her life had changed, but she maintained a dogged determination to work for every opportunity to continue saving every cent that she could possibly get. She would never take good fortune for granted and had always believed that the ultimate outcomes for her family's life rested on the efforts from her own hands, understanding from her mind, and love from her heart.

I used to occasionally visit my mother at her workplace after school. The sweatshop was a mere three blocks from my grammar school, but the distance seemed much greater to a very small boy with a very short stride. The factory was located on the second floor of an old building. The grumpy old Caucasian man would consistently growl at me for forcing him to push the lever that raised the service elevator with the metal grating for a door. His attitude would frighten me to the point where I would frequently try to bypass the elevator and take the stairs to go up. This alternative route would put me in a different jeopardy by forcing me to walk past the Jewish owner of the factory. He would screech out loud that no children are allowed and try to prevent me from reaching my mother's workstation. Only incessant crying on my part, which was not an act because I was by then fearing for my life, would allow me to pass and spend a few minutes with my mother.

I would walk past a maze of tables loaded with scraps of cloth of every color. The route was seared into my brain as I honed in on my mother's position like a salmon finding his way home against the current. I couldn't even see over the tables, but I would pass numerous women hunched over sewing machines. They all consistently looked at me as I pass and would yell out that Suit Ying's youngest son is here. Some would even ask if I was hungry when they offered me portions of their meager lunches. The large room was always buzzing with the noise from the super-fast industrial sewing machines that would be sporadically interrupted by the hissing noise and steam from the large press irons. These were the orchestrated noises that could only come from non-English-speaking immigrants who are working for far less than the minimal wage in order to survive in America. Complaints were nonexistent because they would only cause a painful investigation by the immigration department, who would frequently discover the illegal status of some of the workers and friends. (Unions could never gain a toehold in this type of environment.)

My mother would always look up from her work when I approached. She would chide me for going to the factory when I wasn't supposed to be there while simultaneously greeting me with a beaming smile and wrapping me in her warm, soothing arms. She would caress me and inhale deeply when I buried my face close to her face and neck. After allowing me to sit for a minute on her lap, she would put me down and tell me to sit quietly behind her by the window so that she could finish working.

The two-hour wait with my mother was much preferable to the lonely vigil at the laundry store or staring out the kitchen window at home; besides, I had always enjoyed the palpable glow from the camaraderie among the women at the sweatshop. There was a constant stream of banter mixed with the high-speed buzzing of the sewing machines. All the women helped one another so that everyone would finish their day's allotted workload on time. Occasionally, women would burst into familiar old Chinese school songs, and everyone else would join in. My mother was always injecting encouraging comments and virtually convincing everyone that these were wonderful times because they were all the best of friends and happy to be working together. A few women would sporadically walk up to me to reinforce me for being such a good boy and not demanding attention. They also would offer to share their sweet treats with me. I was usually too shy to accept even though I silently salivated at the sweet/and salty dried plums and chewy fruity candies that the women favored. One slightly older woman whispered to me that she was aware of my mother's bloodline with the fabulously wealthy and generous Chin family. Her sad eyes conflicted with her proud voice when she said that my mother shows great character by working there in the sweatshop without complaint or regret.

"Imagine that, the favorite child of the Chin family and a highly trained specialized nurse now working as a common seamstress under the worst conditions."

She viewed my mother as a remarkable person, who also never mentioned the past and consistently encouraged everyone to work for the future.

Of course, all of this was lost to my very young mind, but I do remember my mother mentioning to me that all the women at the factory were wonderful people. As we would walk back to the projects, with my tiny hand basking in the loving grip of my mother's soft touch, she would continue to describe the personal hardships and tragic situations of many of the women in the sweatshop. Some were educated, and many were not, but all came to America at great sacrifice and personal risk. They arrived in a country where they could not speak the language and were handicapped in every way possible. Their greatest desire was to provide hope and opportunities for their children. My mother greatly enjoyed their company because they lived the precise qualities that very few of the privileged and educated exhibited but should have possessed in abundance. They were all tolerant and accepting of an individual's differences. Kindness, care, and sympathy were first and not last responses. Their life's experiences endowed them with a keen intelligence and insight that rapidly saw through duplicity and deception, yet their hearts were not hardened by cynicism. They applauded the accomplishments of others and never expressed jealousy for another's greater material possessions. In fact, they would be the first to offer to share their own meager food with the wealthier person if they thought that

that other person might enjoy a taste of what they had. I would remember to this day their constant reminder to me to not judge a person by his possessions and style but rather by the quality of their honor, understanding of their mind, and caring of their heart.

A walk along Mott Street with my mother confirmed the substantive feelings that I was slowly developing for my culture and community. The local shop owners would wave and express profuse greetings to my mother. The local grocer would stop his rapid mental math to smile at my mother and me through the store window, where there was also a tank of live swimming fish waiting to be purchased and cooked for dinner by some lucky family. Other pedestrians would yell across the street to my mother and offer general comments of good health and fortune to my whole family. It would be several decades later that I would learn, through acquired relatives, that some Chinese Americans living among more mainstream America would label these marvelous people of character and culture as being too "Chinesey." That label would not be used kindly and also did not need to be further punctuated by the frequently accompanying mocking tone of voice. I have always felt a sense of sadness for these "relatives" who seem unaware that their words and actions are egregious self-indictments that expose a great vacuum in their humanity and insight. I have slowly realized with introspection during my adulthood that I grew up with extraordinary individuals in an extraordinary community during a special time period. Everyone else seems just quite ordinary in comparison.

February 2002

I had flown in to New York for the weekend to perform one of the most painful and heartbreaking tasks of my life. I needed to inform my father that he was suffering from a form of cancer that had no effective treatment, and his death was inevitable in the coming months. Worst of all, there was the necessity to prepare him for the unavoidable and unremitting suffering associated with the predictable manner of his impending slow and tortuous march to death. My mind was simultaneously numb, overwhelmed with grief, and preoccupied with a lifetime of regrets for real or imagined neglects and missed opportunities. My father sensed my unspoken emotional cry and refused to allow me to dwell on sadness. He encouraged me to walk with him in the backyard to enjoy the unusually warm sunny day for that time of year. He employed an analytic tone of voice and distracted me from my sadness by questioning me with a near clinical detachment about the details of his illness in the upcoming months. The conversation allowed me to regain my professional composure as I answered his questions as much as I would to any other patient. This practiced composure, however, deteriorated as my speech started to break down into my childhood Toisanese dialect because this was not just another patient. This was my father. He was the man who bought me a sea captain's hat at the beach and lifted me up onto his shoulders with my tiny hands gripping his forehead as he walked down the boardwalk on the New Jersey shore.

I remember the warm springlike winter sun illuminating my father's face when he continued to reflect and told me that he was still feeling quite well with the exception of some, thus far, minor swallowing difficulties. He wanted to continue with the routines of life as long as he was physically able. He smiled and said that his life had been wonderful and blessed with a nonstop stream of luck. In recent years, he had survived both attacks on the World Trade Center (bombing and airplane collision), bladder cancer, severe obstructive lung disease, a cirrhotic liver, debilitating gouty arthritis, and narrowing of the blood vessels to his brain that was so severe it would have choked a cow. As he looked around the yard and marveled at the growth of the fruit trees, he spoke of my mother.

"Your mother would have loved to see the bountiful yield of these fruit trees. She just loved growing vegetables and fruit in this yard.

"My biggest regret is that she did not live long enough to see the full extent that you three children have prospered. You know, Dai dai, your mother was filled with more love than anyone I have ever known, and she loved her children more than anything else."

His eyes moistened slightly when he continued, "I hope that you three children know that I love you all very much, even when I don't say it. Of course, I have some regrets myself because I am not perfect. I wished I had known what to say and do when your brother was a teenager. All I did was posture because I was at a loss. I know now that he was going through rapid changes that I mistook for attitude. He required understanding and support, and I was too busy to try to comprehend his turmoil. He is my beloved firstborn though. He will always be close to me, and I love him so dearly. Your sister was a darling and precious daughter with a very vulnerable personality. I wished I knew how to relate to girls better, but I left much of the interactions to your mother. My big regret is not visiting her more often and participating more fully in her current family's life. She, like your brother, possesses great talents that are overlooked by others but will hopefully enable them to fulfill their lives. I did not express my love and appreciation for her often enough. And you, my little dai dai, are too serious. I knew I was in trouble when you showed up unexpectedly this weekend. You wouldn't be here unless you had something very important to tell me, something that can only be said in person. I very much appreciate your effort, and I know how difficult this is for you. Maybe it is just your personality, but everyone, especially your mother and I, find it very easy to talk to you. That is why you must be sure you let your brother and sister know how much I loved them. If they hear it directly from me, they might think that I was just drunk, but if they hear it from you, then they will know it to be true. After I am dead, I will continue to love them, and you will say the words that I have failed to say in life."

I enjoyed the rest of that sunny afternoon with my father as he planned out his health care and funeral arrangements for the coming months. It was quite strange for me but a routine for my father to approach the whole situation as if he was matter-of-factly discussing or analyzing a problem to be solved. Plans were made, and decisions were finalized in his mind. He was going to die the way he had lived. He would remain positive without despair. All the variables and practical aspects of the next few months would be anticipated and associated with solutions.

My father's deepest unspoken feelings, however, were revealed when I was leaving the following morning. I had just buckled my seat belt in the car for my ride to the airport when I glanced back at the house. My father was standing at the front door behind the glass portion of the storm door, gazing at me with tears welling in his eyes and a pronounced slump to his shoulders. His eyes did not leave mine until the car was out of sight. It was shattering to leave him, and his tearful image replayed in my heart the entire flight home.

During that grief-filled weekend, I had distractedly noticed that the old neighborhood had significantly changed from my youth. The worn building that housed the old restaurant was probably on its tenth different iteration of a restaurant. Numerous houses had cropped up as far as the eye could see in every direction. Over the years, there had been a nonstop stream of immigrants moving into the neighborhood. Some of the foreigners were Russians, but most were Italians from Brooklyn.

My mind would drift back to far more pleasant times on this same street some thirty-eight years earlier. Mark's Chinese Restaurant had opened to rave reviews and rapidly developed a consistent and loyal clientele. The relatives were still mystified about the sudden availability of financial resources to complete this project. The establishment and success of the restaurant would foment lifelong jealousies among particular relatives. The side street at right angles to the front of the restaurant would be my new home turf. It was so different from the projects that I felt as if I had been transplanted to another planet. The street was only paved to the entrance of the parking lot at the rear of the restaurant. The remainder of the dirt road ended in a field of tall weeds about an eighth of a mile away. Across the street from my house, there was nothing but tall weeds as far as the eye could see. This field of weeds also stretched east and didn't stop until it met the beach that touched the Atlantic Ocean about a mile away. Hidden among the weeds across the street was a small pond, which was home to rats, opossums, and young boys trying to play war. For most of the year, I could inhale deeply and catch a hint of the salty ocean breeze. It was wonderful to discover that stars existed in the sky at night, fresh air was not synonymous with bus fumes, and I could run freely down the street without fear of being hit by traffic or accosted by black or Puerto Rican youth gangs. There were only seven houses on the street, and one had been built by my father solely to provide housing for the restaurant workers who needed it. That street would provide happy memories of running postpatterns, pretending to be Homer Jones while my brother (a.k.a. Y.A. Tittle) threw long bombs with the football, catching countless groundballs but also losing a fortune in baseballs among the weeds, running fast in knee-deep snow to escape my brother's wrath after I had the temerity to hit him with a snowball, and riding my golden-colored first bicycle bought from EJ Korvette even though I never managed to properly assemble/tighten the cheap handlebars (or any other part on that dangerous contraption). I even loved the crisp grayness of the fall after all the leaves had already fallen from the trees. The outdoor life was such a wonderful distracting discovery after the caged existence of Manhattan that I often failed to notice or establish any mental connection between my mother trudging every day and night to and from the restaurant and my opportunity to frolic in the great weedy outdoors of New York City's functional garbage dump disguised as a borough.

Mark's Chinese Restaurant

Over a fourteen-year period, the restaurant provided a physical, emotional, and financial roller-coaster ride for Wing and Suit Ying, and the daily grind of work required continual adaptations. Wing, initially, did not want Suit Ying to work in the restaurant. He outwardly pronounced that he was the man of the house, and his wife should no longer have to work, now that he was successful. Inwardly, he was secretly fearful that his wife would be overwhelmed by the multifaceted demands of a complex business mixed with the needs of three growing children. He quite logically surmised that his wife's total experience in America for the past sixteen years consisted of interacting with a totally Chinese community and honing very proficient seamstress skills. These were hardly adequate qualifications to run a complicated small business with a mostly Caucasian clientele. What Wing failed to factor in to his analysis was Suit Ying's reservoir of self-motivation. After all, she was the crown jewel of the fabulous Chin family empire before China was violently plunged one hundred years backward by the Communists. She was the survivor of the "run" who refused to fail and die. She was the leader who motivated people around her by her intellect, compassion, and integrity. She was the adventuress who was daring enough to give up everything that she had known in her life to start from absolutely zero in a totally foreign land because she believed in love. She was the one who had total confidence in her ability to succeed with no skills or resources because she believed in life; thus, it came to be that Suit Ying ignored Wing's weakening objections and started working at the restaurant.

Suit Ying proved to be a remarkable student. In less than a week, she had mastered the daily needs of the restaurant from vegetable deliveries, meat supplies, and linen requirements to bookkeeping demands. After another week, she had learned to properly mix enough drinks to effectively work behind the bar on the busiest night of the week. This latter accomplishment is all the more remarkable because she not only did not drink alcohol, but she also could not read the labels on the bottles. Within a month, Suit Ying was effectively managing the entire restaurant's operation, and she performed her duties with an effectiveness and efficiency that left her imprint on every phase of the business.

Suit Ying's participation in the restaurant proved to be the perfect complement that even Wing could not have anticipated. Her motivation and meticulous attention to detail dovetailed perfectly with the daily nonstop demands of the business. Wing's natural tendencies were to look at the big picture and he was less observant of the details. Suit Ying's smooth running of the business's infrastructure allowed Wing to do what he loved and did best—that was to impose his personality on the establishment and interact with and entertain the customers. This proved to be a winning formula that attracted patrons in droves for years. They came for my father's magic while my mother enabled the show to go on.

Suit Ying's effect on the workers was profound in much the same way that she affected those around her in China. They did not look on her as the owner's wife. She was, instead, their leader whose concern for their well-being and work conditions was palpable. They never doubted that every decision Suit Ying made was for the best interest of the workers, who had never worked for an establishment that also provided free housing. Suit Ying was their mother figure, confidante, and friend. She worked harder and longer than any of the workers. They, in turn, adored her, trusted her, and protected her. They insisted that she sit and rest whenever possible, leave early with the evening's earnings, and never perform any form of lifting when her back started hurting. The waiters, cooks, and dishwashers all considered themselves part of the Mark family and demonstrated the loyalty and love of family members. Many would return and visit even years after their last day of employment. Some had gone on to college, and others married. All returned to show their pride in their accomplishments and gratitude for Suit Ying's role in their lives.

The restaurant experience also produced unexpected alterations in Wing and Suit Ying's everyday life. Many patrons, for instance, would confuse Wing's surname for his first name that he frequently answered just to the name of Mark. Suit Ying's name was simply phoneticized to the easier-to-pronounce Sue. For the sake of convenience and politeness, Wing and Suit Ying never bothered to correct anyone. The rest of the Caucasian American world just came to know them as Mark and Sue. In fact, they even referred to themselves by those same names when interacting with any facet of the English-speaking community.

Money was another surprising issue—surprising because of the vast quantities of it that kept pouring in on a nightly basis. The restaurant was predominantly a cash-only business, and the rapidly amassing sums were shocking to Wing and Suit Ying, especially considering their previous financial status and reserves (nonexistent) since coming to America. This resulted in daily morning trips to the bank for deposits and the need for financial planning. Even after the restaurant's considerable expenses were all accounted for, the excess money (a.k.a. profits) was substantial. This generated the need for financial planning. That service however, came from a very unusual source.

Doctor Ho was a balding, rumpled-appearing older gentleman who had the unique distinction of being completely incomprehensible to me during my younger days when I was fluent in two dialects of

Chinese in addition to English. His Chinese was Mandarin, which was only spoken by a very small minority of Chinese in New York at that time. His version of it sounded like someone trying to speak Spanish through a mouthful of water. He was also the only Chinese person that I had ever come across who spoke English with a very thick German accent. The German accent developed from his years of study at the University of Heidelberg, where he obtained his doctorate in engineering. So both his Chinese and English exceeded my mental universal translator. I found it fascinating that both my parents had no trouble understanding Doctor Ho, but it also reinforced my position as the intellectual caboose of the family.

Doctor Ho handled nearly all of Wing's investments with great success. Every month, Wing would walk next door, with envelopes fully jammed with cash, to Doctor Ho's office. Over the course of several years, Doctor Ho converted Wing's cash into real estate, office buildings, and apartment complexes. Doctor Ho assured Wing that his financial future was set, and he could walk away from the restaurant business at any time without any monetary worries for the rest of his life. Wing enjoyed this relationship not just because of the resounding financial benefits but because it was based on trust and honor. Any outside third-party observer would have said that a child could see Wing's vulnerable position, which could be taken advantage of without any effort. Wing, however, was not naïve but had always conducted his business and his life based upon the integrity of interpersonal relationships. Doctor Ho also shared that bond and would rather have died instead of betraying Wing. Unfortunately for both Doctor Ho and Wing, they had failed to factor in the one unanticipated event that made all the difference in the world. Doctor Ho did indeed suddenly die and much sooner than expected.

Mama Ho, Doctor Ho's wife, took over her husband's investment business, but her more corrosive and predatory style and philosophy were more aligned with contemporary brokerage house agents who call your home during the dinner hour with can't-miss opportunities. She felt that her client's money was actually her money and, hence, developed a "natural" strong sense of entitlement to Wing's accumulated wealth. Doctor Ho's death, therefore, started a chain of events highlighted by treachery, betrayal, and deception that led to the overwhelming and utter loss of Wing and Suit Ying's fortune that was forged from their blood over decades of spirit-breaking eighteen-hour days for 365 days a year. The millions of accumulated dollars that Wing and Suit Ying had hoped to use to ensure the future of their children and grandchildren not only dissipated like an early-morning dream, but that loss would also leave them in a desperate fight for their financial lives. Total financial ruin awaited them after nearly a lifetime of work. They would eventually only be able to retain the house that they lived in. Everything else was lost. Divine justice was clearly not at work here. If this was God's sense of humor, Wing and Suit Ying were not laughing.

The story of Mark's Chinese Restaurant, however, does not lie in the big picture of its financial success and subsequent failure. It is, instead, buried in the mosaic of millions of tiny details, gestures, and emotional interactions that touched so many lives every day.

Little Help Equals Big Help

The less fortunate patrons were not the only beneficiaries of Wing and Suit Ying's generosity. They touched and were touched by so many individual lives that passed through the restaurant during its lifespan. Howard was one such life.

My earliest memories of Howard were colored by complete awe and intimidation. I was still in grade school and had never laid eyes on such a large and monstrously strong Chinese individual. He was well over six feet tall with biceps that bulged, pecs that strained against his extra large shirts, and a deep voice with a menacing timbre that makes the Terminator sound like a girlie-man. Howard was a walking hard lump of solidified testosterone encased under stretched human skin. I had witnessed him carrying four one-hundred-pound bags (two in each arm) of rice up a full flight of stairs from the restaurant basement to the kitchen. He was the only batter that I had ever pitched to in the restaurant parking lot, which generated a genuine fear in me that the baseball might be hit back at my increasingly fragile, feeling body. Howard, to my relief, usually swung upward to hit the ball high over my head. Unfortunately, the ball was frequently hit so far that I never was able to find it. My brother, Clif (a college scholarship defensive lineman), was the only other person to ever come close to hitting my pitches that far. Howard, at that time, was still a growing teenager.

Beneath Howard's Adonis-like appearance lay the burden of a young boy's heroic struggle against tragic circumstances. Howard's loving father had died when he was young. The trouble started when his mother remarried. The stepfather inflicted years of physical abuse upon the children including Howard and his two sisters. The children recognized that life in that household was untenable, and escape was the only option. At the age of fifteen, Howard led his sisters away from home and onto the streets, hoping to find some means of employment and support. Just as their situation turned desperate, Wing was made aware of Howard's plight and offered him a job at the restaurant, which included housing. This was a life-saving gesture that Howard would appreciate for years to come.

Wing and Suit Ying were not only sympathetic toward Howard, but they were also protective and kind. He was treated like another son in the family. Howard, in turn, returned their affections with loyalty, dedication, and love. Working for Wing and Suit Ying enabled Howard to establish a financial base, which he ultimately used to attend college, receive a graduate degree, and work for one of the world's largest engineering firms. His work to develop a fundamental component of computers for the space program evolved to its adaptation into the infrastructure of every modern computer chip. This work allowed Howard to retire by the age of forty. He currently lectures on national tours about financial issues and on specialized form of martial arts. During a recent telephone conversation, Howard described his beautiful and successful wife and brilliant children who have earned academic success at the highest levels. He also mentioned that he would never forget the helping hand, at a critical moment, from a caring and loving immigrant couple. Life may have steered toward a very different and disastrous direction for Howard and his siblings if not for the seemingly divine intervention of Wing and Suit Ying.

Howard's tenure at Mark's Chinese Restaurant also produced unexpected tangible and very practical benefits for Wing and Suit Ying. Suit Ying's successful handling of the numerous details associated with running the restaurant was greatly handicapped by her inability to drive. The manual skills of driving seemed manageable, but her lack of command of the written English language would never allow her to pass the written portion of the driver's test. Howard tried to help by explaining the entire driver's manual to Suit Ying. She could easily understand the rules of the road when translated, but the great challenge was the test itself, which was in English. There were also four different versions of the written test to prevent cheating. Howard, who was already a licensed driver, went to the Department of Motor Vehicles and sat for the written exam. During the exam, he noticed that the four versions of the test were given out at the same time to prevent copying from fellow examinees. The first person received the first version of the test, the second person in line received the second version, and so on. The cycle repeated after every fourth person. Howard took all four versions of the written exam by standing at a different position in line each time. He had memorized the answers for each exam, which consisted of a multiple choice format. The memorized answers were then given to Suit Ying who, in turn, also committed to memory the answers for all four exams. When Suit Ying was ready, she showed up at the motor vehicles department to take her written exam. She carefully observed her position in line when she was handed her test sheet and correctly anticipated which version was in her hands. Without knowing a word of what was written on the paper, Suit Ying received a perfect score and proceeded to earn her driver's license. There was no happier driver of a squeaking, clanging, belching old gray 1956 Buick Special than Suit Ying, thanks to Howard's ingenuity. Through several decades of driving, Suit Ying would wear out a list of American cars but would never be given a speeding ticket or have instigated an accident.

Christmas 1983

My mother was giddy with excitement as my wife and I drove up to the driveway with our sixteenth-month-old daughter in the baby seat locked into the backseat. She had prepared a vast array of food in the dining area and couldn't wait for us to enter the house because she so desperately wanted to hold her granddaughter again. My daughter was her usual curious self, twisting her head back and forth, wanting to observe everything about her new surroundings with the smiling, warm people who were so affectionate toward herself and her parents. I quietly sat at the dining table and picked at some of the long-forgotten pastries of my youth while observing my daughter flitting back and forth between my mother, with toys at a low coffee table, and my father who was gracefully drawing a mountain scenery with an Asian motif on a child's green chalkboard set up on a small easel. My parents were laughing and smiling without pause for about an hour when my daughter finally tired herself out a bit and settled down to more passive activities. My wife picked up my daughter for some dinner when my mother came to sit next to me.

"Dai dai ah, you make your father and me so happy by spending the Christmas holidays with us." She punctuated her feelings by picking up my left hand and holding it to her chest. "It is hard to imagine loving that daughter of yours more than how we feel inside our hearts. Your wife is also the most loving and kindhearted person I have ever seen. She is truly my daughter, a piece of my own heart. You've made this a very special Christmas for your father and me."

"Mahmee ah, we wouldn't think of celebrating Christmas without you and Baba," I said in a nearly rote manner. I was so busy with the demands of my own career that I failed to even consider that there would not be many more Christmases for us to share together. No one realized that there was a biological time bomb ticking in my mother's liver. In several years' time, Martin and Blaine's holiday standard song "Have Yourself a Merry Little Christmas" would no longer be mere shopping mall background music for me. The verse "Through the years we all will be together, if the Fates allow" will ring in my heart with a special tearful poignancy that I never would have anticipated.

I had glanced over at my father's recliner and realized that it was a different chair. In fact, it looked like a beautiful ornate cushioned antique.

"Mahmee ah, where did you get that new chair?"

"Dai dai ah, that old recliner that you kids gave us during your high-school years was completely worn out from use. Come to the backyard and see what else we have."

I walked to the back door and noticed a new professionally laid pad of bricks that made the old tool shed seem like a palace for garden tools.

"Mahmee ah, why do you spend money so extravagantly when you no longer have the restaurant, and both you and Baba are surviving with minimal-wage jobs?"

She whispered to me even though no one was nearby, almost as if I had brought up a forbidden topic. "We did not buy anything. These were gifts from the godfather."

I was immediately confused. What godfather? She didn't have a godfather. Who is she talking about?

My mother almost read my mind, because after a brief pause, she said, "Dai dai ah, not my godfather, but *the* godfather."

My parents had extended their kindness and generosity to everyone who walked through the restaurant doors. Their sincerity and integrity endeared them to so many people from all walks of life. They even garnered the trust of people from the criminal segments of society though I have never seen my parents prejudge individuals based upon their occupation. I had forgotten that my parents not only befriended powerful individuals from the legitimate infrastructure of society but also those that form the less legitimate but equally powerful elements. I do, however, remember occasional childhood summer days spent swimming in a private ornately decorated large in-ground pool followed by great, big, and joyously loud barbeques that included buckets of fresh iced cherrystone clams on the half shell and huge portions of the best of Italian cuisine against a background of Sinatra's classic melodies mingled with romantic operatic overtures and arias. The delicious memories of those warm, breezy times are also associated with my mother's reminder that those experiences took place at the godfather's private residence as an expression of his friendship, generosity, and respect for my parents. I only incurred the anger of our host on one occasion when I was too lazy to leave the pool to urinate. I believed that I was spared from any real consequences because cement boots did not come in a children's size.

My mother related to me that she and my father had recently spent some time at the godfather's residence. My mother was being entertained by the godfather's wife when my mother mentioned how attractive their living room recliner looked. It was an innocent comment that was mentioned mostly out of kindness. The conversation later turned toward the avocational activities that my mother enjoyed. She proceeded to describe her pleasure at gardening while only casually mentioning the dilapidated state of the tool shed, which mostly suffered from the lack of a proper foundation. The next day, a truck drove up to my parents' home and delivered the godfather's antique recliner to them. Another truck from an established construction firm then pulled up to the house and not only delivered a large pile of new bricks, but without prompting or explanation, the workers also meticulously, quickly, and quietly laid those bricks beneath the shed for a very firm and level foundation. None of the workers made much eye contact with my mother, and they all left without saying a word or presenting a bill for the bricks or their labor. I had learned throughout my childhood that the world works in many ways and along many different paths. I had also learned that many events occurred in my parents' lives as a direct and indirect consequence of their trust, integrity, tolerance, and nonjudgmental demeanor.

Be Good

I used to wonder how so many different types of people could find my parents to their liking. The everyday-working man and his family, the poor, the powerful, the criminals, the businessmen, the thieves, the firemen, the tractor-trailer drivers, the educated, the elitists, the politicians, the condescending lawyers, the TV stars, etc. all felt a bond with this immigrant Chinese couple who did not share any skills or common background with virtually anyone else other than other Chinese immigrants. Were my parents not already labeled as stereotypical Chinese restaurant workers (an occupation that is a close second to the other stereotype of the laundry)? Were my parents (and I) not already subjected to years of racial taunting and generalizations? How could they not be bitter? How could they continue to be positive and generous when others did not view them so kindly? Were they merely feigning goodwill as part of a master plan to manipulate a variety of different types of customers for economic self-benefit?

My mother provided some insight to my questions late one night when I was home for the weekend during my early college years. She had just returned home after an exhausting day and night at the restaurant. She greeted me with joy and never chastised me for slovenly lying on the couch while anesthetizing my cerebral cortex with late-night television. I immediately felt guilty for not relieving her at the restaurant earlier in the evening, but that thought never occurred to my mind, which was more preoccupied with teenage existential angst. My mother's tired, aging arthritic hands reached toward me to caress my hair. After a long moment, she gently held my hand and initiated a discussion.

"Dai dai ah, what is troubling you? You are frowning when you should be rejoicing during this exciting period of your life."

"Nothing's wrong, Mahmee. Why do you think something is wrong?" I was thinking that my mother would never understand and could definitely never offer me any useful insight, so why bother getting into a discussion with her? At the time, I didn't realize that I was suffering from the time-honored teenage delusion that my problems were unique and overwhelming while my insights and worldly observations were thoughts that had never before occurred to the minds of another human being in the history of mankind. (Whatta genius! I gotta remember to preserve my brain for future scientific research after I die.)

"My dear silly dai dai, how can I not sense your conflicts when you are not only from my flesh, but you are also part of my heart?"

With one simple sentence, my mother was able to lower all of my defenses. "Ahhhh. I just don't know where I fit in. The 'white establishment' sees me as Chinese first and last but never as an equal. Meanwhile, the other Chinese students at school reject and ridicule me because I am a *juk sing* [American-born Chinese or ABC] and therefore not really Chinese. I'm too Chinese for one group and too white for the other. How do I deal with *that*?"

She surprised me by answering my question with a question. "Dai dai, how do *you* see yourself?"

I looked at her with my all-too-familiar dumb look and emotionally blurted out, "I just view myself as myself."

My mother smiled without mocking me. Her eyes were slightly sad yet sympathetic. "Do you think the answer was always there in front of you but you failed to recognize it for what it is?"

This time, I was able to match my dumb expression with an even dumber prolonged silence. My lack of vocalization spoke volumes. I had no clue what she was driving at, and she would just have to tell me in plain language.

My mother continued, "Perhaps you are mixing two different issues. Let's separate them and deal with each independently even though both issues are intertwined. There is the problem of race/culture, and there is another problem of generalization. I would prefer to deal with the more important issue of generalization because it is more personal."

OK, she has gotten my attention. I sensed a lecture coming on, but this was one that I may really want to listen to. She is dog tired, sleep deprived, and hungry yet she looks to my emotional comfort before any of her own immediate needs. I had the temerity to think that my mother had nothing to offer me when she had been offering me everything all the time since I was born. Inwardly embarrassed at myself, I sat quietly and listened.

"When I asked you how you see yourself, you could have answered it in many ways. You answered very innocently and honestly, yet it also showed me that you have much insight, intuitive though it may be."

It was weird, but I felt like my mother just insulted me with a compliment.

"You said that you feel some difficulty fitting in with the Caucasian and Chinese elements of society. This difficulty arises only if you think of yourself as a category or part of a generalization. That generalization can be racial, cultural, or financial."

"But Mahmee ah, isn't it a normal human response to generalize or categorize? Wouldn't it be too cumbersome to deal in specifics with everything and everyone?"

"Ah, my silly dai dai, you are even generalizing in your thinking about generalization. Of course, it is natural to generalize. People have the capacity to think and behave in all different ways. Having the capacity does not mean that the expression of that ability is appropriate or correct in every situation. When it comes to human interactions, you must think of people as individuals and not as a group, race, or specific ethnicity."

I was stunned. This doesn't seem to make any sense. It was my mother who has been emphasizing my Chinese heritage since I was born. Is she now backtracking on all those years of indoctrination?

"I can read the confusion of your mind on your face. It is true that you are Chinese, and it is a very important part of that foundation which forms you, but your Chinese culture is only a part of you. It does not define you. It is part of your starting point but does not form your end point. You are more than just your culture. What you finally become as a person will be determined only by you and the choices that you make in life. If you choose to define yourself only as part of racial group, then that is all that you will be. You should and could be so much more. It is unfortunate that those Caucasians and Chinese who reject you have chosen to define themselves and others primarily by their race/culture because they made a deliberate decision to allow themselves to be limited by those very definitions. They have sadly chosen a defined category as an end point or goal to reach for. See yourself not as a member of a group, but see yourself and others as individuals. Your cultural grouping is only a small part of who you are. If you allow yourself to grow as an individual rather than be predefined by the characteristics of a category, then you will be fulfilled, unique, and far greater than the mere sum of your parts. You will also have taken full personal responsibility for your life and your actions. Only then can you begin to find real growth and satisfaction. Those who do not take this personal responsibility will always blame others for their own misfortune or lack of success and will never be able to perceive the right path to free themselves from their self-inflicted quagmire."

At this point, I felt an urge to take notes. I felt the truth of my mother's words resonating in my heart. It did not need the distraction of logical processing.

"My poor dai dai, you have felt the sting of prejudice from both sides—Caucasian and Chinese. That prejudice grows from others who think of you as a group and not as an individual. You are made to feel inadequate because you do not fulfill all of their criteria for either group, and so, you are excluded from their racial 'club.' You are troubled by this because you had unconsciously accepted their premise that a person is defined by their ethnic category, and you are then left to wonder which precise category you fit into. The answer, of course, is that you are a club of one just as we all are. Prejudice is a terrible thing, and I have personally witnessed horrible acts that grew from prejudice during World War II."

I felt a solemn silence because I was aware of the numerous strands of comments from many different family conversations that hinted a terrible experience during the war.

"Prejudice is common, but being common does not mean that it is good or acceptable. We are all capable of prejudice that grows from generalizations about people. That is why you must meet prejudice with understanding and compassion rather than anger. Being capable of prejudice, however, does not condone it. You must make the active choice of rejecting prejudice within yourself when dealing with people. It is a choice that many of the prejudiced would rather define as a natural and therefore a proper or excusable way of being instead of a willful decision. You are capable of good, evil, and all the indeterminate gradations in between. Your character will be defined by the choices that you make in the context of your capabilities."

My mother continued with a hint of sadness in her voice, which slowly faded to a softer tone, "Unfortunately, prejudice is everywhere because it is a part of life, but you don't have to choose to make it a part of your personal life. I know that you will continuously encounter it throughout your life. You will frequently be required to be twice as good in order to be considered just as good as Caucasians in this society. Life will undoubtedly be more difficult for you because of it. But take personal responsibility for your life rather than expending your energy blaming the rest of the world for your problems. If you have to be twice as good, then be twice as good. Succeed rather than succumb to the weakness of anger. Of course, you will feel a sense of injustice, but use that as a reminder for how not to treat others. Become a better person for it rather than allowing it to corrode your heart."

Her voice perked up now. "Your father and I have always treated every customer as an individual rather than a generalization based upon their background, occupation, or prior history. That is why we have gained not only their patronage but, more importantly, their friendship and respect. That is also why we have friends from literally every walk of life. As you know, a few of our relatives frown on our family's association with some people, particularly the less respected members of society. You have hopefully grown up to see how we live our lives by viewing people as individuals and judging others only on the basis of their character. Your great-grandfather learned this and taught me that valuable lesson. You will also hopefully learn to recognize that goodness and heroism are everywhere in life and, in fact, can frequently be found in the most unlikely places. You will also be able to see that some of the most judgmental and privileged people of society are substantially lacking as individuals despite their material wealth."

Now her voice really sparkled. "By the way, Dai dai, don't plan on doing anything during the weekends next month. I'm not sure of the precise date, but I was told that your father was just voted the Man of the Year. There will be a big dinner with hundreds of people, photographers, and a showy ceremony. It is very important for all of the family to be there." My mother then walked upstairs to go to sleep. She said she was too tired to talk anymore and left me to my own thoughts.

I was barely able to digest all that she told me, but I remember asking her more questions during the remainder of the weekend. Since then, I always consulted with my mother about practical matters as well as most of my personal growth questions. My mother, in turn, enjoyed the discussions and the emotional bonding from those interactions. I grew to depend on that bonding and very much enjoyed the mutual understanding. Of course, I knew that I was the greater beneficiary of our talks because it was definitely not an even exchange.

It would be years later before I would realize that my mother had jumpstarted my awakening process that evening with a startling psychological Socratic slap, but it was delivered with a gentle, loving, intellectual hand.

Politics

Life changed drastically after Wing and Suit Ying lost everything but the house. Utter financial desperation seemed a foregone conclusion as their meager resources would not last very long. Previous friends would no longer stop by the house or even call. The nearly palpable absence of people left the impression that Wing and Suit Ying carried an incurable contagious disease. Even many relatives maintained their distance. These were the same relatives who were more than willing to receive financial benefits when the business was thriving. They were also the first ones to show up at every annual holiday meal that Wing and Suit Ying put together at the restaurant for every relative during Thanksgiving.

Some of the more conspicuous absentee individuals, to my mind, were the politicians. Their absence should have been anticipated by anyone over the age of one. Their years, however, of parasitic benefit from my father, coupled with their nonstop singing of hyperbolic praises to him, contrasts so sharply with their total lack of even rudimentary courtesy after my parents' fall that they seemed like caricatures of themselves. Amazingly, my parents merely smiled and knowingly nodded whenever I would bring up this topic. They told me that they held no hard feelings whatsoever.

I asked my father, "Baba ah, why are you not more upset that the politicians, whom you have helped so much in the past, now ignore you in your time of need?"

"Dai dai ah, don't be so naïve. That is the nature of politicians. They actually showed no interest in me during the initial years of the restaurant. We were just considered another island of second-class citizens bringing down the value of the neighborhood."

"Baba ah, how is it that the politicians tried to constantly cultivate your favor? I remember all those trips to Washington DC, the banquets at the Capitol, and even meandering through the empty congressional hearing rooms. Why did they change toward you?"

"Dai dai, what changed were the imaginary lines on the political map. The lines demarcating the voting district for Staten Island expanded because of its relatively low population during the time period prior to the rush to inhabit the island. The new lines stretched north to include the southern portion of Manhattan. New York's Chinatown district also happened to be included in that area. Remember that Chinatown is a very heavily populated area with many, many voters. A politician could literally lose the votes on Staten Island but would still win the election if he won in the Chinatown district because of the vastly greater number of voters in Chinatown."

I finally understood when my father connected most of the dots for me. The last dot was my father. He was so highly respected in Chinatown that his discreet verbal endorsement of a particular candidate to strategic individuals would spread throughout Chinatown and virtually guarantee a huge number of votes going toward that candidate. I thought this was most ironic because the candidates were always Caucasian, and the important bloc of voters were Chinese. Many of the Chinese voters were presumably not only unfamiliar with the candidate but probably also could not even speak English. Armed with only his honor, integrity, intellect, and character, my father became a very powerful man. The more I thought about it, the more impressed I was with my father. I had always loved and honored him because he was my father. Now I was awed by his abilities as a man. It's amazing how my dad improved as I got older.

"But Baba ah, the politicians are not here to help you now. You got nothing out of the years of helping them."

"Dai dai ah, you are still so young [meaning I still don't get it]. The politicians have been, are, and will always be like that. They only work for their own political gain. I was not expecting anything for myself. I was not helping them but helping the people of Staten Island and Chinatown. I only endorsed the best candidates that could help the voters. I was lucky enough to be in a position to ensure that the best was done for most people. It would have been naïve and also dishonorable to have expected personal gain. If I had received some type of obvious reward or public recognition, then I would forever lose the trust that people have in me. Genuine respect and trust are not given away lightly by people and are more valuable and irreplaceable than money."

Very early (5:30 a.m.) the next morning, my father returned to work as a minimal-wage mail carrier for a Wall Street investment firm. Several hours after that, my mother went back to work as an even more minimal-minimum-wage seamstress in a local clothing factory. These jobs were better than their original occupations when they first arrived in this country, but to my emotional eye, they were too similar in tone and clearly undeserving of being inflicted on these two wonderful people. This was, however, clearly my own interpretation because my father always looked forward to work with a cheerful attitude, and my mother greatly enjoyed the camaraderie in the clothing factory. They did not view their current employment as insults like I did. Their lives have, in a sense, come full circle, and they met life with the same positive and optimistic attitude. I could not have anticipated that my parents would continue to contribute to the lives of many new people who would enter their lives in the years to come.

Toilets, Roaches, and
Warm Hugs

For Wing and Suit Ying, good humor ranks with good food as one of the few true pleasures of life. Even during their dark hours, when financial survival was questionable, they both found humor in everyday life. Guests and relatives who visited the house were always treated to a delicious meal punctuated by laughter and happy feelings. To the casual observer, the dinnertime scene at the Mark residence could be interpreted as coarse, loud, and unsophisticated. A more careful observation of the details, however, would reveal delicately spiced, perfectly cooked selections of the freshest meats and fishes on a table surrounded by people from a diversified background sharing good friendships and warmth with each other. The loud speech does not reflect a lack of sophistication but rather a verbal performance by the speaker to welcome and elevate the guests while they try to match it with their own highly voluminous show of gratitude and humility; thus, humor was part of life for Wing and Suit Ying from the grimy projects to quiet suburban life as well as from the dusty sweatshop to the popular restaurant in New York.

Wing always expressed good-natured humor frequently with an inwardly directed laugh at himself and life. This type of humor, coupled with his personality, made him very popular and frequently the focus of attention with other adults. His humor with his children was usually a joyous expression of affection. I can remember many giggle-filled horsey rides on his back and scary-tilting rides on his shoulders. He would usually pretend to feel pain and hurt to defuse my bad moods and create a smile on my face.

Suit Ying honed a slightly offbeat type of humor during her early years in this country because of her inability to speak English. The incomprehensible nature of the language forced her to focus on the nonverbal aspects of the communication and the person. She was able to distill a surprising amount of information about a person's character and intent by simply observing their body movements, forms of gestures, and tone of voice. Her keen powers of observation and analysis allowed her to develop a sharp (frequently borderline wicked) ability to parody unsuspecting individuals. In addition, her mixtures of caricaturized, imitative physical gestures with comedic Chinese voiceovers and whispered piercing editorial comments have frequently given me sidesplitting laughter that could last for hours. The power of her humor was magnified by its utter contrast with her usually reserved presentation of self in everyday life as a polite and unassuming lady. I seem to have inherited part of my mother's unusual sense of humor though I clearly lack her skillful execution. I usually have to substitute sarcasm for her more natural wit, causing me to sound negative and biting while my mother was funny and entertaining.

I remember shopping for cloth with my mother on the Lower East Side of Manhattan as a little boy. My mother always made our clothes because it was quite a bit cheaper since the labor was her own, and she could always bargain for the lowest prices for the material. There was a store on Catherine Street, which sold a large variety of different colored and textured bolts of cloth, that my mother frequented, and I could tell by the exasperated sigh upon entering the store that the Italian shop owner was overly accustomed to the negotiating battles with my mother. My mother steeled herself for a prolonged verbal siege against the merchant after making her mental choice of color, texture, and quantity. When the owner refused to lower his price, my mother turned in frustration to look at me with a plastic smile while she subtly mimicked the man's bushy eyebrow movements and stubbornness. In barely audible Chinese, my mother muttered an unflattering comment about the man's personal hygiene and probable lack of dietary roughage accounting for his rude behavior. This caught me by surprise, but as the man walked by me, the breeze he generated verified my mother's description of his vile odors. When I started to laugh, my mother quickly picked me up and buried my face into her chest to muffle my response. Both of us laughed all the way back to the apartment even though my mother paid the slightly higher price for the cloth.

My mother also used humor to dispel my fears. One such fear involved cockroaches, which constantly infested our apartment in the projects despite repeated and liberal applications of toxic insecticides. Very few experiences can be more effective at disrupting a six-year-old boy's sleep than snuggling under the covers at night and slipping his hands under the pillow only to be momentarily frozen by the feel of a crawling nest of cockroaches scurrying around his fingers and up his arm. That sensation would frequently deliver a startling shock of adrenaline to my nervous system, causing me to jump out of bed and turn on the lights while vigorously trying to shake my hand free of the paralyzingly frightful creatures that are about one thousand times smaller than me. This very action would, in turn, have the unnerving effect of causing all the roaches to dart about more quickly as they tried to scamper out of the light and into the darker crevices of the bed. My mother had the uncanny ability to make light of the whole alarming experience and create a game of finding all the cockroaches that had the nerve to try to sleep on my bed. We certainly administered a scolding that was so thorough that the roaches would assuredly be too ashamed to come back that night. After helping me to eliminate all the cockroaches from my bed (including a careful inspection under the mattress), I was able to sleep in full confidence that none of the creepy, crawling, antennae-moving, prehistoric creatures would try to crawl up into my nose, my mouth, or my ears as I slept. It was difficult to feel any more anxiety after a warm, comforting embrace from my mother that reassured me that I was protected, and all was well with the world.

My mother's background in health care and her early years spent in a culturally rich yet poorly infrastructured country such as China caused her to be quite vigilant and insistent about proper personal hygiene. She would usually use humor to punctuate her many lessons to me regarding cleanliness. That humor was an effective teaching tool but may have also had the unintended side effect of causing my childish mind to overemphasize the more trivial details of personal care. I believe she was the person inadvertently responsible for making me aware of (or fixated on) the unpleasantly wet and cold tactile droplets on my buttocks from the rebound splash of repugnant toilet water that accompanied the discharge of large plopping stools during bowel movements. That awareness spawned a tendency that motivated me to avoid the use of public toilets and bathrooms belonging to people with dubious personal hygiene.

We may have been relatively poor with seemingly limited options during our time on the Lower East Side, but I never felt poor or deprived because my family's vibrant attitude toward life would not allow it. In fact, my memories of that time period still ring with a tangible warmth punctuated by my father's beaming smile, my mother's sparkling voice, my brother's cuddly stomach, and my sister's gentle eyes. It is only now when I revisit Manhattan's Lower East Side without my family that I can recognize the depressing gray atmosphere and deep physical despair of the projects.

Tours

I was lying in bed and staring out of the window in the very early-morning hours just as the sky faintly lightened, enough to enable me to see the outline of the adjacent roofs and chimneys of the surrounding buildings. The sun had not yet peeped over the horizon on this quaint yet touristy city in the Loire Valley of France. I had some difficulty sleeping for an entire night in an uninterrupted fashion, but it has been like that for me for the past fourteen years. Some would say that I am firmly entrenched in the depths of my middle age and have started to sprout the early symptoms of the elderly. I know, however, the deeper truth for my disturbed slumber, and its roots are connected to my parents and their passing from this life. I've managed to hang on, though just barely, because of the comforting love of the three people sleeping with me in this hotel room. My wife and daughter are sleeping in one bed while my son and I are using the other. The windows were open all night because of the uncharacteristic stifling heat for that time of year in this part of the country. Besides this charming bed-and-breakfast hotel, completely and efficiently run by a very friendly local French couple, cannot afford the luxury of air-conditioning. I can barely see their outlines in the darkened room, but I thank God for the three resting individuals in the room with me. Without them, I could have easily degenerated into a self-centered, pleasure-seeking philistine who, over time, would merely grow older without getting any better. This would have doomed me to join the minions seeking an elusively inappropriate perpetual youth instead of welcoming the peace and enlightenment of age. I could also have adopted the airs of a cultural dilettante who could provide seemingly eloquent lip service to society's ideas without possessing even the tiniest morsel of understanding, substance, value, meaning, and fulfillment.

I looked over at my wife, who was engaged in her recent sleeping habit of quietly inhaling through her nostrils while making a slight puttering noise with her lips during exhalation. She is usually very deeply asleep during this portion of her nightly ritual, which I find very endearing. I looked at her and wondered how I can be so fortunate to share my life with her. I could remember feeling as if I had been holding my breath my whole life waiting for her to come into my life. How is it that she enables me to feel like I am the center of the world even though everyday life tells me otherwise? Throughout the decades of our marriage, she had never kept a mental record of my innumerable wrongs and always listened to me with an attentive ear even as I was becoming bored by my own repetitive verbal ramblings. Her unfailing love has allowed me to sleep with dreams and hope while awakening from my slumber feeling like a man without faults. She never asks for anything and consistently gives me all of herself. She can listen without judgment and speak with words that resonate from the heart when I am in need of advice but am too proud to ask and too clouded by pettiness. Love and comfort palpably radiate from her every gesture. I feel most fortunate to be the choice of her life's efforts, but I am truly blessed because she has given the priceless gift of enabling this limited man to love in an unlimited way. I look over at her quietly sleeping form and am just thankful for the privilege of being her husband.

My two children have become an admirable young woman and man. Where have the years gone? They are still cuddly toddlers to my mind's eye even though their intellect, compassion, and physical prowess have long exceeded mine. They may not realize that my first impulse is to hold and hug them every time I see them, be it first thing in the morning or when they come home for the holidays. I only refrain myself to spare them the embarrassment and protect myself from permanent physical injury because they are no longer small enough for a nightly "horsey" ride on my back. I often wonder how my children can exert this profound emotional effect on me. Their very existence transformed me into a person whose life is filled with magic. They have made me a father.

My daughter is sleeping on her stomach, with a wisp of hair covering her face. She held this same posture when I used to stare at her for long moments after she was asleep in her crib. It seems to me that she is deeply asleep, dreaming about the idealism, self-discovery, and love that motivate her awake inner world. She had been living in southwestern France for the past six months prior to the rest of the family joining to meet her for the return home. I've discovered that all those who came in contact with her have developed strong positive connections with her. People here, as they do in the States, seem to readily respond to her compassion and sincerity. She is a remarkable young woman whose dancing is as enchanting as her personality. It is a personality that also allows her to exercise a piercing intellect with a gentle touch that does not threaten the insecure. Her attraction toward the aesthetics and idealism of the arts, literature, and languages is a part of her joy in life. That very joy is infectious and visibly affects the world around her. I've often wondered how she had developed into such a wonderful person without being tainted by my all-too-frequent moods of cynicism and sarcasm. My little girl, who slid across the floor in her moon chair, pulled herself upright on the playpen netting, and closed her eyes in exhilaration (when I threw her up in the air in the pool), had more loving resources than I was able to inadvertently exhaust. Her sensitive adolescent mind that I fed with morning cups of tea and sliced raisin toast with butter evolved faster than I could follow. She may have thought that I initiated long talks on psychology, theology, and philosophy with her during the morning drive to school to further stimulate her questing intellect, but I really did it for the more selfish purpose of needing the love and emotional bonding with my firstborn child.

I note with irony that my son is sleeping on the very edge of the mattress of the bed that we are sharing. This is quite a contrast to when we slept together during vacations when he was much younger. He used to be what I silently described as a nocturnal gyroscope in the form of a small human being. He could start off the night asleep on his back, progress to using my stomach as his pillow, then drape his leg across my chest, face the complete opposite direction, and return to a right sided-up position while breathing on my neck. I used to be afraid to move during the night for fear of waking him. It was an unnecessary fear because he always managed to sleep soundly and awaken well rested and impatient for breakfast. I, on the other hand, faced the beginning of another vacation day, clouded with fatigue and desperate for a cup of coffee.

Over the years, my son had developed into a mature, caring, and sincere young man who is quite protective of me. In fact, he slept the whole night without moving a muscle on the edge of the bed to create more room for his overweight father. In consideration for him, I had also slept on the edge but on the opposite side of the mattress. This had the amusing net effect of creating a sizable space between us that neither one took advantage of. This is so typical for the wonderful young man he has become. This same compassion led to his spending the previous summer digging latrines in the impoverished mountainous countryside of the Dominican Republic to significantly improve their public-health infrastructure. He returned looking a bit gaunt, having continued to work despite being ill, yet he would have been willing to return in a heartbeat. He is just at the beginning of his path toward self-discovery, but he already exudes integrity, respect, and sympathy. His conspicuous lack of flagrant self-centeredness is atypical for his age and is one reason why others are drawn to him as a leader on the athletic field. His quick intellect is strongly enabling, but it is also coupled with a silent but deeply passionate side that peeks through in the arts. He is a man of virtue, charity, and gravitas: clearly a contributor to the world around him.

I look at my two children and can only be thankful that I have been allowed to be their father. My heart resonates twice because they have accepted and welcomed me in that role.

Their grandmother, Suit Ying, would have been very proud.

That pride, however, would have been more than just grandmotherly pride but would reflect a deeper theme that she often repeated to me when I was my children's age.

Arts

I used to wonder what made my mother proud of me. My teenage mind defined parental pride only in the context of achievements. In other words, parental pride could only be parceled out like Pavlovian reinforcement for correct or outstanding behavior. This outcome-based or quantitative view of the world seemed logical but was a deeply unsatisfying and incomplete explanation of my daily experience of life. My mother's interactions with me were always a deep communication from heart to heart rather than just mind to mind. Her words were more than mere ideas and insights to be shared. They were cradled within the rich textures of the emotional blanket that bundled the ideas. That emotional blanket was woven from her choice of phrases, inflection of voice, soft gestures, comforting touch, and always kind eyes. She not only taught me about life, but she also bestowed me with her hopes and dreams. This provided me with a daily source of psychological and spiritual sustenance that could only be felt, never measured.

This cognitive dissonance urged me to better define my mother's parental pride. I guess I also needed to know if her feelings were genuine or merely gratuitous. After all, I was now old enough to realize that I was not the center of the world: lots of people run faster than me, my strikeouts exceed my base hits, girls don't even know I exist, and my grades can only be generously described as average. I only need to look at my older brother and sister to expose all of my inadequacies in every category of life using any standard of measure.

My mother was busy washing and chopping some delicious weedlike Chinese vegetables (*tung ho*), which she had picked from our backyard garden during a brief break from the restaurant, when I startled her by blurting the beginnings of a tangential conversation.

"Mahmee ah, does it bother you that I am not attending an Ivy League college like the children of so many of your proud friends and relatives?"

"Dai dai ah, why do think that bothers me?"

"Well, my not getting into one of those schools means that I am not as smart as the other children."

"So you think that I am less proud of you for not getting into those schools and I would, therefore, be more proud of you if you had gotten in? Is that what you are saying?"

Every time she succinctly summarizes what I say better than the way that I've just said it makes me feel like the guy who realizes he has just stepped on a land mine the split second before it explodes.

"My dear dai dai, you will understand better when you have your own children. My feelings toward my children are not so shallow as to be based upon outward achievements such as gaining acceptance to the 'top' schools."

My mother put down the large Chinese cleaver, wiped her hands, and walked over to the small round table where I was sitting.

She placed her hands on my shoulders and gently sniffed at my hair like she always does. Then she sat down beside me while gently stroking my forearm.

"Dai dai ah, I want to tell you so many things, but I especially wish that your great-grandfather were still alive so that you could benefit from him as I did. Let me first tell you that I believe that many people, including most of my friends and relatives, have silly notions about schools. They tend to think that getting into the Ivy League schools is a form of a contest. Those who get in are the winners, and those who don't are the losers. So getting in becomes the goal rather than the means to a goal. I think that most believe that merely having a degree from those institutions will gain their children acceptance into and access to the glory and inner power structure of America. As my grandfather would say, this is delusional and shallow thinking. When getting into an Ivy League school is a person's only priority, that person will often fail to get educated. 'Education,' in the true sense of the word [to open, awaken or draw out], can only come from within. An institution cannot do it for a person. A school can only provide either a compatible or incompatible environment. That type of environment for learning is independent of the perceived prestige of the school. It is instead an individual experience that is only temporarily related to the chance intersection of a particular student's psychological makeup with the teachers/students of a particular school. That fortuitous overlap of common need and nurturing environment can occur anywhere with anyone at any institution if the match-up is compatible. For instance, Dai dai, how many relatives have you known who attended the top universities and remain internally unaltered by their tenure there? In fact, how many of those are still waiting for and expecting good things to happen to their lives merely because they have a degree from those schools?"

I paused and considered my many brilliant relatives. There were many who fit my mother's description.

"Dai dai ah, I think you know what I am saying. School is not like a board game to be won. You don't win by working the system to your success. School is also not a place to merely show off the cleverness and skill that you already possess. It should be, instead, a place to cultivate the maturity, insight, and wisdom that you don't have but hope to possess."

She continued, "Your great-grandfather would have told you that school is a sacred place of contemplation and learning and not a place for job training. He always told me that I should learn merely for the integrity of learning. Similarly, I should work for the integrity of work. He used to tell me to learn for the sake of learning and not as a means to make money. Quite the contrary, money should be made so that learning can occur. Without education and the accompanied personal development, a person is merely a wild animal though he can be a very wealthy animal wallowing in material goods. A degree should signify that the holder possesses right mindedness, right speech, and right actions. This learned person would possess personal values yet remain open minded to the differences within others without feeling threatened or compromising his own values. He would understand the propriety of polite behavior but still understand the burdensome anxiety that impedes the enlightenment of the rude. This person would also possess the skills and potential to fit into a wide spectrum of society even as he is actively being excluded from certain segments of that very society due to ignorance and prejudice."

At this point, I was silent for longer than a moment. I not only appreciate this insight, but I also realized the deep rich traditions of my family history. Those traditions are not rooted in rituals or styles of dress but rather in the intangible but more remarkable tapestry of values, insight, and personal development. Somehow, it felt comforting to know the direction of my ancestors. It provided me with a sense of a moral compass to direct my superficially marked different life on the other side of the world. It would also be a legacy that I could leave for my children after me.

I wasn't sure if my mother had answered my original question but I, nonetheless, proceeded to asked her another question. "So Mahmee ah, you are not disappointed that my interests lie more in the direction of the arts and social sciences?" I asked this knowing fully well that my mother had been hearing for years how the sciences and engineering were the only "real" or substantive areas to study in college. After all, these are the only subjects that require objectively measurable intelligence. These areas will also lead to well-paying positions after college.

"Dai dai ah, I will return to what my grandfather taught me. The arts and sciences are only different sides of the same coin. You must be familiar with both to be complete, yet an emphasis on one does not diminish the other."

My mother paused to gather her thoughts and continued, "What is the purpose of any society? Is it to make money? What is the purpose of money? Is it still to make more money? Build tall buildings? Beat down your competition? Sensual gratification? What is the point of academic accomplishments? Collect another trophy diploma for your wall? Self-glorification? Prove your intellectual superiority? What is the ultimate point of anything? Do you care about anything other than yourself?

"I learned from your great-grandfather that all the arts and the sciences attempt to discover the truth, the truth that is within ourselves and all around us in the universe. Money and accomplishments are hollow without enabling the continued search for truth and the pursuit of self-discovery and artistic expression. The arts and the social sciences are part of that process. I couldn't be happier that you are pursuing your interests in these areas because that is why your father and I work so hard. We slave away in the restaurant so that you don't have to. We slave away so that you can reap the fruits of what money is able to provide in the world. You are fulfilling what we want for you. If you, instead, wanted to continue working in the restaurant solely to make the type of money that your father earns, then I would be disappointed because you would have wasted those very opportunities that we worked so hard to obtain.

"So you see, Dai dai, I am proud of you not because of your outward achievements but because of your inward development. Your very act today to seek me out and address this line of thought speaks volumes about your character. This is a much higher and a much more valuable accomplishment than any acceptance letter from a school."

Twelve years later, I would mentally revisit this conversation with my mother. At that time, I would be developing an unanticipated and unlikely scientific career. As I walked through the hallowed corridors of one of the oldest Ivy League institutions in America, I would be totally unimpressed by the institution's name and only focused upon the truths that I could discover. I did not harbor any expectations of secondary gain from my association with this institution. My only expectations were directed at myself and my integrity.

3-J's

To this day, I still get the urge to pick up the telephone every day between 10:30 and 11:30 a.m. when I am at work. This was the time period when I used to call my mother every day even though I was halfway across the country from where she lived. I also knew that she would usually be waiting by the phone, anxious for my call. I developed the habit of calling her, even for a brief five-minute chat, during those dark years after she and my father had lost the restaurant and the entirety of their hard-earned financial fortune. Those calls took on an entirely different emotional context after she was diagnosed with liver cancer years later. During the first year after her death, the late mornings continued to evoke emotional reflexes both painful and nostalgic. It was not unusual for me to seek the temporary peace that comes from the physical isolation behind the locked door of my office. The concrete walls, however, were insufficient to deter the tears that would discover my hidden heart and blur my vision.

After the discovery of her cancer's malignancy, my mother used to thank me at the end of every one of those telephone conversations. She explained that the conversations meant the world to her, no matter how brief. I used to ritualistically ask how she was feeling, and she would ritualistically reply that she was constantly fatigued but happy now that I was talking with her. Tears would well through her voice toward the end of every conversation when she would add, "Dai dai ah, my daily talks with you deeply satisfy my spirit even though there is no hope for me. You are the heart from my heart. Your every call is reaffirming to me. I know you must live your life, and I wouldn't have it any other way. I am just glad that you remember and care. My life is now complete and fulfilled." Those words would crush me during the last few years of her life because I was a physician, and I couldn't help her. My own mother, whose unfaltering love sustained and nurtured me, was beyond my help. I continued to be astounded that she found comfort in my daily dose of inadequate words delivered by an impersonal electronic technology. Her words always managed to reach beyond the telephone receiver to grab my heart.

Nowadays, I still glance at the phone in the late mornings. I also look around my office at all the trappings of the academic life. The books, official-sounding memos, schedules, research proposals, and scattered lecture materials create the façade of a life busy with important activity. I even sporadically glance at a dusty old makeshift award given to me years ago as the faculty member who heaped the most abuse during the academic year on the residents and fellows who were training within my department. After dealing out the assignments to the residents and fellows under my direction for that day, I frequently make time during the late mornings to retreat to my office. I look around and can easily remember how it all got to be this way. I am also filled with regret for no longer being able to share this with my mother via the usually late-morning telephone calls.

I remember being home during a crisp fall evening filled with some degree of anxiety about an idea that I wanted to present to my parents. Business was slow in the restaurant, and my father suggested that my mother and I accompany him to his friend's restaurant, appropriately named, "3-J's." I believe the three owners were relatives, perhaps brothers, who were named Jay, Jay, and Jay (or perhaps it was John, Joe, and Jimmy). Only in Staten Island could such things happen, I thought to myself. It was a modest-sized restaurant that was decorated with the typical Italian motif popular during the early 1970s. Actually, I couldn't quite tell whether the décor was more of a reflection of Italian culture or the '70s. Most of America seemed caught in transition between hippie haze and disco cool. It was not uncommon, during that time period, for some establishments to have waitresses dressed as the whole Mother Earth while trying not to bump their heads on the gaudy, reflective ball hanging from the ceiling. The cooks exuded pride in the strong natural odors of their hippie (nonexistent) hygiene while the bartender looked at you with the sloped stare and coiffed hair of a fat middle-aged man stuffed into a tight white open-collared shirt, exposing the heavy gold chain around his neck. This particular restaurant was different because the workers were businesslike and attired in a neat but attractive style. As usual, the owner greeted my father with open arms and a hug, much like in every restaurant that we patronized. My father would shout "*cugino!*" and engage in a beaming cheerful banter with the owner for several minutes before we were shown to our table. Menus were discarded as unnecessary because the owner would insist on ordering for us. The food was frequently a nonstop parade of off-the-menu, delicious Italian delicacies that could sustain us for a week. This particular culinary experience at the 3-J's was no different.

While halfway through the meal, I paused to assess my parents' mood and decided to dive right in and broach a topic that would have profound ramifications. I mentioned that I was halfway through college and had already completed the requirements for my major area of study. The past two years had been spent immersed in Freud, Erickson, Jung, Frankl, Piaget, and Skinner. They probably believed that I was going to announce my intention to apply to graduate school in the same area. I, instead, surprised them by telling them that I wanted to change my area of study. I could tell by the look on my father's face that he was set to lecture me on the cost of my indecisiveness. Before either of my parents could speak, I continued by saying that I realized that I am just an average student but that I wanted to attempt a radically different direction that would be excruciatingly long and probably doomed to failure after years of study. I wanted to go to medical school. I would still complete college in four years, but it would require my taking courses every summer and filling my regular schedule with an unreasonable (or irrational) burden of the highly competitive required courses. My time would be completely filled, and my odds of success would be remote, but I wanted to try. I fully acknowledged that I had never before demonstrated any interest or aptitude for the rigors of medical study. I also accepted that this course of action can be easily viewed as foolish and doomed to end in ego-crushing failure. If a miracle would occur and I managed to perform well and gain acceptance to a medical school, then it would be followed by the horrific burden of a prolonged financial drain because of the training that would not end until I've become a middle-aged adult. In other words, my reward for achieving the impossible would be an extra helping of academic and financial punishment. During all this time with no guarantee of success, I would require my parents' financial support—bottom line.

I think my parents stopped chewing during my brief monologue. Their shock, however, was one of joy rather than recrimination. They both mentioned that their financial support of my seemingly unpromising gamble was assured, and they were proud of my honorable intentions. My mother did mention the obvious; that is, I would have to prove myself worthy of the noble profession of medicine. I would be attempting to participate in a process that is far greater than me and that the attempt should not be violated by cheap motivations of self-aggrandizement. She wanted to be sure that I was doing it for the right reason—to honor the field. There is, then, no disgrace in failure.

One factor that no one anticipated was my parents' total financial ruin during my early years of medical school. The financial burden of medical school, therefore, became completely my own. I think my parents always felt a sense of regret for being unable to fulfill their promise of financial support for my training. I, on the other hand, felt proud to shoulder my own financial responsibilities rather than adding to the undeserved troubles of two wonderful people. They never discouraged me despite the irrational nature of my plans. They never mocked my intentions or attempted to diminish my self-confidence. They were only proud that their son chose to try to contribute to their vision of America. I believe my great-grandfather would have cracked a small smile on his stern-looking face.

There is never any doubt in my mind that the plaques on my wall, invited lectures given nationally and internationally, and clinical insights that help patients were and are possible only because I am standing on the shoulders of my parents.

Music

Suit Ying never gave up hope or a sense of idealism during her years in America. This was true even during the more difficult early period when money was extremely tight and the financial demands were great. The needs of her family back in China only magnified her sense of guilt as well as burden. The guilt grew from her decision to pare back on the material goods of her own immediate family in order to regularly send some money, no matter how seemingly trivial, to China. There was one aspect of life, however, that she refused to compromise even though it came at great financial cost for that time period. That aspect was culture and artistic self-expression, which came in the specific form of music.

I slowly recognized the depth of my mother's conviction and passion regarding this topic years later when the family was already doing well in the restaurant business. I remember stopping by the restaurant after a typical high-school day and sitting in the customary booth just in front and to the left of the bar. I was sipping some piping hot vegetable (*tung ho*) soup with small chunks of tofu mixed with several scoops of cooked rice on the bottom. I thought that was a meal for a king because it always produced a richly satisfying feeling without the bulk and eventual nausea of greasy meats. It was my comfort food. That particular vegetable only grew during a short period of the late summer and early fall, so I tended to savor every drop in my bowl. While I was luxuriating in the warmth and aroma of the *tung ho* soup, my mother took the opportunity to sit opposite me while she just watched me eat with a slight maternal smile on her eyes and lips. After a while, she spoke up. I, of course, would filter her words through my coarse-teenaged psychotic mindset and interpret the words as nagging.

My mother would say, "Don't forget to practice your piano tonight after you get done with your homework."

I did my usual grumbling through a mouthful of food. I was annoyed that I couldn't even have ten undisturbed minutes to enjoy a nice bowl of soup without being hassled about assignments. I was beginning to detest and resent piano, so I decided to skillfully rebel by questioning my mother. "Mahmee ah, I have quite a bit of homework tonight, and I have to keep up with my training program for sports, so I don't know if there will be enough time for piano; besides, why does piano matter so much? It's not as if I will ever be a concert pianist. In fact, I am probably the most inept of all the family's friends and relatives who play piano."

I think I hit a nerve because my mother's kind eye lost that benevolent aura and looked at me with a steely stare. Yikes! My mother has multiple personalities, and I must be speaking to the evil mahmee now. Her voice grew in volume when she said, "You of all people should know better. Didn't you ever wonder why we made the grossly extravagant purchase of a piano when we had so little money during our time in the projects? Are you that dense?"

I was too big to crawl under that table, so I thought the wisest choice was to remain silent and limit the damage. I just waited for my mother to continue because I could tell that she was going to explain everything to me one bitter morsel at a time.

"Do you really think that your mother views music as a form of job training for a professional career as a musician? Perhaps you even think that your mother is so shallow that I would have you and your brother and sister learn to play the piano only to show off how superior they are to other children?"

I reminded myself to remain silent and not to move a muscle on my face.

Her voice became less strident when she continued, "Why do you think your father and I struggled so hard for so long? If it was only to provide you with money and material goods, then it would not be worth it. Our children would only grow up to be spoiled brats. You should know, if not before then now, that the whole point of struggle and work and money is to provide the opportunity for personal enrichment. That personal development comes from engagement with the arts and music. In the world of music, the piano can be considered a universal instrument and a good starting point for any type of music. You don't have to play well. You just have to play. The process of playing and not the end performance is the point of it all. The appreciations for melody, rhythm, and structure are only the tools for self-expression, which is so important for every individual. Artistic self-expression, no matter the quality, is as necessary for life as breathing. That type of self-expression is not for public consumption or commercial benefit but to develop and maintain the integrity of yourself. The self that I am referring to is not the physical person that you see in the mirror but the real self that is in your mind and your heart. That is the most important part of you. It is the part that is the most difficult to understand and cultivate, yet it is the most valuable component because it defines you and gives meaning to your life. Finding an outlet for your inner self, therefore, is essential. Finding an artistic outlet for it is divine. It allows you to momentarily raise yourself above the mundane reality of existence. When that happens, a person will be capable of hope, idealism, and charity. Many people who are not given the opportunity for that type of growth or are opaque to its real value when they possess those opportunities are frequently doomed to a life centered on material accumulation, selfish pleasure seeking, and petty jealousies."

My mother had a momentary faraway look in her eyes but continued, "When we lived in the projects, I insisted on having a piano because it was a symbol of hope despite our surroundings. For me it was a hope for my children that they will ultimately find benefit from our struggles. I refused to believe that my children will not realize the most important reasons for living and working. I refused to have our poverty reduce my children to a shallow and unfulfilling life even though that life can be financially successful. Having a means of self-expression would open the door for a whole world of other wonderful possibilities that would otherwise be shut out of your life. Music would enable you to feel emotions in a way that would be difficult, if not impossible. This, in turn, would enable my children to explore their potential to love, to sympathize, to cry in joy, and to care. They would feel a sense of both deep personal development and attachment to a process that is far greater than themselves. It would be like having the awareness to look up at the starry night sky and feeling both inwardly blessed as well as outwardly small and awestruck.

"So, Dai dai, don't you ever dare question why I made you take piano lessons and forced you to practice all these years. It is one of the few activities that truly makes you a human being."

When she mentioned that, I immediately thought back to those very early years in the projects. My mother would monitor my piano practice while we both ignored the irritated banging on the wall by the older family who lived in the adjacent apartment. I remember her listening to me while stringing the beads that would bring a few coins per string. She would make me practice each brief finger exercise five times before I could be excused. She would keep count. At times I noticed that she would nod off to sleep as I played. I would usually try to slink away to play, but she would invariably awaken as soon as I moved even a half of a buttock off the piano bench. I would also realize in the years that followed that my mother took advantage of my inability to count during my first year or so of piano lessons. She frequently kept repeating the count at three and four without ever reaching five before my fingers and attention span were exhausted.

Years of piano lessons did very little to improve my digital dexterity. This flaw is probably not congenital but rather the result of all the times I banged my head into the small living-room end table, trying to imitate the bulls that I saw on the cartoons during Saturday mornings. Everything my mother told me, however, did come to pass despite my physical limitations. Music changed my life. It created a place within me that is always beautiful. It is a place that no one can touch, damage, or ever take away. Piano playing, therefore, is much more than just a physical skill. The superficial observer will only see the amateurish clanking of a marginal player, but I do not hear my misplayed keys or clumsy inaccurate rhythms. My playing creates inner moments where life feels wonderful. Music, as my mahmee tried to tell me so many years ago, was just a small part of the larger mosaic that she wanted to create for me. It was and is a mosaic that spells hope. It is a broad sense of hope where life is allowed to be an adventure, every breath feels fresh, and outcomes are always uncertain. This feeling can happen only because she made me feel that anything is possible in life. I'm not talking about material accumulation or vocational achievements. I am talking about having the hope that I will be able to see with my heart's eye, walk with the peace of a crisp autumn sunset, search with a tolerant but analytic mind, and most of all love. Being given this gift of love enabled me to love and allowed myself to be loved. This type of hope allows me to believe that I can reach beyond myself to rise above the selfish and hateful tendencies that rule the majority of our lives.

Lyme, New Hampshire

M y medical training consisted
of many stages with the four long years of medical school defining
only the initial launching site. One of those stages was a memorable
tenure in the upper valley of the Connecticut River. This beautiful
area, nestled between the Green and White mountain ranges, sits
on the border, separating Vermont and New Hampshire. I had the
option of returning to my medical alma mater in New York City,
but the allure of the upper valley was irresistible because the physical
and cultural environment was entirely different from my prior
experiences in New York and St. Louis, and that difference was the
deciding vote in my mind.

My wife and I found housing in the small village of Lyme,
which seemed to me to be the living manifestation of my mental
vision of the Shire. I had visited places with taller mountain vistas,
broader expanses of open countryside, and more dominant
geographical characteristics. Lyme, however, seemed to me to be
the perfect balance of gentle hills, rolling streams and rivers, and a
beautiful mixture of stunningly colorful foliage. We lived in a small
clapboard single-story house that was built around the turn of the
twentieth century with a rock-filled trout stream that ran along its

side. That stream would turn into a constant thundering roil every spring during the thaw of the heavy winter snows. The most startling sensations, however, emanated from the air itself. The air absolutely sparkled. I couldn't tell if that sensation was due to the elevation in altitude or was merely a figment of my wishful thinking. That sensation added to the magic of the town during the Christmas season with the numerous pine trees laden by a heavy, silent white blanket of snow, crystal-clear strikingly blue skies, and the cold, crisp sparkle that accompanied every intake of breath. One needed to have a heart of stone not to believe in Santa Claus in such an enchanting place.

Lyme also proved to be my parents' favorite among the many places where I would live. They loved the physical surroundings in just the same way that my wife and I did. They too felt the magic of the environment. We all felt so vibrant and alive. Mere strolls to the general and hardware stores were experiences to embrace and remember. I would also have the opportunity to take my parents to visit nearby attractions, which included activities such as cave explorations and hiking along the Presidential Mountain Range of the White Mountains. It was during this time period that my mother informed me that this type of hilly, mountainous terrain was her favorite. She liked it not only because of the heights but also for all the other attributes that one can feel in Lyme. This was a feeling that she cherished since her days of living in China where she would always look forward to outings in the surrounding hilly countryside. The crispness of the New Hampshire air, however, augmented the feelings in a way that the humid and warm southern Chinese climate could not match.

During the third year of my tenure in the upper valley, my first child was born. It seemed appropriate that such a wondrous event in our lives would occur in a magical place. My parents, of course, were overjoyed beyond description and eagerly drove the long hours from New York City to be with their first grandchild. It is difficult to forget the beaming look on my parents' faces when they cradled my daughter in their arms. My mother's smile radiated a happiness that exceeded all the other joyful expressions that I had ever seen on her face. It was apparent that this grandchild was a culmination of her life's desires. This was the beginning of another generation upon which she could bestow her hopes and dreams. Karen had also become a second daughter to my mother. They shared their hearts' feelings and affections for each other. A child from my wife coalesced dreams that my mother would not have thought possible when she first arrived on American soil.

My mother would finally ask me a rhetorical question, "So, Dai dai, what name have you picked out for your daughter?"

I looked at her somewhat puzzled and said, "We decided before she was born that she would be called Lauren, which is the name on the birth certificate."

"I don't mean her American name. I am speaking about her Chinese name."

It had been a tradition in my family to give separate Chinese and American names rather than merely phoneticizing the Chinese name. My parents felt strongly that we are Americans, and we should completely assimilate into American culture beginning with an American name. This is not meant to disregard or forget my Chinese heritage but to engender a feeling of full participation in this wonderful country though I would also have the added benefit of Chinese cultural augmentation.

I replied, "Mahmee ah, I leave that up to you and Baba. It would not only be more appropriate for you two to do it, but I am completely inept with such as task, as you already know; besides, I believe you already have a name picked out, isn't that right?"

My mother gave a small smile, knowing that her son had anticipated her. She said, "We had to come up with a name that not only reflects our feelings toward her but would also engender the magical aura that fills this place that she is born into. Your

father and I searched our memories of Chinese literature and came
upon a perfectly appropriate literary expression. That phrase
expresses the feelings of physical and spiritual exhilaration much
like the sensations that arise from looking out from the top of a tall
mountain range. We took the first and last words from that phrase
to be our grandchild's Chinese name, Sum Yee."

How appropriate. I would not know that my parents would
perform this same feat of literary insight and provide an equally
appropriate Chinese name for my son three years later.

I will forever remember Lyme for the soothing spring rumbling
of the stream that comforted my daughter's sleep. I will also
remember it to be the place where my daughter listened for my
footsteps on the creaky old kitchen floor every morning, hoping
that I would come to pick her up and smile with her. Most of all,
Lyme will remain in my memories as a place of physical and spiritual
exhilaration for my wife, my daughter, my father, and my mother.

Dean's Convocation, 1999

My wife was seated next to me in the amphitheater-styled auditorium of the newly built portion of the medical school. This yearend gathering of the faculty of the medical school provides an opportunity for the dean of the medical school to look back on the past academic year and summarize the achievements of individual faculty as well as the institution as a whole. I came not only because my department chairman was going to address the whole assembly but also because I was one of several faculty members to be recognized for our promotion to the academic rank of full professor. It was satisfying to feel the warmth of my wife's hand during the ceremony. Karen has been with me every step of the way and shared my hopes and ideals. There was never any second guessing about my career decisions because they were always joint decisions. The comfort of her heart beating synchronously with my own created a life that is greater than I could have imagined. My achievements, therefore, are her achievements. I've heard these same words used before as part of marital rhetoric, but regarding Karen, I can feel its resonant truth, which moves through me with a substance that defies easy definition or casual reduction to a simple platitude.

The imposing physical layout of the auditorium, the procession of the administrative entourage dressed in colorful academic regalia, and the somber intonation of the institution's litany of investigative and educational accomplishments generated an atmosphere of idealism, altruism, and ironically, pride. Oddly, I found that the academic incantations did not affect me as I thought it would have or should have. I, instead, felt vaguely uncomfortable being recognized or honored merely for doing my job. It also struck me as somewhat incongruous that physicians, who have taken a specific oath and are part of a specific altruistic culture, should engage in activities that seemed to be designed to spawn self-promotion and satisfaction. Perhaps I should not have been so critical or cynical. After all, pomp and circumstance have been a part of the academic tradition since Plato. In addition, those same traditions have enabled me to live a comfortable professional and personal life. Do my feelings, therefore, reveal me to be unappreciative? I prefer to interpret my feelings more in the light of the age-old clash of reality and idealism creating a messy big ball of cognitive dissonance. My initial lack of recognition of this dissonance drove me to early distraction and frustration. My mother's insight later allowed me to dissipate this inherent contradiction in virtually every facet of life. She was the first to introduce me to the concept of duality as an integral component of experience.

I can remember my mother looking at me with pained but sympathetic eyes when she first witnessed my adolescent idealism splattered against the steamrolling radiator grill of daily life outside the cocoon of youth. She, after all, had a scorching personal experience with the unlimited potential for cruelty that a human being can possess. Her wish had been to provide a safe environment for her children where they could see the human potential for good and have the opportunities to choose to pursue those positive avenues. She told me that she did not want to see my idealism crushed because the world was different from how it should be or how I wished it to be. She survived that same fight when her joyful schoolgirl bloom was permanently tarnished by the brutality of Japanese artillery. I needed to remain a human being, she mentioned, and not be reduced to an animal with the appearance of a cynical person. She went on to say that I must recognize the simultaneous coexistence of the positive and the negative in every experience and learn to accept the reality of the negative without giving up the difficult ability to choose the positive.

I remember asking myself, how do I do that and how does this apply to specific examples of everyday life?

My memories creased a smile on my mind as I sat in the amphitheater. Life is both different and the same for me now. The issues are the same though the players and fields are different from life in the projects. The educational institution that I work for pronounces an idealistic mission statement, but the working reality reinforces self-serving behavior. This, however, is not an accusation but merely an observation of the nature of the work that affects every similar medical institution. "Success" is measured by tangible standards—generally financial in nature. The more successful individuals are the ones who manage to coral the most research grants. The more prestigious grants are from the traditional funding sources such as the government. Those who are unable to run that race obtain second-tier funding from commercial sources such as drug and equipment manufacturers. The risk associated with this choice of venue is losing one's academic credibility because selling one's soul to be a company man inevitably labels the person as a strident shill for the sponsoring company. The personal and departmental financial gains are huge, however, because of the abundant resources of industry. In addition, the secondary benefit of trying new technologies can foster the illusion (delusion) that a person is on the cutting edge of the field. Those who are unable to obtain significant funding from any source resort to the mindset of the municipal worker. They attempt to maximize personal and professional benefits while minimizing personal risk and effort. Every academic institution contains an array of opportunities to take advantage of, such as using trainees to do your work, holding administrative positions, accumulating titles, working on committees, strategic posturing toward the next highest buttocks, etc. The academic world is rife with peripheral, high-profile opportunities that can lead to regional and even national recognition without actually requiring substantive knowledge of much real science. The common theme that binds all these individuals is the term "self-serving." The natural tendency of most people is to create and then protect their own little (or big) professional empire. Their own self-interests are the top priority, and the effective services to individual patients are just a byproduct of that higher priority. Of course, everyone would use indignant posturing to claim otherwise. These same individuals would skillfully engage in highly sophisticated obfuscation and specious argumentation. After all, they are the intellectual and educational elite. They can conveniently redefine motivations, observations, interpretations, and events. The rationalizations and manipulations are world class because these are Olympic-caliber sophists. In the words of a former colleague: "They can piss on your head and convince you that it's rain." It stands to reason, therefore, that the successful individuals in this setting are those who are able to bring great prestige and financial benefit to themselves and the institution while simultaneously generating the mirage of altruism.

Those who perform predominantly clinical work are viewed as the mules of a department. They take care of the essential duties, which are handled with disdain (at worst) and dismissive attitude (at best) by the upper-echelon investigative types. It is quite ironic that these same individuals, whose investigative activities are designed for ultimate patient understanding and treatment, would consider clinical work to be an inconvenient interruption of their investigational activities. Shouldn't the clinical work be the ultimate expression and fulfillment of their investigations? In an ideal world, that would be true, but in the real world, their investigations are more designed for career advancement than altruistic contributions, which may be regarded as helpful but unessential if present. The reality of the academic world is that obtaining research funding becomes more important than the research itself because one is primarily judged by the funding and only secondarily by the work that the funding produces. The projects, hopefully, will generate just enough intriguing data to justify further funding. The art of obtaining funding has become a full-time profession in itself, and the more "successful" individuals are those who excel at this art.

The private sector has a more honest and a more straightforward mercenary approach. The clinical work is merely a means to an end. The short-term goal is to live from vacation to vacation while the long-term goal is to retire as early as possible. Of course, the dichotomy between the academic and private sectors is not so clear anymore. Many people in the academic world also function with the private mentality while trying to create the veneer of an academic life. This can be likened to sniffing at the crotch of academia hoping to find an errant bone tossed in one's direction. Ironically, even individuals with highly developed clinical acumen can be seduced by the dark side. I have seen too many superb clinicians use their finely honed skills predominantly to carve out an empire for themselves. The final payoff may be political, financial, celebrity, lifestyle-related, or psychological, but the priorities are mostly self-serving. Once again, the ultimate goals can hardly be considered as altruistic. Despite a professional oath and an institutional mission statement, the human condition prevails. I continue to see nasty-grasping children all around me, only they are disguised as adults with a highly polished and sophisticated form of educated posturing, baroque verbiage, convenient specious rationalizations, and Machiavellian intrigue. The motivations of people remain the same be it at the Fulton Fish Market or the hallowed halls of academia. The only differences are in the players and the styles.

My living conditions have also significantly changed for the better since my childhood. A house with some surrounding property in a quiet residential neighborhood surrounded by protected wildlife properties and rolling acres of farmland can easily give the impression of the lifestyle of a comfortable country gentleman. The escape from overt crime, the unremoved human waste, and the feeling of chronic vulnerability is also a dramatic improvement in daily life. One would assume that those who are fortunate enough to live in such an environment would appreciate life's generous bestowment of comfort and safety. A closer examination of this more fortunate segment of the population would reveal universal flaws. Just as I am often surrounded in the workplace by people filled with professional jealousies and self-serving motives, who parasitize from the idealistic lifeblood of the institution, many people who enjoy an envious lifestyle degrade that experience by their unconcealed display of a sense of entitlement. They vaguely imply that material advantage is a reflection of some sort of a genetic superiority. Their sense of entitlement is also displayed in their disregard for the needs of other pedestrians and cars on the road when they drive or are engaged in their daily gentleman's constitutional. I always thought that their lives must be a tedious continuum of competitions against equally comfortable neighbors. There seems to be a need for continuous comparison using an unending choice of weapons that range from their children's accomplishments to political insight. There is a never-ending need to flaunt one's superiority in intellect, aging athleticism, conversational witticism, breadth of superficial knowledge, career accomplishments, and material possessions. They even have to show that they can be more humble than others as if humility was a contest to be won. This usually translates into a gross display of false humility that sounds too much like the condescension from which it arises.

In later years, my mother would say to me, "So what? What are you complaining about? Did you expect people to change simply because they have money?"

I replied, "Of course not, Mahmee ah. I am just a bit disappointed that people who have the benefit of more education, money, and opportunities would not behave better. A better life did not seem to translate to a better person but just another person [I thought but didn't say—schmuck] with more resources to draw from."

My mother reached up to touch my furrowed brow. Then she stood behind the chair that I was seated in and leaned down to place her face near the top of my head. After inhaling and rubbing my shoulders, she sighed and whispered, "My dear dai dai, you are so disappointed that others don't share your idealism when you have worked so hard to get to where you are at this point in your life." She said this not so much as an impersonal declaration but more as a sympathetic observation. My mother reseated herself opposite me at the kitchen table.

"Did I ever tell you that my grandfather used to have me dress up in Western clothes and insisted that I eat a Western-style meal with him every weekend?"

The puzzled look on my face not only revealed my never having heard this story but that I was also completely unclear why my mother was mentioning a seemingly irrelevant topic.

"He, too, dressed up in a finely tailored Western suit. We frequently ate meals consisting of the finest steaks, delicate appetizers, and mouth-watering English cakes and cookies. He insisted that I learn the rudiments of proper Western utensil usage as well as table etiquette, posture, and comportment.

"He would ask me, 'My sweet Suit Ying, why do you think your old grandfather treats you to a grand Western-style meal every weekend? After all, we live in China and not England or the Golden Mountain [a.k.a United States]. In addition, we have the greatest cuisine in the world [Chinese], and I have hired the best chefs in the province in my household. Why would I bother with any other style of food or clothing that would be inferior?' He would smile benignly as he waited for my answer, and I would stare at him, maintaining his usual erect posture and consistently meticulous attire, be it Chinese or American. He always adhered to a strict personal regimen of discipline and propriety in his entire demeanor. His diction was carefully constructed, but his tone of voice and his eyes always rained sunshine and affection whenever he addressed me.

"I smiled impishly and said, 'Of course, we do this so that I can learn to appreciate different cultures, is that not correct, Yeh yeh?' I followed my statement with a giggle because I thought that I had correctly anticipated the standard pedestrian response that my grandfather wanted to hear from his little granddaughter.

"He surprised me this time by pressing the issue instead of allowing me to rapidly proceed to politely gulp down my deliciously sweet dessert. He asked me, 'My dear little Suit Ying, what is the point of knowing about other cultures? After all, there are so many, many different cultures in the world, and you will probably not have contact with 99 percent of them; besides, you already know how to properly use a knife and fork, so what is the point in repeating the exercise every week?'

"At this point, my young stomach was growling with frustration, but his questions also intrigued me, and I found it difficult to formulate a correct response. My silence was his signal to continue.

"'Ah, my favorite granddaughter, you are very inquisitive and remarkably bright, but what I tell you now you may not understand until you are older. I can never be totally sure with you, though, because you have frequently surprised me with the breadth, depth, and speed of your learning despite your young age.' He paused to gather his thoughts, straightened his already straight back, and continued with a stern and formal voice that was countered by loving and gentle eyes. 'There are many people who would learn Western ways as a means to display their worldliness on their sleeves. This is merely pretension and completely unworthy of you or our family. Others learn Western ways because they believe it to be a superior lifestyle. This is ignorant and quite insulting to the formidable development of our culture over thousands of years. There are, after all, both good and bad elements in every type of society, and to glorify one over another is to be blind to the truth. Perhaps you think that I want you to familiarize yourself with

Western ways to allow you to be able to move within any society and be comfortable with many cultures and customs. This is a practical reason and indeed has substantial value, but by itself is not enough to be the only or even major justification. I would like you to think of learning the ways of the West or any other culture very much like learning another language. There are practical advantages, but knowing the mechanics of a culture or its language is only the first step. That step is the first of the many steps you have to take to more deeply understand what a culture or a society cherishes or values. In other words, what does a society aim for? What are its ideals? What concepts does it hold dearest? Is it something ephemeral, shallow, and concrete such as material gain, physical pleasures, and profit? Or is it something entirely abstract and unconnected to the realities of daily life? Every society has good and bad points including our own. Every culture also prefers to boast about and define itself by its achievements. The essence of the soul of a society [and an individual], however, lies not in its accomplishments but where its aim is or what it is shooting for rather than what it has done. My wish for you, my dear Suit Ying, is to understand another culture by knowing how to look at it. Search for its ideals and what it hopes to be. Learn about the aspects of another culture that are good. Learn how to incorporate it into and enhance what is good in your life.'"

My mother would use this same logic with me years later as she tried to tell me that I have quite an advantage being Chinese American. Instead of viewing myself as being burdened with being an imperfect fit within American and Chinese culture, I should benefit from all that is good that comes from being both American and Chinese. The combination of both will exceed that which is from each individual culture alone. Instead of confusion, I was frequently able to draw strength and unique inspiration from the combined virtues of each.

My mother would also mention that my great-grandfather's high regard for my father, despite his humble background, was derived from my father's ability to have a vision. In other words, my father was able to judge a society by its dreams and what it cherishes. My father then had the courage to pursue those ideals for his own life by going to America. My great-grandfather viewed my father as the lucky one despite having no financial resources. He also viewed most of the comfortable and well-to-do around him as nothing more than moral peasants.

So my mother brought the conversation back to my own cynicism. "You see, Dai dai ah, there are good and not-so-good people everywhere in every society. They have a variety of motivations for every act in life. Do not judge others by what they have done. Their real characters will be better revealed by looking at what they aim for. Everyday life forces people to do many things that are incorrect or morally suspect. Everyone must do what they must to survive. What you are so disappointed in, however, are the disappointing choices that some people willingly embrace when they are not compelled to make those types of choices. See this in others and learn from it. Remember it and know how to better run your own life. Keep your focus on why you are doing something and keep your aim steady toward a good and idealistic dream even if you never achieve it. The effort is its own reward. You will be defined by what you aim for more than what you have done."

I sit here reminiscing, with my wife at my side, while being honored for attaining the rank of full professor. I wished my mother was here. I could tell her that I kept my focus on my ideals and the responsibilities that accompany the great privileges that have been granted to me as a physician. I did not allow myself to become distracted by enticing secondary gain, I've never pressed the advantages that I've had, and I've always tried to maintain the spirit and integrity of my position even at substantial, unrequired, and unacknowledged burden to myself. I have discovered that the effort to maintain an idealistic professional and personal focus was indeed a substantial inner reward by itself. It was the only reward that I ever really wanted. In the end, however, within this auditorium, with Karen's hand intertwined with my own hand, they also gave me the prize.

The First Noble Truth

In the early spring of 2002, I revisited New York to spend some time with my father after informing him of his fatal diagnosis during the late winter. He had returned from a desperate trip to China, hoping that unconventional treatments with ancient Chinese herbal medicines could at least temporarily stay the lethal hand of his cancer. It was a trip that he was lucky to have survived as he barely managed to return to New York after requiring intravenous fluids just hours before his flight. His collapse in a Shanghai bathroom on the day of his departure greatly alarmed his dedicated travel companions and generated the fears of a worst-case scenario. My father's wish, however, was to make it back to Staten Island. If he were to die, he wanted to die in his own house where the urn containing the ashes of his wife lay on the decorated altar arranged in his bedroom. My father's sheer determination and the constant caring ministrations of Tingke Wang, who has been his savior for the past twelve years, enabled his safe return.

When I entered the house, I gently walked down the stairs to the basement, which had become the default family room since I was a child. I discovered my father sitting in a slumped fashion on a chair by the dinner table, but his eyes brightened at my presence. He was lethargic and struggling with every wheezing breath. I realized that the cancer was beginning to narrow his windpipe and every breath, of every second of every day and night, would be a struggle for him. He had lost considerable weight, and the shadow of emaciation and death was clearly upon him. By this time, he already had a gastrostomy so that he could be fed some nutrition via a tube inserted through a hole made directly through his abdominal wall into his stomach. The poorly executed gastrostomy resulted in constant leakage of acidic gastric juices through the hole, causing intense burning and chemical excoriation of his skin adjacent to the surgical site. My father was also coughing every thirty seconds or so because of his difficulty in swallowing his own saliva. Any attempts to swallow invariably led to his aspiration of his saliva into his windpipe, which triggered severe fits of coughing and spitting. The upper portion of his esophagus could not be completely emptied because of the cancer. It was constantly filled with oral secretions, liquids, and residuals of foods, which did not pass beyond the obstructing cancer. This led to frequent spitting of mucous and brown sediments between the fits of coughing and persistent wheezing struggles for breath. Sleep became a fruitless exercise. The unremitting pain and suffering superimposed upon perpetual sleep deprivation exceeded the imagination of even the most sadistic Hollywood screenwriter. Pushed beyond his considerable endurance, smothered without hope of relief, and utterly broken, my father, Mark Wing Soon, persisted. I could not hide my sad eyes and the aching pain in my heart shattered with tears when my father looked up at me and smiled.

How could this man know so much love that it could overcome his worst nightmare of suffering toward the end of his life? In his darkest hour, he found a reason to smile. It was a pure smile untainted by hidden bitterness, sorrow, or rage. He found some spark of happiness in my presence. I, the flesh from his flesh, the person trained to heal and now unable to heal him. I, the son who failed his mother thirteen years earlier and was now about to fail his father. I, the son and physician who could not heal or comfort either parent while watching them both slowly die. He did not ask for a miracle. He did not ask for comfort. He did not even ask for momentary respite. He was just happy to merely see me.

I looked at my father's slumped form, which spasmodically rose with each attempt at a breath, with great pain. He did not, however, want to see too much sympathetic sorrow on my face because it would only reinforce his desperate condition and begin to elicit tears in his own eyes. This dying, tortured man had always been the living embodiment of the willful refusal to acknowledge that life only consisted of suffering. He was still defiant and preferred to concentrate on the positive potential of his next moments, no matter how small the experience, rather than dwell on past hurts and regrets. He did not despair at his disease but instead was waiting for the next small moment when his tumor would allow him to temporarily swallow a modest sip of a watery, nutritious Chinese gelatin mixture made by Tingke. He would even make several daily futile attempts to climb up the stairs from the basement. When I asked why he persisted in this ritual despite his inevitable failure, he would always put a small smile on his face and squint slightly at me while he answered, "To test my legs, of course. I have to try to maintain and perhaps even slowly increase the strength of my legs. It is very important to maintain my ability to walk." He can barely remain seated upright in a chair, yet he insists on cultivating a sense of hope and progress. I have seen this trait in him throughout his life. It is not derived from a delusional mind in denial but rather from a calculated complete refusal to submit to despair. This is simply raw courage. This is an extraordinary courage exhibited on an everyday basis that will not make the newspapers or be exaggerated out of all proportions. It is the substance of my father. He whom I have loved my whole life.

His positive signature outlook never wavered during the many trials of his life including his final greatest trial from which there would be no recovery. He always preferred to look for solutions rather than dwell on problems. My father, for instance, never allowed the loss of his lifetime's accumulated financial fortune to affect his attitude even though that loss came about by nefarious means spiced with additional helpings of malice and betrayal. He still maintained a genuine positive outlook on everyday life and on people that he encountered. His new work as a mail or bond carrier on Wall Street was not considered a menial minimal-wage occupation but rather a new adventure with new possibilities. My father always managed to find joy in everyday experiences. In other words, he personified the Taoist concept of the uncarved block.

This attitude infectiously influenced his otherwise monotone workplace in the bowels of Wall Street. His supervisors had come to expect to see him already at work before all the other workers arrived. His ability to organize the day's duties enabled all the other employees around him to start the day with constructive structure and direction. It also greatly simplified his supervisor's responsibilities. There was never any resentment because my father not only did not ask for special compensation or recognition, but a quick discussion with him would reveal his methods to be a superior and a more efficient strategy to run the department. In other words, he made everyone's job much easier. The practical influence of his presence, however, was the least memorable of his many contributions to the workplace. Everyone had grown accustomed to his energetic presence with the warm early-morning greetings, fresh donuts and bagels that he would share, and cajoling of less enthusiastic colleagues. Many people had turned to him for advice on a variety of issues ranging from organizational logistics to career decisions and personal tragedies. Everyone had come to learn that my father was a very wise and compassionate man who could be trusted with the most intimate secrets. His broken New York—accented English could not conceal his knowledge, experience, and insight. Most of all, he was recognized as a man without a personal agenda other than his wish for the happiness of all those who had contact with him. He was even able to outwork his much younger fellow workers by completing tasks by 10:00 a.m. when those same tasks would take the other workers all day to finish. Most people tended to forget that they were talking to an elderly man nearing the ripe age of eighty. His attitude and physical comportment created the impression of a man of undefinable age with a shock of gray hair. A sunny disposition, treats of spicy cheeses and summer sausages from Wisconsin, and an unerring work ethic endeared my father to many, but his more significant contribution was as a friend, confidante, and advisor to all those around him. This was most evident to me during my father's funeral when a group of his colleagues came to pay their respects. Most were so emotional at the loss of my father that they were unable to verbally articulate the words in their hearts as their faces were drowning in their tears.

My father's uniquely positive attitude not only inspired those around him, but it also seemed to have endowed him with an uncanny physical resiliency. I had never seen him take up a regular (or even irregular) exercise regimen, and his total physical activity seemed to consist of how far he could raise a bottle of scotch. Yet, he never needed to limit any of his physical activities during work or vacation because of fatigue, weakness, or lack of motivation. His smoking and drinking habits were developed since his early teenage years leading to emphysematous lungs and a cirrhotic liver, but he was still able to engage in any and every recreational physical activity that he desired. I remember witnessing my father suffering through years of debilitating gouty arthritis, but I also remember him being able to hobble back and forth to work despite the excruciating pain.

I used to wonder if his stamina was due to fortunate genetics or an old-war injury to the centers of his body that enables him to feel pain. I knew that he was not immune to the ravages of disease and self-induced abuses to his own body. He hinted at the answer one day when he was suffering from a particularly bad episode of the gout. He was shuffling and hobbling down the stairs to the basement to put on his shoes to go to work when I asked him, "Baba ah, why are you still going to work when you are obviously in severe pain? How can you stand it?"

He slowly eased himself down to sit on the long basement bench, which my mother had used to store many of the fabrics from which she made clothing for herself. She had continued this frugal lifetime habit despite, at one point, having more than enough disposable income to buy any type of designer clothing of her choice. My father sighed and said, "Dai dai ah, why don't you come here and help me get this shoe on my foot with the painful toe while I tell you a short story."

As I tried to slowly insert his foot into his firm leather wingtips, my father cried out, "Ay yah! Dai dai ah, I don't think this will work well. Too painful. Take off all of the shoelace and just slip the loose, floppy shoe on my foot." I did as he instructed and he continued to speak to me. "You remember, Dai dai, I told you that I went back to China after the war? You also remember that *Ah mah* [paternal grandmother] was in the hospital and Mahmee was taking care of her? Well, I don't think I ever told you why Ah mah ended up in the hospital."

My father was looking straight at me as he spoke, but I could tell that his eyes were focused on another time, place, and emotional cauldron. "I used to think that I had it bad during the war, but it was nothing compared to the people, civilians, who had to live under the Japanese occupation of China. It was especially terrible in my home village. When the Japanese soldiers came into the village, they simply took whatever they did not destroy. My mother, your ah mah, had to give up all of her food to the invaders. I will never understand why they went out of their way to abuse a helpless old woman. Most of the villagers stayed alive by picking at bits of food that dropped from the bowls and mouths of the soldiers. A few lucky villagers had hidden or buried some food before the soldier's arrival, but they were unwilling to share their booty because survival was at stake, and it was a situation of every man for himself; besides, once the soldiers discovered that some villagers had small hidden stores of food, they made a public spectacle of beheading those individuals after defecating on their meager food supplies. On a regular basis, the soldiers would force all the villagers, including your ah mah, to kneel in the center of town. Those who refused were executed without discussion. Your ah mah was forced to kneel in the red baked dirt for hours at a time. Those who were too weak and fatigued to stay in a kneeling position were beheaded where they lay. Others were just randomly beheaded for no apparent reason. Everyone lived in fear for their lives during the entire war. With her knees destroyed from kneeling, body wasted from malnutrition and starvation, and stripped of clothes, tools, and animals, your ah mah became desperate. She managed to survive by eating insects, which were attracted to the yellow night lantern, and slowly sipping from contaminated puddles of water that randomly formed on the fields after raining. All types of illnesses rapidly ravaged her body, but she hung on. She refused to die. Her only wish was to see me, her oldest son, again. She believed that I would come back to save her. I was shocked when I saw her in the hospital after the war, but I tried to hide my emotions behind a casual façade. Your ah mah was nearly bald from having her hair pulled out by the Japanese as they dragged her in the streets. All of her teeth had fallen out from malnutrition and decay. Her knees looked as if they were macerated by a butcher, and her kneecaps were just about protruding through her wafer-thin skin. There seemed to be no muscle mass on her. It was just the skeleton of my mother covered by a thin layer of sun-browned skin. I barely recognized her. Still she persevered. Her face still lit up into a ghoulish, toothless beaming grin when she saw me." My father's blank stare had turned into a misty pool covering his eyes.

He continued, "I told myself, at that time, that I will never again complain about my own suffering. I will endure whatever I must endure. I will carry whatever burden that needs to be carried. I will persevere no matter what. Most of all, I will never give up hope. That is the gift that my mother gave to me through her years of horrific suffering during the war. This is the gift that I would like to pass on to you and for you to pass on to your children."

As I watched my father spitting mucous while struggling for each breath, I was reminded by something that he told me years ago during a late-night lull on a busy weekend in the restaurant. I was leaning against the counter to rest my weary knees after standing for ten straight hours, and my father was still on an adrenaline high after hours of entertaining patrons. My father looked over at me and said, "You know, Dai dai, there were a lot of customers tonight who were very depressed about their own daily lives. I helped them to forget their troubles for just a few hours to enjoy a good meal with good company. Mostly, I treated them with respect and charity. But you know, Dai dai, I wasn't really being all that generous because it cost me next to nothing but a few drinks and some time. Remember that it is easy for a person to be magnanimous when it costs them nothing. A wealthy man is not being generous when he gives you a nickel. When a poor man, however, gives you the only nickel that he possesses, that becomes an act of profound generosity. In other words, the true measure of a person's character tends to be revealed when they are stressed. It is how you conduct yourself when your situation is hopeless. It is your attitude during your darkest hour. Can you maintain hope and honor when all is lost? This is what I learned from my mother."

My father was slowly deteriorating before my eyes during my days with him in the basement of his home. He was gradually becoming unable to tend to his own bodily functions without assistance. The cancer was inexorably dragging him to his grave. I could tell that hospitalization was just around the corner. My father continued to futilely stretch his legs, choke down food that he could not realistically swallow, and maintain a semblance of personal hygiene. He thought that every day was a gift, and he didn't waste any more time by reminding me that he had loved my mother, and he loved me. He also wanted me to remind my brother and sister that he also loved them dearly. I could see that he was intent on making his last hours to be his finest hour.

A Walk in the Park

It is generally quite easy for me to hide my embarrassment when the next septuagenarian laps me as I hobble along at a snail's pace around the indoor track at the local health club. Deception, duplicity, and a frankly innocent stare come quite naturally to me after years of cultivating the practiced habit of blaming my siblings for my own mischief and malice. As I am a recently qualified member of the AARP (American Association of Retired Persons), those early skills become quite convenient though it troubles me that they can be so easily revived. My control over my autonomic functions astonishes even me as I prevent my face from flushing, render my labored breathing inaudible, and prevent leakage from my bladder while the next group of female octogenarians takes a break from their bridge club to flaunt their cardiovascular vigor for the afternoon by passing me by while engaging in a running conversation. My wife and I had recently joined the club after our last child had left for college. We now have the motivation and the opportunity for this type of essential activity, which we had neglected for years. At the beginning of the processing of our membership, my wife was tested to assess the current status of her fitness. Of course, she was found to be strong, flexible, and lean while qualifying for the top ten percentile for women in her age bracket. All this without the aid of a regular, dedicated exercise regimen. It must be superior genetics. Despite my wife's urging, I refused to be tested. The overhang of my abdominal fat over the already loose beltline of my baggy sweatpants was proof enough for me regarding my level of fitness. (I don't think "fitness" is a word that I would use when talking about my body habitus for now.) Besides, they don't make calipers big enough to measure my percentage of body fat. My wife is quite enthusiastic about using the various mechanical devices designed to develop specific muscle groups, but I believe that I need to significantly improve before I can initiate that type of real exercise. The mere simple act of walking and swinging my arms would leave me with two days of pain in my knees and ankles as well as a strained rotator cuff. As you can see, I really don't need an assessment to establish my physical baseline. I will need years of exercise so that I can get to a baseline that can be measured.

My thoughts frequently return to my father, who had died just last year. His life had not only inspired me, but it also enabled me to look at life through a different and richer filter. This health club, for instance, is filled with people that I now interpret with a different standard than I would have applied as a teenager. One corner of the room is filled with massively muscled men who grunt and strain at clanging barbells while they continue to add to and chisel out their already steel-like physique. Other women, having already been furiously working on training machines for over an hour, continuously drip sheets of sweat over their lean bodies that look as if a quarter would bounce on their rippled abdomens. These are the people whom I would have admired as an adolescent. I would have been envious of their physical prowess as well as their discipline and effort to reach and maintain such heights of physical development. I imagine that it is somewhat similar to a child looking up to a sports hero. My attention nowadays shifts toward the struggling, gray-haired middle-aged individuals who can barely rotate the elliptical trainers or pump the stair climbers. These are the people who are given dismissive glances of fleeting disdain by the toned and trim bundles of cardiovascular aristocrats who seem capable of energizing the air around them to defend against bad cellulite karma. I sympathize with the struggling club members not because I am also one of them or I want to embrace physical neglect and deep fried fast food but because I see different lives and reactions to the call of responsibility. Instead of wrinkled endomorphs who need better circulation around enclosed body parts, I see someone who may have sacrificed every waking moment of each day, for decades, working two jobs to provide the opportunities for their families to fulfill themselves through education and personal development. I see someone who had willingly sacrificed themselves for years for the greater good of the family. Perhaps the overweight, vaguely unkempt lady on the exercise mat actually spent the prime of her life caring for demanding, unappreciative, and ultimately demented parents while sacrificing her personal activities and health. The puffing, red-faced man, who casts furtive glances while he pretends to be reading a book as he "power walks" may have been suffering from years of undiagnosed and untreated agoraphobia, leaving him afraid to leave his house while observing the rest of the world through the television set. Life is frequently cruel and quite unfair, and people are just left to deal with the consequences. These people have reached the same end point though the route they had traveled to get there may have been quite different. They all share the same admirable quality of having decided to deal with their problems, no matter how hopeless it now seems. They, in my eyes, are then the real heroes. Perhaps the health club's workout junkies are the ones who have had it easy. They have had the means and the opportunities to obviously devote at least a regular if not a major share of their daily lives only to themselves, hence their fitness level. The tiresome rationalization of their narcissistic indulgence by invoking the top priority to the maintenance of their level of fitness only underscores the fact that they may not have been required or even willing to sacrifice themselves for another person or a higher cause. I admire the people in the club who had made that type of sacrifice at the expense of their health and now take the additional step of addressing those health problems after a lifetime of the proper and conscientious discharge of those voluntarily shouldered though costly responsibilities. I have my parents to thank for this perspective simply by the manner in which they lived their everyday lives where self-indulgence was always a secondary priority at best. There was very little tolerance for immaturity, and a premium was placed on honor and duty.

"Is that not a very Chinese characteristic?" I once asked my mother.

She replied, "That is only a proper mindset for any human being of any culture. My grandfather was the first to make me aware that these ideals can be found in many cultures scattered around the world, and the Chinese do not hold a monopoly on wisdom and principle even though we already have a vast and highly developed history regarding these traditions about life and its meaning. These are also the criteria by which a person should be judged regardless of their background and skin color. These virtues do not come naturally to anyone. They must be learned, cultivated, and practiced. This, in turn, occurs only with discipline and understanding."

I remember seeing my mother sitting on some covered crates stacked against the wall at the end of the bar in the restaurant. Her head would be barely visible from the other side of the bar. My mother would sit there in every chance that arose. Her back would give her terrible pain, which caused her to bend over and grab her flank. She did her best to hide her discomfort from the customers and create the illusion that all was well. She would recruit me to fulfill the bartender duties and complete the takeout orders whenever possible as her pain was unremitting. I was the only person that she confided in regarding the severity of her discomfort. Years of this type of pain did not sway her from marching back and forth to the restaurant every day and night. The daily firestorm of details that demand immediate attention in the routine operation of a restaurant all continued to be expertly and authoritatively dealt with by my mother. The business never skipped a beat, and my mother never complained. I urged her to see a doctor, which she ultimately did. Those visits, however, only resulted in the marginally helpful X-rays of her spine and the unsatisfactory explanation of some degenerative arthritis as the cause of her suffering. Treatments were only symptomatic, and the mild relief was temporary.

Years after the closure and the loss of the restaurant, my mother's back pain slowly and miraculously dissipated. A routine medical evaluation for an unrelated issue revealed that one of my mother's kidneys had autoinfarcted. That was the cause of her years of back pain. The relief from that pain came only after the kidney completely finished its own process of self-destruction. A painfully slow disorder that would have debilitated most people did not stop my mother from carrying on with her daily work routine. Was this foolish? That depends on your perspective. I now more fully understand her mindset and marvel at her stamina and devotion to duty and service. Her immediate and extended families enjoy opportunities and advantages that came at a very costly and painful price, yet she never asked for gratitude from anyone. She just never anticipated anyone to betray her affections and devotion, but that is a different story. I, who have witnessed her years of suffering, was hurt when she was hurt, and shared her anguish sparked by old and predictable sources of familial intrigue. I also understand that her heart's burden was further complicated by another ruthless episode in the historical changes of twentieth-century China.

The Communist takeover of China occurred soon after Suit Ying left China with her Chinese American husband. The physical destruction of China during World War II had metastasized from ugly to satanic after the war because of the inhumane machinations of a madman that turned the Chinese people on each other. Japan destroyed the landscape of China, but Mao's insanity destroyed the mind and spirit of the Chinese and their ancient culture. The wealthy were immediately vilified, and a vengeful revolution demanded immediate bloody retribution. The great Chin family became one of the biggest and the most visible targets in southern China. Suit Ying's grandfather had died well before the revolution,

and her father had luckily died not too long before the Communist
hordes had invaded the Chin property. Her father died of the
relatively common disorder of appendicitis, and later reconstruction
of events would lead Suit Ying to feel relief that her father did not
live to see the depraved humiliation inflicted upon his wife by the
Communist mobs. Suit Ying learned that her mother was subjected
to regular abuse by mobs of people. She was routinely dragged out
of her house to be ridiculed or "criticized" in the center of town.
This "criticism" in Communist China does not possess the same
meaning in America. The verbal insults and attacks were
humiliating and insulting. The beatings and gang assaults, however,
were the most injurious parts of the "criticism." My grandmother
was regularly contemptuously dumped on her knees in the center
of town with her hands tied behind her back. She was made to
bow and kiss the filthy dirt smeared with human excrement while
the mobs taunted this "unrepentant capitalistic whore." The
physical blows to her face and body would cause permanent
damage. The dragging of her torn body by her hair through town
would result in a nearly completely bald old woman that I would
encounter in 1960 as a young boy. Perhaps the vilest abuse occurred
when the Communist mobs decided to dig up the decayed corpse
of my recently deceased grandfather. They then forced handfuls of
the rotting flesh into my grandmother's mouth. They celebrated
this nauseating consumption of the corpse in front of the mobs by
simultaneously chanting, "You who have lived and feasted off of
the blood of the people will now receive a just dose of your own
treatment! Eat your own blood as you have taken from the blood
of the people!" Somehow, someway, she survived. She did not only
survive, but she managed to escape by swimming across shark-
infested waters to Hong Kong a decade later.

My mother would only occasionally recount bits and pieces of
those horrible and incomprehensible events to me over the course
of years. Her voice would sound far away, and the sorrow in her
heart would be palpable even to this spoiled and typically indifferent
and self-centered Chinese American boy. I guess this is another
reason why she never complained about her own pain or let it

interfere with her daily duties. This must also have been why she never stopped thinking about or working to make regular financial contributions to her family back in China even if it meant nights with little or almost no sleep and barely enough resources for her own children and husband.

Personal pain and suffering were also constant companions for my father. You would never know it, however, from casual observations of my father because he always projected an aura of ease, friendliness, and competence. He usually dealt with pain and suffering with the same universal response for every other problem in his life. He merely smiled and said, "No problem." I knew that he was not immune to pain as I have witnessed his suffering up close. I also knew that he ruminated over the welfare of his mother and siblings. I think he just refused to be defeated by pain and life's misfortunes. A promising outlook was an integral part of his personality. It seemed as if he went through life with total confidence that everything will always work out. Even during the excruciating times when he could not even touch the skin over his toes because of the severe inflammation of gout, my father always believed that relief would soon arrive. He only had to hold on for just a little while longer. I always sensed that victory was just around the corner every time he had a problem, even when there did not seem to be any available options for a solution. This sense did not grow from superhuman powers, an immunity to the laws of nature, or an overbearing attitude of hubris or entitlement. Instead it was cultivated by a mindset that he, like my mother, would remind me of from time to time. "Dai dai ah, life is not about victory. Life is about effort and endurance. Many misfortunes can occur in your life. Some are obvious, and others cannot be anticipated. How you deal with misfortune including physical suffering is the only thing that is important. Talent can be insufficient, and victory can be capricious. The only thing that you should find unacceptable within yourself is the lack of effort and the unwillingness to endure. A person is not entitled to anything in life. Life is a gift, and nothing is guaranteed. Success is frequently a product of luck, and suffering is everywhere. Your only expectation of life should be from yourself where you voluntarily choose to take this gift of life and put forth your fullest effort to live it with kindness and value while willingly enduring whatever suffering comes upon you until the very end."

This determined embrace of willful effort and endurance allowed my father to be mentally flexible enough to change jobs several times, learn new skills, exhibit great physical stamina, and withstand several severe illnesses and surgeries without affecting his daily work into his eighties. The honing of this psychological edge also enabled him to survive the great emotional devastation of his later years with the death of my mother. It should not have been that surprising, therefore, to see my father not only weather the humiliation of being a minimal-wage earner on Wall Street but to accept ownership of the new position. This motivated him to perform his tasks with dedication and energy while applying his life experiences to make the work more efficient and inspiring for his much-younger colleagues. My father seamlessly transitioned from decades of standing at a bar to walking more than five miles a day. Many workers, from the local street vendor to secretaries in different offices and executives in high-profile companies, began to look forward to their daily interactions with this cheerful elderly Chinese American courier from the mailroom of one of the local stock companies. My father not only withstood the physical rigors of a new lifestyle, but he did not even let his slowly deteriorating health affect his duties. He never told me, for instance, about his fatigue and darkening urine until he came to visit me for the Christmas holidays, and my wife discovered blood in his underwear while doing the laundry. This led to the diagnosis of bladder cancer and multiple treatments with chemotherapy. He never, during this time period, let his illness disrupt his work and assignments. After surviving his cancer, he was unfortunate enough to be in the World Trade Center the first time terrorists attempted to destroy the buildings with a bomb in the garage. My father simply walked out of the building and continued on his way. He was doubly unfortunate to be but a few blocks away when the two towers of the World Trade Center crashed down after being hit by the terrorist-hijacked airliners. He said that he felt as if he was transported back to World War II and was being bombarded by the Japanese. The bright blue sky turned midnight black as the sun was blotted out, and he was covered by a thick mantle of gray dust. What did not translate in the news coverage was the intense heat of the experience, which my father likened to being thrown into a blast furnace. He described the sensation as being very similar to the concussion and the heat of exploding artillery shells. The crowds in the street around him seemed utterly shocked and tried to swarm away from the catastrophe toward the nearby Staten Island Ferry terminal. My father would later tell me of the tragedy of seeing so many people, especially elderly women, being trampled beneath an unstoppable avalanche of mindlessly stomping shoes during the surging wave of mass panic when people tried to escape the collapse of the Twin Towers. He was standing by the water's edge at the very southern tip of Manhattan island and was prepared to jump into the polluted greenish waters of New York City harbor should there be another unbearable blast of heat and dust. Desperate men began leaping from the pier at the departing ferry boats. Those who managed to barely reach the boats endured the thirty-minute ride by dangerously clinging to the outer rim of the overcrowded ferries. The others disappeared beneath the murky dark green waves. My father persevered and managed to stagger home many hours later, similar to millions of other New Yorkers during that dark day in history known as 9-11.

There would be still more for my father to endure. He, for instance, had always attributed his growing fatigue with walking his five-mile courier route to chronic emphysema from decades of smoking and a cirrhotic liver from hard liquor during those same restaurant years. The source of his growing weakness was finally traced to his severely narrowed carotid arteries. This led to emergency surgery, which he not only endured with good humor, but he only allowed it to minimally interfere with his routine daily work and lusciously satisfying simple vacations. He simply carried on with his life with heavy bandages on his neck and more frequent pauses during his daily rounds to rest and recover. My father continued to be a positive source of inspiration for all those around him even as they looked upon his physical wounds with sympathy and concern. He still listened compassionately to others with lesser personal problems, shared his lifetime of clarity and insight with his friends who were struggling with difficult decisions, and elicited a brief smile from those on his route who were weighed down by the burdens of everyday life. In other words, he continued to provide others with those seemingly small moments that bring happiness to an individual life when all is said and done.

To Never Falter

I prefer to describe my late teenage years as a period during which I actively engaged in my heuristic development by constantly raising questions of an ontological nature and exploring my epistemological assumptions. In other words, I was trying to grow up. During those troubled years, I, incredulously, struggled with basic questions about who I was and wondering how I fit in the world. In my arrogance, I believed that my every insight was original, unique, and profound. I was too ignorant to realize that my strident pronouncements of life's truths were banal and derivative. My "profound" logic, usually only managed to produce conclusions, which I failed to recognize, were merely tautological constructs of an idiot who didn't realize that he was an absolute git.

My mother, however, maintained an unwavering faith in me. I thought, at the time, that my mother carried her normal maternal biases to an irrational extreme because she seemed to be in denial about the realities of my thoroughly confused adolescent mind. She stubbornly remained undeterred in her belief that I will resolve my metaphysical angst, become a productive member of society, and develop the skills to fit into any portion of society. Her intentions were always benevolent even if they consistently ignored my obvious shortcomings.

Those good intentions, born from her total faith in me, caused her to coerce me into attending a party one balmy sunny summer afternoon weekend. The party was being held at the home of a wealthy Chinese family, who were distant relatives of my father. That family had long established roots in America compared to my parents. Their first ancestor to come to this country became a medal-winning war hero during World War I for the American army. The subsequent generations of the family parlayed that accomplishment into a financial empire in New York's Chinatown, which, in turn, created opportunities for the family to truly blend into American society through the well-heeled traditions of obtaining the best education at the finest academic institutions. Culture, money, education, and real skills are powerful enabling factors. They can also be accompanied by the insidious development of a sense of entitlement and superiority. Seduced by their family's never-mentioned-but-assumed coronation as Chinese American royalty, they usually treated my parents with a patronizing smirk. After all, the members of that family were college-educated and well-connected real Americans whereas my parents were "right off the boat." I believe that an invitation to this party was extended to me only from their sense of noblesse oblige.

I used to have difficulty understanding how my mother was able to suffer the interactions with these relatives. I later understood that my mother did not harbor resentment or ill will. She, in fact, did not even interpret their actions as thinly veiled insults. They were merely relatives with eccentric ways but still deserved all the affections and loyalties reserved for relatives. In this light, my mother saw no malicious intent behind this invitation. She only recognized an opportunity for her youngest son to mix with the "proper" and successful elements of society. Never mind that I had no inclination to attend the party, and my natural tendencies were (and still are) to be alone. I had enough issues with myself just trying to grow up. I didn't feel that I needed an extra helping of humiliation to complicate my life at that point. My mother would not tolerate my objections. She insisted that I go and expressed total confidence that I will acquit myself well in that exalted company. So off I drove to the privileged neighborhood that nested in one of the most exclusive enclaves of Long Island all the while mumbling to myself that I will probably be as welcomed as a turd floating in the punch bowl.

As I pulled onto the circular driveway, which framed the entranceway to a palatial home, I couldn't help but notice that all the cars lining the edge of the driveway were high-end German automobiles. The majority of them were Porsches while the remainder consisted of BMWs and Mercedeses. I chose to park my family car in the street to prevent the squashed domestic bugs on the Chevrolet Impala from being scraped off the car by very expensive Teutonic paint. I must have dawdled in the driveway for at least fifteen minutes, admiring the line of magnificent automobiles that I had only read about in car magazines but had never seen up close in real life.

As I entered the house, I remember thinking that this must be how the other half lives. I was surprised to find that I was warmly greeted at the door and ushered toward the large common room where music could be heard in the background. I walked past expensively adorned Western-style rooms with tasteful Chinese accents. The décor exuded a harmonious Gestalt that was a perfect expression of their American success while still maintaining a small tribute to their Chinese heritage. I had never entered such a home in my young life. I was much more accustomed to the vaguely organized clutter of a typical Chinese immigrant family. The usual scatter of cheap Chinese trinkets, slightly dingy surfaces, and hint of food in the air were replaced by impressive plaques celebrating professional and academic accomplishments, sparkling surfaces that gleamed with polished wood and leather, and finely conditioned air that was refreshing to smell and soothing to feel. It would have been so much easier for me if my hosts were sarcastic or condescending. They were, instead, pleasant, polite, and generous. Try as I might, I could not vilify or dislike these people. I also could not bring myself to feel envious of their success, which was

well earned and deserved. I was happy for them though I also felt
distinctly separate from them.

The differences that I felt in my heart were almost cultural in
nature even beyond the obvious material upgrade of their lives
relative to mine. I remember walking into a slightly darkened hall
where a large group of college-aged students were gathered. They
were all meticulously dressed and well groomed. Even their casual
attire exuded a designer chicness. All were well mannered and
pointedly social. The males were mostly students or recent graduates
of Ivy League schools or other upper-echelon institutions such as
Stanford and MIT (Massachusetts Institute of Technology). The
females were all slim and attractive like fashion models with their
long and styled hair. Their conversations centered on the recent
sorority activities on their Seven Sisters campuses. They all tried,
at some point or another in the afternoon, to engage me in
conversation to promote a sense of inclusion for me, but it was
more awkward for me than for them. How can they relate to my
high points during the past year at a local New York City college,
which has no real campus other than the grimy streets of the city?
Why can't I stand comfortably in my discount-store-bought pants
with the coarse seam that chafes me in a deep body part that should
never see the light of day? How do I communicate with people
whose casual use of the language exceeds my formal and
premeditated attempts in either English or Chinese? Everyone was
discussing their plans for professional schools or high-paying
executive positions in corporate America while I was struggling to
decide if it was still meaningful to keep my hair at shoulder length.
Anyone care to toss the football around in the backyard? I didn't
think so.

Style is what I lacked and was so clearly genetically ingrained
in everyone else at the party. That style is what I used to label as
"AA" or "affectations of the affluent." Body stance is the first
impression. It must be mastered to convey an air of formality and
a relaxed demeanor as if proper posture and behavior is the result
of nature rather than nurture. Next are the eyes. Prolonged direct
eye contact would only reveal oneself as an uncultured thug. One

must instead be able to look at a person while giving the impression that the eye is instead turned inward to concentrate on the power of your thoughts rather than the person you are looking at. As a bonus, looking without seeing deflects any embarrassment from the other person in case she is blighted by an obvious physical deformity or a distractingly hairy large wart perched on the end of her nose. If the eyes are windows into a person's heart, then one must use the eyes to project the most impressive image possible. Last, but not the least, is the extravagant display of oratorical skill to demonstrate the power of one's intellect. This is the most potent of all the affectations because words can be wielded like a weapon to injure, handled skillfully like a paintbrush to show artistry, or merely sloshed around like a cathartic to expel noxious mental vapors. The individuals with highly developed oratorical affectations can frequently do all three simultaneously so that they can artistically insult an individual in such an entertaining fashion that the targeted person cannot feel or at least admit to injury. Killing with a light touch demands consummate skill.

I noticed, however, a distinct difference in the oratorical styles between the parents and their offspring. The highly educated children were obviously influenced by their immaturity because their tempo of speech was much quicker. There seemed to be a need to instantaneously follow every statement with a witty or an insightful retort. Every conversation became a fencing match with every quick thrust met by an even quicker parry. Victory was awarded to the person with the last say. The more aggressive attacks came in the form of questions. Query every statement with probing interrogatives disguised as an innocent need for more clarification on a topic that you slyly claim ignorance of. The aim is to expose the speaker's shallow knowledge about that which he is pontificating. This would be analogous to slashing with the sword to maim rather than to merely score. The parents, on the other hand, having progressed past the stage of life dominated by surging testosterone, driving the quest for the title of alpha male, tended to be more sedate but equally consistent. They all preferred to speak slowly with that mushy quasi-English/F. Scott Fitzgerald accent from early Hollywood movies meant to convey an aura of culture and high society. The content of their conversation was uniformly narcissistic with a tortuously slow articulation of every minutia of their everyday thoughts. They seemed so enamored of their own self-image that they probably believe that the listener is truly interested in their mundane mental activities. Every observation was presented as insight and announced as if they were reading from tablets descended from Sinai. My, how clever. My, how perceptive. I found myself pretending to be attentive out of politeness when I was asking myself if this was the end product of success and education. Their company grew quite unattractive to me with each passing hour. Surely, my mother did not wish for me or actually thought that I would even want to fit in with these people.

Beneath the shallowness of their affectations, however, lay the spirit of immigrants no different from the "uneducated" grocer in Chinatown trying to sell his fresh leafy *bok choy* and fragrant dark orange persimmons. Both are striving to succeed and merge into the flow of the American dream. Both are insecure about their own and their children's proper acceptance into American society. Both respond to respect, honor, and kindness just as any decent human being would. Meeting the standards of American and Chinese definitions of personal excellence are high priorities for each group. Unvoiced concerns for their children lingered in the air of each group's conversation. Both intuitively recognize the fragility of financial/material success and the intangible nature of the still powerful requirements of personal development. They also understand that each of these achievements must be simultaneously developed for survival in this world as a respected Chinese American. The successful Chinese American must demonstrate both inward and outward success while having the good graces to be modest about both.

Over the course of that warm summer afternoon, I found myself looking past the style and responding more to the substance of my hosts and their guests. I discovered familiar territory in what initially looked like a foreign country. I began to address the concerns of their hearts rather than the wit of their verbal jousts. I felt and expressed my sympathy and kindness for the hidden pain behind their trivialization of seemingly mundane problems. I chose not to take more than token advantage of their readily offered abundant resources of food and entertainment so as not to indirectly insult and cheapen their home and efforts by an attitude of entitlement or expectation. In other words, I tried to respect them for who they are and not for what they have or the image that they tried to portray.

At the end of the day, the host wished me a very warm farewell, which was a far cry from the good riddance that I was anticipating hours earlier. Many of the other students also gave me their addresses and numbers to maintain contact over the coming academic year. They all seemed to overlook my ill-fitting, sweat-stained clothes and aging family chariot. The patriarch of the house came up to me as I was opening the creaky door of the Chevy. He held me with a piercing, unwavering gaze and thanked me for coming while shaking my hand. He also told me that he had known my parents a long time and had admired them as truly wonderful people. I drove home slowly, basking in the balmy summer breezes blowing through the car windows, which I had rolled down. As I was crossing the Verrazano Narrows Bridge, I couldn't help experiencing the odd feeling of having passed a pop quiz.

When my mother returned home that night after another exhausting day/night at the restaurant, she immediately asked me how the party in Long Island was. I muttered my typical abrupt teenage answer, "All right, I guess." She smiled a knowing smile and mentioned that the host had called her earlier to tell her how much he was impressed by me. She had total faith in me even when I didn't have faith in myself. She didn't want me to adopt or fit into the shallowness of style but rather to recognize and respond to the substance of people, who are all the same no matter what their economic or educational status. She never faltered in her belief in me as she hoped that I would "fit in" just as easily with the grocer as with the corporate executive.

Years later, I would fondly recall that summer afternoon after having just woken up from a nap to see the sunrise through my window in the first-class cabin of a jumbo jet flying over the Atlantic. The insecure and clueless teenager from that summer could never have anticipated that he would someday be invited to comfortably fly to Germany to deliver a lecture. That lecture would occur in an impressive amphitheater in Berlin with simultaneous translation into multiple languages. A curved screen that wrapped around the semicircular walls of the lecture hall would show a variety of ever-changing dramatic scenes from the very recent fall of the Berlin Wall. Those inspiring images were matched to the pounding rhythms of Beethoven's Ninth Symphony in a stirring tribute to celebrate that historic event and the triumph of the human spirit. I felt comfortable in this international gathering of selectively invited physicians just as I felt comfortable in empathizing with the plight of the German people at that time. This immigrant's son from the Smith projects fit in because his mother never faltered in her faith in him. He also tried to never betray that faith in his ability, but most of all, with his willingness to distinguish the fundamental differences between substance and style.

Always Hoping

My mother was able to relate to me with a polished experience, but her interactions with my brother could be more accurately described as a work in progress. He was, unfortunately, the firstborn child. Similar to every firstborn child, he was handed over to the care of parents with no prior experience. I, on the other hand, benefited from the hard lessons learned by my parents from two prior children. I have teasingly described my brother and sister as trial runs while I was the finished product. The truth of it was that I felt hurt whenever my brother and sister felt hurt, and their lessons were also my lessons.

Like many first (or closely second) born children, my older brother and sister were showered by an inconsistent mix of affection, irritation, discipline, and overprotection. The affection arises naturally for many mothers, but my mother's level of intensity left the children with an impression of an unending and an uncompromising source of love. Irritation is another natural consequence for novice mothers whose lives are interrupted with constant around-the-clock demands that any prior life experience could not have prepared them for. Most mothers develop a sense of guilt for feeling irritated at their children. After all, how can these bundles of joy and love also become simultaneous targets for blame as a cause of unhappiness? Discipline is an unending behavioral pattern for many parents that starts with their children's initial expression of their inner urges to the world around them and extend well into old age as parents continue to try to judge and shape how their children run their lives. Discipline becomes an easy habit and an initial response particularly when children seem to have a natural predisposition toward rambunctious behavior beginning early in life, like my brother. Overprotection is another natural response of parents who know all too well the dangerous realities of life and see the potential for psychological and physical injury to their precious children. That overprotection can easily tip over toward excess as it can also stifle a child's ability and desire to explore the world around them as well as develop the courage and skills to effectively interact with that world outside of themselves.

For most mothers, unfortunately, there is no one correct formula for dealing with and raising their children. Child rearing is further complicated by the unique individual qualities of each child. Therein lay the thorn for my brother. He was actually quite fortunate in one way for being the first to be born. A male child is highly desirable in the traditional Chinese family, and a firstborn male portends very good fortune indeed. Clif was therefore showered with unrestrained affections but also, unfortunately, unrestrained expectations. My parents' anticipation for a perfect child in the form of this male firstborn was reinforced by Clif's childhood physical attractiveness and piercingly precocious intellect. Furthermore, his curiosity knew no bounds as he sought to develop an understanding for everything around him. What an auspicious beginning for a first child! The ancestors must have been working in unison to produce such perfection. No expectation, therefore, should be too high for this son to reach. His potential is prodigious, and every niche of that potential shall be fulfilled. The very laws of physics will bend around the contours of this mighty personage. What a tremendously unfair burden that no mere mortal can fulfill. My mother, in her inexperience, believed that only discipline would be required to properly harness all of that potential. The more my brother deviated from that path of perfection, the more vigorously my mother applied the discipline. She failed to see that her precious interactions with her number-one son were slowly condensing into a futile test of wills. This was a typical novice mistake.

Both my brother and sister, but perhaps more so with my brother, seemed to resonate with an elemental spirit. My father's robust vitality and my mother's profound passions undeniably fused within my siblings. They seemed, to my young eyes, like beautiful mountain songbirds yearning to soar free and high. When they sang, their talents produced pure melodies that were so luscious and singularly perfect that the whole world seemed to stand still to listen. The delicate beauty of that essence, however, required nourishment and cultivation and would not tolerate being caged. Without an avenue for expression, any restriction would ruin their souls and destroy that which defines the spiritual beauty within them. My brother, especially, fought against a controlling hand not because he was genetically predisposed to belligerence but because he was fighting to be what he was meant to be. He was only seeking to preserve the viability of who he was through the fulfillment or actualization of that inner self. He needed to fly high and sing. I, on the other hand, took kindly to the hand of discipline. The general chaos, random Brownian motions, and indolent particles of my psyche were a natural fit for a disciplining structure in order to create any sense of purpose and direction (or consciousness). I was attracted to discipline like a positive ion to a negative one whereas my brother reacted to the hand of authority like a killer T-cell to a bacterial infection.

It was years before my mother recognized and accepted these nuances. She continued to hope that my brother would conform to her wishes without realizing that that hope and its implied expectations were essentially pernicious because the desire for him to change and the resultant disappointment from the unwillingness or inability to change was hurtful to all parties. My mother would tell me during the last few years of her life that she gradually understood that my brother was only fighting for his life: to merely be who he was. Her greatest regret was the long delay in reaching this realization. She wished she could have avoided the decades of confrontation through grammar school, high school, and college. Throughout my brother's life, however, until my mother's death, the one unwavering constant was the enormous depth and persistence of my mother's love and support for my brother. She would mumble to me during late-night discussions that her persistent hoping for my brother was born from love and not from intransigence. It broke her heart whenever life did not turn out the way that my brother had hoped for. His disappointments became hers because of her affections for him. She emphasized that this type of dedication is not a mother's blind bias for her son. She did not deny my brother's faults or excuse his responsibility for his actions. She loved him for who he was, which included all his faults and great virtues. Late in life, she understood that he did not need to fulfill her expectations but only his own.

In the end, the constancy of that love was the one lasting residual of my mother's relationship with my brother. He was there for her every time she suffered debilitating episodes during the slow course of her disease toward death. He was there at the end when she finally collapsed into a coma from which she would never recover. He was there for her when she effectively died, literally in his arms. He was there for her as she was always there in her heart for him. In the end, my brother did not falter.

Winners Finish Second

My sister, Cynthia, was involuntarily placed between the horns of the dilemma at birth. She was born an innocent and greatly talented female second child in a Chinese family. Females are generally regarded as second-class citizens in the Chinese mindset. Their status would be further reduced if they happen to follow an already perfect firstborn male child. My sister's intellectual vitality, however, constantly searched for outlets of expression and opportunities to grow. Those opportunities, furthermore, would always be viewed through the lens of female expectations. This is not to say the opportunities were limited, but she carried the extra burden of needing to be mindful of the proper attitude and behavior of a cultivated Chinese girl. How can a talented though fragile bundle of potential find full expression when constrained by convention and cultural expectations? The very expression of that potential would violate cultural convention unless the very fine limits of female acceptable behavior were observed.

These were the types of issues that my mother struggled with. She wanted so much for her baby girl. She wanted her only girl to be perfect in every sense of measurement, but she also wanted her baby to benefit from the unlimited opportunities that she herself was granted in her early life. These idealistic desires, however, ran head on into the reality of her dearth of economic resources during her early years in America. Money was nearly nonexistent at home, the apartment was barely fit for human habitation, and two babies were born fairly close together. She was accustomed to a privileged life and found herself in this predicament without any useful domestic skills. Life, at that time, was a challenge, every minute of every day and night. Crying babies during the day and night, seemingly constant washing of soiled cloth diapers in a rusty sink, rats attacking any exposed foods on the table, and guilt-producing letters from family members in China crying for financial aid all conspired to solidify any sense of despair. My mother, however, refused to succumb and concentrated on reducing her burden to a series of small concrete tasks. She then proceeded to perform those tasks one small step at a time. Only then was she able to manage, learn new skills, and keep her family alive.

My mother would discuss those early years with me, years later, while I was sitting in the family restaurant eating a hot bowl of soup poured on top of white rice. That soup was a particular favorite of mine because the light green broth was made from a delicious, seasonal, and aromatic leafy green vegetable with small white flowers—*tung ho*—mixed with tofu. I was barely paying attention to my mother even though she was speaking with a softly serious tone of voice.

"I have many regrets from those early years before you were born, Dai dai. Life was very difficult, and I could not give the attention that your sister deserved." She sighed and then added, "That she *needed*.

"I had two very young babies on my hands with each of them in diapers. Those 'diapers' were actually discarded soiled napkins retrieved from the restaurant garbage bin by your father. Your brother and sister reused the same napkins over and over. Life was so hectic, we needed so much, and we had so little. As you can imagine, your brother was constantly in need of supervision and was demanding in his inquisitive, precocious, and energetic way. I was just glad that your sister was a very good baby, who was very quiet and passive. It became easy to ignore your sister because of her undemanding nature, especially since there were so many immediately pressing issues presented by your brother and other day-to-day obstacles. That attention that I did not give was precisely what I should have made the time to give. It was exactly what your sister needed as I now look back on the past.

"Your sister would have benefited from more nurturing guidance. She was like a very rich soil capable of growing in a multitude of ways if only the time and effort were spent to care for and cultivate the land. I could tell that her quiet, self-sufficient ways only enabled me to treat her as a secondary consideration. After you were born, I was even more preoccupied with my two boys and newfound work in the sweatshops. Your sister's passive nature and the events of life at that time only made her withdraw slowly into herself.

"Of course, I tried to make up for it in other ways such as providing her with ballet lessons, music lessons, and all the clothing that I could make for her. The attention that I did give, however, was overdone just as I had overreacted to your brother. I was too controlling and tried too hard to make her the perfect girl. I never stopped to consider where her natural desires would lead. I defined what she wanted and how she would achieve her goals. I was, also, overly critical of any initiative that she took on her own especially if it disagreed with my own perceptions. This is one of the regrets that have weighed heavily on my heart over the years. I should have, instead, viewed her initiatives in the perspective of what was appropriate for her age and merely enjoyed her growth rather than subject it to a critical eye and an even sharper tongue. Your sister was a gentle soul who needed more affection and care. Her very sensitivity made her more vulnerable to my impatience. Life did not grant me the opportunities for reflection and proper understanding during those early years.

"Over the years, I could see that your sister was developing a sense of hesitation and uncertainty. This seemed to produce a continual need for me to guide her. She was always looking over her shoulder for my approval." My mother sighed and added, "Perhaps it would be more accurate to say that she grew timid because she was always anticipating another critical remark from me."

I slowed in my slurping of the hot *tung ho* soup with rice because I realized that my mother's self-castigation had adopted a more somber and reflective tone than I had expected for a casual afternoon chat. I started to feel the beginning twinges of guilt and shame. Did my very birth and existence contribute to my sister's relative neglect?

Before I could add my own self-centered guilt to my mother's swallowed sorrows, she continued her reflection of her past perceptions.

"I held on so tightly when your brother and sister were young. I was so inexperienced and had no guidance. We were, after all, all alone in this strange country. This is not meant as an excuse but merely a statement of fact. My actions did not accurately reflect my intentions and affections, but daily life did not allow me the luxury of the contemplation that accompanies wisdom. Your father and I were in a constant state of physical and emotional exhaustion. The physical burdens were work related and the emotional burdens came from pleas for help from China through heart-rending letters written by surviving family members."

I can recall the many evenings I spent as a very young boy standing guard by the kitchen window to watch for my mother's return from the long hours at the sweatshop. She would always greet me warmly and energetically when I ran to her by the apartment door. My heart was at peace, and I was content to just sit at the kitchen table to watch her clean up and prepare the evening meal for the whole family. Her work, of course, never ended with dinner. After caring for the immediate physical needs of the three children, my mother would grill us on any hidden misadventures of the day and preparations for the requirements of the following day of school. She would continue to clean the rest of the house and do the laundry while preparing us for our nightly baths. I would always emerge from the tub with wrinkled skin because of my prolonged immersion in the increasingly dirty bath water. As usual, I had spent more time playing with the soot-encrusted bath toys, which I kept by the bathroom window, than washing myself. My day's accumulation of grime was simply replaced by newer window soot. I would still be half wet (or half dry) when I would search out my mother, expecting another lavish helping of affection for having completed the monumental task of bathing without calling for help. She would frequently be sitting in the living room half asleep while stringing beads for mere cents per piece. She would do this for hours after I had gone to bed to augment the money that she could send back to China for her suffering family. The casual observer may conclude that the small remuneration was not justified by the disproportional effort on her part, but my mother never considered effort to be relevant. She never allowed herself to relax her dedication and effort while clinging to the belief that every penny would be well earned and spent. So long as the children did not have major problems to be addressed, Mahmee was happy because so much was needed to be done. Somewhere in the cauldron of daily life, my quiet sister watched and waited.

"I wanted so much for your sister. She was my only daughter, and I wished for her life to be full of possibilities. I wanted her to be accomplished, educated, and independent. I also wanted her to simultaneously be polite, humble, and graciously giving. These all required a development of person and skills. In retrospect, I believe that my desires for her were probably interpreted as merely being driven. It would seem to a child that I pushed and pushed. What I really wanted to communicate to her was the depth of my love for her and my wish for her to have a fulfilling life."

From my own point of view as a younger sibling, I thought my sister was wildly successful in achieving my mother's wishes for her. Over the years, I observed my sister exhibit outstanding athletic ability and razor-sharp academic acumen. As an undergraduate mathematics major, she was asked to work in the lab of a Nobel laureate in physics to assist with the mathematical challenges of ongoing investigations. She succeeded in every endeavor that she undertook. I can remember that her description of her thesis for her master's degree in mathematics was so foreign to me that it seemed that she was describing an automobile engine. Her desire to teach led to another master's degree in education. Her skills in explaining complex mathematical theory in easily understandable terms not only attested to her depth of understanding but also put her in a position of being highly sought after. Her later ventures in the corporate business world provided her with rapid and lofty advancement in the banking industry, all accomplished with relative ease. Outward success was merely a puzzle to be mastered.

What could not be seen with the superficial eye were all the self-sacrifices throughout the years. My sister initially voluntarily attended a less demanding high school in order to provide familiar company for relatives. I would always remember her choosing to attend a state university to minimize the expenses for my parents when she had the ability to attend any prestigious university in the country. I also remember her ready willingness to help with any problem in the college dormitory during her years of tenure as a resident assistant. It was her job to help, but her easy and friendly demeanor as well as her effective problem-solving skills made her an invaluable cog and a focal point in the daily lives of many college students. In short, she was a leader—a very good and natural leader.

Of course, I had personally benefited from my sister's altruism. There were too many times that my older sister patiently led me out of the tangle of grammar school's social studies problems. She never chastised me for being unable to solve rudimentary academic problems because I wallowed in a lethal mixture of self-indulgent laziness and innate stupidity. It was her concern for my stunted adolescent social skills that motivated her to coerce me into accompanying her to a variety of social and recreational activities. Several included outings that involved activities such as horseback riding, picnics, and swimming. Often, I was outclassed by the company, which frequently consisted of Ivy League graduates with professional degrees and beautiful young Seven Sisters women with elegance and style. These young and highly accomplished Chinese Americans were usually part of prestigious Chinese fraternities and sororities. I was part of nothing, but I was always treated warmly with a sense of inclusion because I benefited from being Cynthia's younger brother. My sister always watched out for me and never ever patronized me or left me with the impression of being a burden for her. She treated me with so much kindness despite enduring my horribly psychotic preteen years when I would regularly inflict premeditated, unprovoked torture on her just for entertainment. How much more perfect can anyone expect their older sister to be?

It made me happy when my sister was happy. I remember the times when she positively glowed. She returned from a trip to Hawaii, with my mother during her late teenage years, with such a glow. She stunned all those around her with her presence during the trip. It even culminated in a marriage proposal from a respected Chinese professional who was dazzled during his short time with my sister. There also seemed to be a continual parade of male friends who visited my sister every holiday and summer during her college and graduate school days. They ranged from graduate to professional-school students. My sister was merely flying and singing, with the others entranced by her song. Those times, however, were relatively brief as Cynthia would frequently put her own needs secondary to the needs of others.

To this day, my sister has devoted her life to serving her husband and daughter. It pains me to see her regularly swallow the bitterness and disappointments of others without recognition. Her skills go untapped as she voluntarily closes the gate to her cage in deference to others.

On more than one occasion, I have had good reason to cherish the memories of support from my older sister. She looked after me without prompting or expectations of reward. She looked after me as she has sacrificed for others at her own expense. Every time I stand at a podium, I can feel my sister's encouragement and strength behind me. I have not forgotten that my brother and I received much attention while my sister stood by the side and waited.

Three West,
St. Louis Children's Hospital,
1978

Emergencies, by definition, occur suddenly and without warning. Emergencies are difficult to prepare for just as it is difficult, if not impossible, to prepare for every type of emergency in any and every type of situation. Emergencies are the most dreaded situations for every newly stamped doctor straight out of medical school. The most dreaded emergency is the "code," which was short for a patient who had stopped breathing and whose heart had stopped beating. A code usually generated frenetic activity and huge panic-inducing adrenaline surges because the clock was ticking, and time is against you and the patient. Every second that passes without revival brought the patient a second closer to death. Most patients only had a grace period measured in minutes during a code before their fall becomes irretrievable. A physician is acutely aware that there is zero tolerance for failure, and the patient pays the ultimate price for mistakes.

A code was called not twenty-five feet away from my position at the nursing station. I was in the midst of completing chart work for the patients that I had been caring for. It had been a very difficult past several months for me since I had graduated from medical school. The difficulty did not arise from my chronic lack of sleep (I had already been working for thirty-six continuous hours), numerous overnight admissions, mind-breaking multitasking (simultaneously caring for fifteen acutely ill patients), and the painstakingly detailed concentration that was required for the care of patients with diseases that were so complex that very few similar cases were even reported in the literature. My medical-school experience had prepared me quite well for these types of demands. The greatest difficulty for me lay in the psychological weight of my responsibilities. Failure is not an option. I carried an overwhelming responsibility for the health of many children, the final greatest resource of any individual and society. I carried the weight of nearly impossible lofty expectations for any graduate of my particular notable medical school. I carried the weight of expectations of this particular hospital, which has a century-old tradition of caring for the sickest and most difficult pediatric patients from around the world. I carried the weight of expectations of this pre-eminent pediatric training program, whose director chose to give this son of an immigrant a chance to train with the best. Finally and most personally, I carried the weight of all the hopes and dreams of my parents. Under these conditions, I glanced up from the chart I was writing in to observe a nurse cradling a limp female toddler in her arms while rushing into the nearby central treatment room on this cardiology ward.

I hurriedly entered the treatment room through a nearby door at precisely the same moment as the rest of my fellow residents and interns converged through a door at the opposite side of the room. The cute blond-haired girl lay limp on the examining table while many voices spoke simultaneously.

"Somebody speak to me! What's going on?"

"What's the girl's blood pressure?"

"What's the diagnosis and reason for admission?"

"Anyone get a pulse?"

"Where's the pulse ox?"

"Someone listen for breath sounds."

"What medications is she taking?"

"Any known allergies?"

I tended to stand back and let the present senior residents handle the situation because I was not only a lowly new intern in the hierarchy, but I was also among the least experienced in the group. As the seconds ticked by, however, I felt a rising cascade of anxiety and overwhelming worry. They're taking too long in the assessment. This girl is becoming quite pale and fading fast. Her life will soon end unless someone takes concrete action to save her. I couldn't take it anymore and jumped in while speaking softly but authoritatively to everyone around me.

I looked at the experienced nurse beside me and asked for the tongue blade and the endotracheal tube. I calmly but quickly slipped the life-saving tube into the girl's windpipe to establish a patent airway and started to help her breathe while I simultaneously instructed a nearby senior resident to start an intravenous line and hang a bottle of LR solution after a bolus of sodium bicarbonate. I had another resident continue bagging the girl while I instructed the nurse to put cardiac monitor leads on the patient. I turned around to charge the defibrillator paddles while awaiting the cardiac monitor to register the EKG readings. It was immediately apparent that the patient's heart was not beating followed by short periods of asynchronous rhythm. I applied the paddles and jolted the girl's heart with a short electrical pulse. Sweat had started to pour down my forehead as I anxiously stared hopefully at the monitor. A sense of relief swept through me as her heart began to establish a normal beat. She was less pale, and her blood pressure rose to a more normal range.

The little girl had been revived. She wasn't even my patient, but I gave her assigned intern a list of blood tests to run after transferring her to the cardiac intensive care unit. The whole experience seemed like it had occurred in slow motion, and I found my undershirt drenched in sweat, which chilled my whole body. I didn't think that the girl would survive because we took too long to revive her. I would later discover that what seemed to be an excruciatingly long, traumatic event endured for perhaps thirty minutes had, in fact, lasted precisely two minutes and thirty-five seconds. The classic experience of prolongation of time during times of extreme stress was entirely produced by the flood of adrenaline washing through my body. It would not subside until several hours later when I was walking home. Total exhaustion would overtake me that evening over dinner with my wife of two years. She smiled at me as I fell asleep sitting up in front of my dinner plate. I get to start the whole cycle all over again at 6:30 the following morning.

The next day, I received a page to go to the program director's office after morning rounds. I was sick with worry. What did I do now? No one had ever been paged to go to the director's office in the middle of the workday. Did he change his mind about my position and feel that I was unworthy of remaining in this elite training program? Will I have to return to New York in shame and disgrace? How can I face my wife and my parents? Will I ever be able to get into another training program anywhere else in the country after my disgraceful dismissal here? What will I do?

As I exited the elevator at the top floor of the hospital, I was struck by its entirely different ambience. The place exuded the aura of an executive suite. Lush, soft carpets softened my steps so that I had to strain to hear myself walking. The walls were lined with richly polished woods and a line of portraits of distinguished individuals who had previously walked these same hallways. Some of those figures had the face of former Nobel Prize winners. The entire atmosphere intimidated me as I walked toward the end of the corridor toward a smiling secretary. She volunteered that the program director was waiting for me, and I was to go right in. My palms were drenched in sweat as I opened the door and stepped toward my inevitable beheading.

My heart was still beating rapidly as I emerged from the office five minutes later. I was still in shock over the experience. No only was I not dismissed with disgrace, but I was actually officially commended. Apparently, the senior nurse during yesterday's code had written me up for commendation for my actions during the code, which resulted in the saving of the toddler's life. She was impressed that a new intern had the calm presence of mind and intellect as well as procedural skills to direct, perform, and coordinate the handling of the cardio-pulmonary emergency when relative chaos and delay were compounding a dire situation even in the presence of more senior and experienced physicians.

As I retraced my steps toward the elevators, my heart calmed from a state of life-threatening panic to a mere sprinting rate. In fact, I felt embarrassed. I know in my heart what was going through my mind yesterday. It was sheer, heart-rending worry for the child that compelled me to action, which overstepped my lowly boundaries. I was no hero, and I certainly felt that recognition for merely doing my job was a bit too generous. Moreover, I was actually a little concerned that my more senior colleagues would take exception to my assertive demeanor, which did not carry an appropriate and necessary degree of deference during the code.

Where did I get the nerve to jump into action yesterday? It seems so atypical of my usually passive personality. These are uncharted waters for me because no one else in my family is a physician. What possible role models could my unconscious have drawn inspiration from?

Leadership

During my teenage years, I used to marvel at my mother's ability to inspire loyalty and devotion from the hired help at the restaurant. This petite middle-aged woman, who every morning donned a tiny hairpiece to cover the thinning at the top of her head, was able to direct all the workers (young, old, handsome, gruesomely ugly, gentle, and temperamental) to do her bidding to the point where they collectively ran the restaurant. She was even able to convince them to help her do some of the chores around the house and garden. They took delight when she was satisfied with their work and redoubled their efforts if anything was amiss or incomplete. They very much did not want to disappoint my mother. Many of them would express concern over my mother's long hours and growing fatigue. It would not be unusual for the workers to compel my mother to sit and close her eyes while they tended to their duties at the tables as well as my mother's chores behind the bar.

Their feelings for my mother did not end with their tenure at the restaurant. Many would leave to complete their education. Others would leave for higher-paying jobs closer to their apartments. Still others would leave to get married and start a family. Most would return to show my mother their new college degrees, new wives, new children, and new cars. My mother expressed her pride in their ability to improve and progress in their lives just as if they were all her own children and relatives.

Her secret, I learned, was that her feelings were genuine. She related to people not by her outward actions but inwardly with her heart. She always told me that the most important development for me would have to occur in the inside—within my heart. That is where I should concentrate my efforts. I knew that she focused mainly on her inner development, and the results were very tangible and concrete. She cared and possessed no hint of duplicity.

"Dai dai ah, your father and I are the owners of this restaurant, but we carry the special burden of being the leaders of this enterprise."

I thought she was saying the obvious and didn't see what the point was.

"Leadership requires special insight and character development in order for that quality to exist. Many people mistakenly believe that leadership is automatically granted to the person who possesses the money to start a business. Ownership merely creates a boss with workers, not a leader. People who do your bidding because you pay them are only defined within the constraints of the financial arrangement with you. Such a business will struggle to thrive because it treats people, including the owner, as mere commodities. Any organization is only as good as the people in it. Any organization is defined by its people. The people are not and should never be considered as interchangeable parts."

It sounded like a pseudo-insightful aphorism to me, but I still didn't get her point.

"Do you see how everyone works so conscientiously? They don't have to do that, yet they not only do it, but they do so willingly. You see, Dai dai, leadership is not a position of privilege. Leadership is a burden of responsibility. We have the responsibility to serve those who work here."

Now I really didn't get it. Doesn't the boss get to count his money in the limousine while the workers slave away at the assembly line? Isn't this the whole American idea of capitalism?

I believe my mother was supplementing my father's thoughts about conducting business. I learned that any relationship defined only by money is merely another form of prostitution. Of course, society uses many convenient euphemisms to disguise, even from itself, the bare nature of a business relationship. In the final analysis, multinational transactions on the ninetieth floor of awe-inspiring buildings can be no different, in essence, from those that occur on the grimy street corners of Forty-second Street in Manhattan.

My mother continued, "Real leadership cannot be fabricated, purchased with money, or conferred with ownership. It can only come from within a person's character. The more developed that character is, the better the leader will be. This is because a leader must care, truly care. I'm not referring to a semblance of caring for the workers so that they will work harder. I'm talking about the genuine absence of ulterior motive and secondary gain. This requires a person to see the workers as individuals and not as workers. Seeing others as individuals does not allow you to reduce them by impersonalizing them. You will see them as people who possess worth and value. They become your responsibility and deserving of your care. That is why your father and I provide free housing and food for all the workers. That is why we encourage many to go on and improve their lives. That is why we treat everyone here as an equal. Helping someone to cultivate a sense of pride and integrity is a powerful gift that can be unforgettable for the recipient."

My mother waited to see if I was absorbing what she was trying to tell me. "Most people without a heart of complete stone would tend to respond positively to kindness, to well-wishes, and to good intentions. When they realize that you are looking out for their well-being, people would want to respond in similar fashion. They will also come to realize that your motivations are pure, and they often will begin to adopt your causes as their own. If you take actions only from a desire to improve the restaurant, they too will want to help you to achieve that goal. They will not take advantage of you because you will have shown that you are not trying to take advantage of them. A business or an organization can then progress to be greater than the sum of the individual parts. All the members of the business will want to add their collective enthusiasm, ingenuity, and sweat to create a product that would be beyond the abilities of just the owner[s] alone."

I realized that this wasn't just parental mumbo jumbo because I've seen it work every day at the restaurant.

"You must start to develop your leadership skills by developing yourself within your own heart. A leader does not take charge. A leader does not tell others what to do. A leader cares enough to serve and does not expect to be served. Very few people understand the true nature of leadership and even fewer possess it."

I would realize years later that this was what I was drawing from during my reaction to the code in St. Louis, which was so far away in every sense of the word from that conversation in Staten Island. Others responded to me because they realized the purity of my intent. My only concern was for the recovery of the child, and my only focus was accomplishing all that is needed to be done to achieve that end. Everything else was not only secondary but was nonexistent. I had also simultaneously realized the panic in the room and tried to reassure everyone through my actions and attitude that everything was under control and all will be well.

To this day, I have tried to maintain continuity with the role model that my mother provided for me. My daily professional priority centers on a clarity of focus and motivation without being tainted by secondary benefit. Some consider this type of idealism to border on naiveté. For me, however, every decision and action flows naturally without hesitation from an undisturbed heart. There is no alternative but to be concerned with the welfare of all those who work with me, from the fellows and residents to the nurses and technologists. I keep them focused on helping the patient to safely navigate through dangerous and difficult examinations of their brain and spine while I conducted myself in a way that also strives to minimize their stress while engaged in these intrinsically threatening activities. No panic. Any well-intentioned mistake is correctable. No finger pointing and no yelling. I assure the patient and my fellow colleagues that all is well, and we will all work to get through this together. I promise this, and everyone is willing to go wherever this son of immigrants will lead.

My mother did leave me with one caveat on the matter of leadership or more specifically, the appearance of leadership. "Dai dai ah, as you gain more experience in the world, you will come across many clever people who are adept at portraying and cultivating the image of benevolence and care. They are skillful at drawing attention to their calculated performance of overtly observable kind acts without betraying even a hint of the complete absence of kindness in their hearts. Remember that acts do not sanctify the person, but it is rather the quality of the individual that sanctifies the act."

I was surprised to hear my mother paraphrasing Meister Eckhart because I was quite doubtful that she had ever heard of the man, no less read the literature about him (unless it had been translated and then taught in Cantonese at a specific girls' boarding school in southern China during the years before World War II, which seems even less plausible). This medieval Catholic mystic of the Dominican order sermonized his parishioners to be less concerned about what they do and be more concerned about what they are. In other words, they should be less concerned about doing good deeds and be more concerned about improving their inner selves. He taught that deeds do not sanctify the person, but it is rather the person who sanctifies the deed. To hear my mother echo these same concepts, arrived at solely by the strength of her own character and intellect, reinforced her formidable image in my young mind. The memory of it is still impressive to this currently not-so-young mind, whose wisdom would be far more dependent on books were it not for the decades of guidance from extraordinary parents.

Air-Duct Conversations

I continue to be surprised that parents, including myself, are so unaware of the extent of confidential family information that their children already know. There are no family secrets. Children seem to know everything that we try to keep from them. In fact, there appears to be an inverse proportional relationship. The harder we try to hide secrets from our children, the more determined they become to find out about them. This tends to dramatically increase the amount that our children know about those precise facts that we don't wish them to know. I plead guilty on all counts for being the type of deviously saucy child who was constantly drawn to taste from the forbidden fruit of knowledge. My determination to know the answer to all secrets would have even defeated Santa Claus's deft arrival at my house. Pity, I didn't apply that determination to my school work.

My own parents used to think that their conversations were safe from me. After all, they tended to engage in their most serious conversations after my father would return home from the restaurant between one and three in the morning, which would be hours after I had already gone to bed; besides, they would be talking in the basement while my bedroom was upstairs, separated from the basement by sound-proofing foam tiles. My brother and sister had already left the house to attend college, which significantly decreased the amount of random activity around the house at all hours. My own routine was regular and predicated on the demands of a rigorous high-school schedule. My movements were, therefore, quite predictable or so my parents thought.

Two forces worked against my parents' confidentiality. The first was the persistence of my congenital need to know everything, especially concerning family matters and particularly parental opinions. The second was a physically designed element of our house, namely the air ducts. The house was heated and cooled by central units located in the basement immediately adjacent to the kitchen area, which, in turn, was in very close approximation to the basement dining area. The ducts of the ventilation system were designed to carry hot or cool air from the units in the basement to the entire house. This was also a very effective means to carry the sounds from any conversations near the basement kitchen and the dining area to the bedrooms upstairs. I spent many nights lying awake in bed, listening to my parents' "private" thoughts and conversations.

Their mundane concerns about the day-to-day operations of the restaurant were the least interesting to me even though my lifestyle greatly benefited from those "boring" details. I did learn, however, that those same details created a grueling routine that exacted a harsh physical toll on my parents, particularly on my mother. It broke my heart to listen to my mother's graphic descriptions of her daily discomforts. I never realized because she never told or exposed her suffering to me because she did not want to burden my young life with what she considered as inappropriate concerns. My life at this time, she mentioned, should be about dreams and possibilities, whose pursuit should not be hindered by the twin psychological burdens of worry and guilt. It was one of the first times in my life that I began to develop a clearer understanding that the opportunities that I enjoyed and assumed with a sense of entitlement in my everyday life were painfully extracted for me at considerable cost with interest. My awareness of that cost did not become so much a hideous spiritual burden than a source of inspiration, which motivated my silent oath to never violate the integrity of my parents' gift to me by striving to live a life with honor. This, in retrospect, seems naïve but, perhaps, an appropriate form of idealism for a high-school teenager whose parents showered with encouragement and support. Little did I know that the murky, convoluted, and ethically ambiguous details of real life would later test and superimpose hesitancy to that conviction time after time with obfuscation, rationalization, and seductive secondary gain. In the end, however, it would be that very conviction that would help me make very unambiguous choices. That help would prove to be a pivotal influence in my decisions regarding the direction and tone of my personal and professional life in the years to come. Proper action requires clear vision, which can only come from clear and right-minded thoughts. Eastern platitudes, like Sunday sermons, though, are easy to verbalize and to listen to with nodded heads but extraordinarily difficult to live up to. My parents, however, provided a very concrete directional beacon for me merely by how they lived their lives.

Occasionally, my parents would broach topics that gave me a glimpse into their innermost selves when they would discuss their concerns for us, the children. I, like other children, found it amusing that my parents still referred to my brother, sister, and me by our childhood nicknames and personality traits when in fact, we were physical adults and two were of legal age. I, also, currently exercise this habitual parental right even though my youngest towers over me. During more than one late-night discussion, my mother expressed a desire to show us our ancestral home in China.

"Wouldn't it be nice to be able to show our children the beautiful Chinese countryside and the estate where I used to live?"

In an unexpectedly slightly brusque tone, my father would ask, "Why would we want to do that?"

"I'd like to show them the grandeur of their history. I'd like them to see that their parents come from backgrounds that would defy belief. I'd like to show them where they come from."

I would recall this segment of the conversation in the fall of 1991 when my family and I were sitting in a restaurant, eating that establishment's specialty of flash fried leafy vegetables. That restaurant was located in what was then called the New Territories just outside of Hong Kong. I had been invited as the featured speaker on a lecture tour through four countries along the Asian perimeter and my wife and I decided to bring the children along with us on this unique opportunity. It was a pampered experience for us with limousine services everywhere and gourmet meals every evening. The vegetables were like none that I had ever eaten. Every mouthful was delightfully light and airy without any expected heavy hint of grease despite it having been deep fried. The spices were wonderfully aromatic, yet they did not hide the underlying taste of the vegetable itself. The satisfied smiles on the faces of my wife and children warmed my heart. Their happiness is my raison d'être. It was then that I remembered my mother's words. Here I sat, not on a three-hour drive from what used to be my mother's house, but this was an opportunity that had come too late. My mother had died only two years earlier. I believe the same wave of sadness that washed over me would also wash over my father as he would later join us to share some time in Hong Kong.

My father answered, "What is there left to show them? The China that we knew no longer exists. Your family mansion has been converted into a three-story school. Chinese culture has been reduced to only a shell of itself with everyone wearing the same monotonous peasant jackets and waving that little red book as if it was written by God. Everyone spies on everybody else. Children are reinforced if they turn in their own parents for 'counter revolutionary' thoughts! There is no more of the real China to show our children, and our family roots have been destroyed by a genuinely evil person with the cultural limitations of an ignorant peasant." After a slight pause, my father continued, "Our children are American. They are Chinese American, and America will be their proud history."

My mother then asked, "But what will we leave them about their Chinese history? How will they know what it means to be Chinese?"

This question brought to mind another dinner that I participated in several years earlier. It was a delicious ten-course Chinese wedding banquet held in New York's Chinatown. I used to love the abalone with oyster sauce, dark and crispy roasted squab, and savory bird's nest soup that were fairly standard but expensive items for most of these types of exquisite banquets. The thought-provoking surprise of that warm summer evening for me was the groom's speech. I was initially shocked when I saw him at the microphone because he was a "loh fahn" (a not-so-complimentary term for Caucasians). The bride was clearly Chinese, and both the bride's and groom's parents seated at the head table all looked Chinese to me. I was even more puzzled because a glance at my mother revealed a smile on her lips rather than shock in her eyes. How could my mother look so approvingly on this obviously mixed marriage? This type of mixture even seemed dubious to my own American-born eyes. My mother whispered to me that she had known the groom and his family for years. The groom had carried quite a reputation for being a very good son. How could an unruly loh fahn be considered a good boy in a normally civilized Chinese family? My mother saw the puzzled look on my adolescent face and told me that the groom's biological parents were Italian from nearby Little Italy, and he was adopted by this dear and caring Chinese family when he was a very young boy. As the groom began his wedding speech, I was stunned that he did not speak English as I had anticipated. He, instead, spoke in perfect Cantonese, even better than I could have managed. He spoke politely and eloquently with perfectly formal diction that was beautifully punctuated by a palpable sincerity in his voice. I remember him taking the effort to thank the guests for sharing this joyous occasion with him. He was effusively appreciative for the generous gifts given by the guests. The most memorable part of his speech came at the end when he looked at his adoptive parents and gave thanks for their love and support. He thanked them for taking him into their family so many years ago, and he felt that he owed his very life to these people—his parents. He made a few self-effacing comments and joked about his loh-fahn appearance. Then he turned his eyes from his parents to the audience and said that he was hugely grateful to his Chinese cultural upbringing in a loving family within this close and warm Chinese community. In his heart, he emphasized as he finished, he saw himself as Chinese and would, therefore, always consider himself as Chinese. With these final words, the whole audience of several hundred guests stood up and burst into wild, thunderous applause. It was a touching moment as his whole family embraced him, in a culturally uncharacteristic but irresistible public display of affection. The emotions flowed throughout the room without restraint as tears filled the eyes of everyone in the wedding party as well as the simultaneously cheering audience. I left the celebrations that evening feeling both elated and inspired. The evening, however, also provoked deeper questions. What does it really mean to be Chinese? Does it mean being born with the genes and physical appearance of someone Chinese? Does the ability to speak the Chinese language qualify a person to be called Chinese? Does the inability to speak Chinese disqualify a person? Can a person who only studies Chinese language and culture through books be considered Chinese? Is it only people who look Chinese and can speak Chinese considered Chinese? Am I really Chinese? I had always been referred to in the Chinatown community as "juk sing" (empty bamboo or American-born Chinese), which was often said in jest with a hint of condescension, but it also carried the connotation of being less than fully Chinese. Again, I asked myself how was it that I considered myself to be Chinese and what were the requirements needed to qualify as Chinese. What exactly is the nature of my legacy?

These were some of the same questions that my parents addressed during their late-night conversation. What does it mean to be Chinese? Does waving a red booklet and paying homage to a balding fat fascist with poor personal hygiene qualify as Chinese? Does the ability to recite Chinese history and quote from Mencius make an individual Chinese? How about the poor and illiterate, who labor in virtual slavery and suffer from racial discrimination in America? Do they qualify for consideration as Chinese? Does the wealthy white New York lawyer's expert knowledge about the history and the quality of Chinese jade and porcelain qualify him as Chinese? Despite these ambiguities, I would venture a guess that not one person at that wedding banquet would have disputed the fact that the groom was Chinese.

My father would say, "What exactly are we leaving the children? Is it Chinese culture? If so, which one are we leaving because it has been changing throughout its history and has especially evolved into a hideous form in the middle of the twentieth century? So what is the point of showing them the old country, which no longer exists? What is the point even if it still exists?"

My mother added, "My grandfather made the same points to me when I was a little girl. He said that Chinese culture and its language, like any other culture, was essentially fluid, which changes and conforms itself to the times. It is, therefore, difficult to accurately define in a fixed, concrete fashion while ignoring its relative nature though some academicians can make careers of that task. It is also only the most superficial, though visible, aspect of a persona. Chinese culture could be a significant part of a person's makeup, but it is only a *small* part that does not [and should not] completely define that person. Anyone who allows them to be defined only by their ethnicity or culture does a great disservice to themselves. The placement of such fundamental limitations on a person's most basic sense of self and potential is very shortsighted with dangerous long-term ramifications. Those limitations contribute to the planting of the very destructive seeds that can give rise to the formation and acceptance of the mental and moral quicksand that is racism. The ability to exceed your own culture, on the other hand, is also within everyone. The realization of that potential enables substantive and fundamental forward progress to occur for the individual and society."

I can remember both of my parents discussing what they wanted the children to feel and understand about their links to their past. That past would enrich and be a part of what they are, but it would not define or predetermine what they are or will be. Over the course of many nights listening to many conversations, I would come to understand that the nature of those links does not consist of historical facts, languages, or customs. Those links across generations were fabricated entirely by the love and affection spread from one generation to the next. It was the affection that formed the glue or connection between the groom and his parents. That affection also closely linked the groom to everyone at the wedding banquet despite a total lack of physical resemblance between the groom and anyone else in the room. My father wanted us, his children, to start our own traditions here in America, but we would be linked to my parents by their love for us just as they, in turn, were linked to their parents by their affections. We would ensure that continuity by generously sharing our affections with those that come after us either through birth or marriage. This feeling of being part of a long line of people is quite powerful and enabling. One never feels alone, even when living by himself, because he become part of something that is greater than himself. The generations of support is always there and becomes almost physically palpable. This type of legacy across generations cannot be defeated by distance, time, or force. It cannot be limited by narrow definitions, genetics, or cultural biases, yet for each individual in the chain, it is also a unique experience because of the singular connection that finally goes through himself.

Over the course of several years, I would slowly develop a greater appreciation for the nuances of my parents' thoughts. I would understand that their legacy to my siblings and to me was richer than cultural habits, customs, or anything else I could have anticipated. That understanding allowed me to grow very comfortable within myself, and I had no problems simply describing myself as Chinese American without any sense of doubt or need to explain and clarify. The term is merely a mixed ethnic description that doesn't even remotely approach my vast and unique position across generations of affection. My father and great-grandfather's beliefs shared the sentiment that it is a person's heart and character and not his cultural familiarity that would define and honor his heritage. This mindset enabled a traditionally raised Chinese man to learn from and accept Western traditions, a Chinese boy from the countryside to fight for the American army, and an Italian-born boy to be considered and be accepted as wholly Chinese.

The "Bed" in the Basement

My mother survived for two years after her initial diagnosis of liver cancer. A growing sense of fatigue motivated her to see a series of doctors to determine the cause for this slow and insidious feeling of debilitation. In the beginning, it was difficult to distinguish her complaints from her chronic baseline fatigue, which accompanied her decades of overwork and little sleep. She knew, however, that this additional fatigue was different. Several visits to a final authority in Manhattan would reveal that the liver cancer that had taken root. This was the final lasting, ugly insult from the horrors suffered during World War II. The cancer was probably a long-term complication from the hepatitis that afflicted my mother during the "run" in China while trying to escape the leading edge of the Japanese devastation as they marched through that country.

The gradual failure of her liver to remove the daily accumulation of normal bodily toxins from her bloodstream was the cause of my mother's slowly increasing sense of fatigue. She found herself in an unfamiliar territory with the irresistible urge to take naps during the middle of the day and then capitulating to those needs and actually taking those naps. She would rationalize that the luxury of napping was affordable because it would not interfere with everyday duties. After all, it had been years since the family had lost the restaurant, and she had also given up her work at the sewing factory after the restaurant's closure. She would, however, continue her lifetime ritual of preparing the evening meals for her husband as he returned from his new employment as a mail courier for an investment firm on Wall Street. My mother was initially worried that my father would consider the new line of work to be too menial considering his past lifetime of accomplishments, but she thought that the work would be an improvement over the unending days of moping at home. Much to her surprise, my father felt rejuvenated by the work and approached the job with his old gusto and enthusiasm. His character inspired her even as the creeping shadow of an acidic fatigue dampened any lasting sense of joy.

Life was, initially, relatively normal immediately after her diagnosis. My mother greatly enjoyed the support and the comfort of her new friendships developed during this later stage of her life, the most memorable of these friendships formed with the loving person of Regina. Regina was a very good friend even before my mother's diagnosis, but they became the best of friends after the diagnosis. At a time when "friends," relatives, and other acquaintances slowly and embarrassingly, though revealingly, dissipated during the years following the loss of the restaurant and now her health, Regina not only remained a steadfast friend, but she also redoubled her efforts to comfort my mother. Regina was the loving and the devoted sister whose mere presence greatly enhanced the quality of my mother's last years of life. She was a guardian angel or a saint sent to shed some light for my mother during her darkest hours.

My mother initially made the acquaintance with Regina several years before her illness. They had shared the same working environment, but my mother was immediately drawn to this pleasant, engaging woman who was at least a decade younger than herself. Regina was also an immigrant, but my mother recognized the spark, the intelligence, and the compassion of a kindred spirit.

Not since her schoolgirl days had Suit Ying felt this connection with another sister of the soul. Work became less of a daily chore than of a social occasion because of Regina. Their interactions at the factory were scented by a continuous stream of insightful, energetic, and always humorous conversations. Their admiration was a mutual experience, and they quickly became frequent companions during and also after working hours. Suit Ying's weekends were often punctuated by Regina's good company with her departure during the evening hours necessitated only by her duties and responsibilities for her own husband and family.

The slow but unstoppable progression of Suit Ying's cancer eventually forced her to cease working at the sewing factory. Regina, however, maintained her almost daily interactions with my mother. It would not be unusual for Regina to visit my mother after work before going home during the week while bringing luscious treats of Chinese delicacies and specialty dishes to her on the weekends. Regina's spirit and genuine affections were highly cherished by Suit Ying, and her visits soon became the highlight of her day.

My mother's growing fatigue not only forced a stoppage of work but also made it difficult for her to move around the house. Most of her days were spent in the basement, which had always been used as the de facto family room—primary living space. Nighttime was, of course, spent in the bedrooms upstairs. Suit Ying soon found the short climb up the stairs to her bedroom to be excessively taxing on her rapidly dwindling small reserve supply of energy. For this reason, she converted the basement couch into her bed. With some creative padding, strategically placed blankets, and additional cushions, the couches became a sitting area by day and a conveniently located bed at night. The bed in the basement also allowed my mother to cook and clean with minimal effort as the basement was equipped with its own kitchen, the laundry facilities were also downstairs, and guests usually congregated in the basement. The bed in the basement became my mother's final resting place at home. It was where my brother cradled my mother in his arms as she fell into a coma. It was where my father would lie down to sleep during the years following my mother's death.

The basement bed also provided another convenience, which became quite important for my mother and me. It was within a short arm's reach to the telephone, which was positioned on the coffee table next to the bed/couch. Over the years, I had developed the habit of calling my mother during the late-morning hours. That time was convenient for me because it occurred during a lull in the professional activities that required my direct personal intervention. I would have just finished reviewing and assigning work to the radiology residents and neuroradiology fellows, who were training under me, and there would be some time before they would be ready for another bolus of work from me. I had made an extra effort to regularly call my mother since her diagnosis of cancer was established. With the end of her life crystallized from an intellectual abstraction to a concrete and imminent event, my mother used her remaining time to unburden her heart to me. She did so on a daily basis during these daily telephone calls that she looked forward and I still cherish so very much.

When I called, my mother would frequently pick up the telephone while napping on the couch/bed. Her voice would sound a bit groggy to me, but her mind was alert. The conversation would usually start with her grasping for some sign of hope from me.

"Dai dai ah, I am so very tired. Is there something that I can do about it? Are you sure that there are no effective treatments? Can't I get a liver transplant?"

I would then repeat the story about the information I gathered from my personal and professional resources. I also repeated our past discussions about the choice to preserve the quality of her life in the remaining time instead of opting for debilitating, aggressive treatments with a low chance of success. After a sigh of resignation, my mother would change the topic and begin to relay some of her heart's regrets.

"Dai dai ah, you know my heart. You realize that I am dying too soon. I wish I could live to see some of the major milestones of my grandchildren. My heart would have overfilled with joy if I could have attended the college or high-school graduation of Lauren and Ian. My fate will prevent me from even seeing them finish grammar school."

After a long pause, I could hear my mother weeping while she continued speaking.

"I know that Lauren and especially Ian's memories of me will rapidly grow so faint that it will finally disappear over time. How will they know the depth and the intensity of my love for them? It would break my heart if they were to forget me. Please, Dai dai, don't let your children forget me."

"Please keep your mind and heart at peace, Mahmee ah. I promise that I will never let my children forget. They will know through me. They will know by how I live my life. My life and who I am is a direct reflection of you and your love. You will show your love to them through me. My love for them will be your love for them," I said.

I stifled my own tears and slowly whispered, "I will also try to write your story, as much as I can remember. The facts will be less important than your feelings. I will let my children and my children's children know you, love you, and always cherish you. They shall hold you in their hearts as I will always feel you in mine. Your memories can never die. Love as great as what you feel for us lives forever."

Eleven o'clock Tea

I had come to consider my daily late-morning conversations with my mother as a short break in the middle of the day. It was a time to "visit" her and spend a seemingly suspended thirty minutes or so "chatting over tea." The differences between my conversations with my mother and the prototypical afternoon tea, however, were substantial in content and form. My mother usually did the majority of the speaking, and I listened with sympathy. I learned fascinating tidbits of family history, many of which were completely unfamiliar to me. I learned about significantly hurtful events that my parents endured without ever burdening me with their pain. The depth of the betrayal of some lifelong "friends," business associates, and relatives stunned even my own innately cynical personality. How my parents managed to maintain a sense of optimism and idealism after the ruination of their lives and emotions by those betrayals is beyond me. Again, I relearned that my parents exceed me in every way. Despite the baring of many painful topics, my conversations with my mother were very good times of communion with her. Most of the conversations yielded rewarding insights for me. When a person realizes the end is near, the everyday random clutter of life becomes irrelevant. My mother spoke with an uncommon clarity of vision and understanding. She frequently addressed the bare essence of life, its values, and its relationships. It became soothing for both her and me to speak plainly from heart to heart. After all, there was no time left to do otherwise.

I, like every child who had benefited from deeply caring parents, felt that I knew everything about my mother. After all, I had known her my whole life and could easily anticipate her words and reactions to many situations. I spent a lifetime seeking her approval, memorizing every line on her face, interpreting every subtle movement of her eyes, basking in the warmth of her embrace, and holding my breath while I waited to hear the music of her laughter. When knowledge of the coming finale removed the masks of everyday life as well as the invisible but impenetrable armor of psychic defenses, I was still surprised to discover the additional depth of my mother's emotions. This expression of her profound feelings of love and gratitude for her children and grandchildren was a consistent theme of our conversations.

My mother also mentioned my wife, Karen, whenever she spoke about her children. After all, she considered Karen as her own daughter. I always sensed the connection since the very beginning. At first, my mother automatically put Karen under serious scrutiny because she knew that Karen was very important to me. Over a short period of time, I could tell that my mother began to heavily invest herself emotionally in my wife. Karen became her daughter in every important sense of the word. She even protected and defended Karen as if she was the flesh of her flesh. As with her own daughter, my mother gave materially and affectionately to Karen without limits and without conditions. There was no mental tallying of the balance sheet, and she never asked for anything in return. I could also see that Karen responded to my mother as I had throughout my life. My mother's warm, nurturing, and embracing effect encouraged a spontaneous dropping of psychological masks, a nonthreatening exposure of the heart, and a cathartic welcoming sense of being home. The reciprocal emotional attachments occurred rapidly because there was never a sense of impending betrayal or manipulation. My mother's heart was aching to love Karen, and Karen was, in turn, waiting her whole life to be loved like that. My mother's awkward combination of Toisanese, Cantonese, and broken English did not hinder her communication with my wife. They spoke to each other through their hearts, and I often found them immersed in sparkling conversations that were usually punctuated by spontaneous laughter because of the striking similarity in their insights and feelings about the everyday events of life.

It would not be uncommon for my mother to say to me, with a fatigued voice during our eleven o'clock "tea," that "You are indeed fortunate for having Karen to share your life. Most people can go through several lifetimes and not find someone like Karen. Her heart is golden. Your great-grandmother was right. You have your father's lucky spirit. It is unusual but perhaps also revealing that her own family fails to recognize her value and virtues. Their inability and/or unwillingness to acknowledge what is so evident to the rest of the world, that Karen is the diamond of that family, is quite unfortunate. Nonetheless, it does not matter. She is within our loving circle now, and she is *my* daughter now. I appreciate and cherish her not just because she treats my son so well but because she is that rare person who lives with sincerity and goodness in her everyday heart. The selfishness and the duplicity that corrodes the soul of too many people has no ability to taint or take root in the purity of your wife's personality."

I noticed that my father agreed with my mother's assessment through his actions toward Karen. He would usually vigorously defend Karen's position during any decision process. He would also acquiesce to any requests that she placed on him. Those requests were never about what he could do for her but almost always about him capitulating to what she wanted to do for him. My father, for instance, would have preferred to build his entire diet solely from choices based on the different types of flavorful fatty meats. (He was the ultimate Atkins warrior before the publicized birth of the diet. By the way, this diet directly contributed to his severe atherosclerotic disease that required life-saving surgery later in life.)

He would, however, force himself to consume quantities of fruits and vegetables that Karen would insist on placing on the table for him and for his own good during his visits with us. It was also my wife's insistence on doing my father's laundry that allowed her to notice the bloodstains on his underwear. This attention and care on her part led to the early diagnosis and, ultimately, successful treatment of my father's bladder cancer. At that time, my father preferred to dismiss the stained underwear and alarmingly bloody urine (alarming at least to me) as trivial and not worthy of notice or discussion. Karen's determination to provide service to my father over his protestations, therefore, literally saved his life. My parents, like everyone else including the schoolchildren that she teaches, recognized that Karen never placed demands on others based upon selfish or controlling motivations but did so out of a sense of altruism, genuine affection, and compassion. I also know my own nature all too well, and I am fully aware of and bear full responsibility for the unattractive impulses, which govern my natural baseline tendencies. I have also become adept at rationalizing, disguising, and concealing these destructive traits from most people that I encounter. That is why I am constantly grateful for the privilege of being Karen's husband. She has allowed me to rise above myself and do what I could not do alone. I think my parents agreed with me on this point. They also felt blessed to have Karen as their daughter in the most important sense of the word. They, like I, felt that it was a privilege to have the opportunity to love my wife, Karen, and to receive her love in return.

My father was another repetitive topic of my conversations with my mother. She was constantly concerned for him and his care after her death. She could think of no optimal solutions and felt consistent pangs of guilt for abandoning her husband during his greatest time of need in life. On more than one occasion, she insisted on hearing me promise that I would look after my father when she was gone.

"Dai dai ah, you must take care of Baba after I am dead. Baba will be lost though he will never admit it because he is a proud man. I fully understand the difficulties that I am asking you to immerse yourself into because your father's life is rooted in New York just as yours is firmly established in Wisconsin. If you take Baba out of New York, you would doom him to a life in limbo where he would wake up every day only to wait for his own death. This is an unacceptable existence for anyone, especially for someone like your father, who is so full of vitality and loves the thrust and the parry of daily life. Yet I still ask this of you because you are his son, and it is your duty to take care of your father. Children cannot abandon their parents, or they are not their children."

I could not help but interpret that last sentence as possessing a slight accusatory tone. The rising well of guilt within me reminded me of my years of knowing preoccupation with my own career. I understood from the very beginning that medicine was a very demanding mistress, which forced a compromise with my family and my parents. I rationalized my life's direction by unconvincingly telling myself that this was the nature of life, and there was no other alternative. All this, however, failed to prevent the flush of shame and guilt that washed over me. My impotence was more nakedly exposed than ever before during this time of my parents' most desperate need for my assistance.

I would usually whisper, "Don't worry, Mahmee. I'll take care of everything." As those words would leave my lips, I would have absolutely no concrete idea about how to fulfill that promise. If money were the only issue, then solutions would be possible. Both of us knew, however, that caring interactions with family, emotional sustenance, functional purpose to life, and clearing simple everyday logistical hurdles were his greatest challenges, and he mostly depend them on my mother.

What I did not anticipate were solutions from unexpected sources. My father and I would be extracted from the horns of the dilemma by a deus ex machina in the short term and the long term. Regina, who was my mother's companion, comforter, and life saver during the final years of her life, reached out to also support my father after my mother's death. This divine lady, who always lavished gifts on my children whenever we visited New York, would continue to regularly call and visit the Mark household to check on the status of my father. Her attention, unwavering care, and loyalty sustained my father during the most difficult months immediately after my mother died. Regina would also provide a steady supply of Chinese delicacies to ease my father's physical and emotional deprivation. Regina continued this service for more than a decade until my father's final illness. Here was a person whose personality and actions were motivated by a heart that was touched by a divine hand.

Another completely unforeseeable event occurred to save my father. A young lady from my father's Chinese homeland came into his life to grant him a second life. Tingke and her later family would care for my father with the devotion and affection of a loving daughter. She and her family would enable my father to embrace life once again and to once more function as the patriarch of another young family. In other words, my father was given another chance. He took full advantage of this opportunity to relive his life over the next twelve years as a doting grandfather, a loving father, and a supportive father-in-law. Tingke was truly an angel sent from heaven. More will be mentioned about Tingke later.

As comforting as my conversations with my mother were, there were also heart-wrenching moments. Her greatest regret was being unavailable during the most formative years of my children, Lauren and Ian. She would frequently weep quietly when she spoke during these moments.

"It is most disappointing for me to be unable to give my most valuable gifts to Lauren and Ian, ah Dai dai. I only want a few more years to love them and hold them close. Most of all, I wanted to be able to bequeath to them all my hopes and dreams when they are slightly older and able to understand better."

After a slight pause, she would continue, "Ah, Dai dai ah, you have to love them for me. You know my heart. Give that heart to them. Be sure they grow up to stand tall and strong. Be sure they are proud of their great heritage, and they become good, productive people with good values. Everything that I have ever wished for, every idea that I ever strove for, and every dream that I have ever cherished for, I leave to them. Please enable them to fulfill themselves. Allow them to be more than they thought they could be. Help them then to be true to themselves as they find their way through their lives. Allow my love to fuel their growth and search for answers. Hold them for me when they yearn for my embrace and comfort. This is my wish."

Once again, I said, "Don't worry, Mahmee. Every time I caress their furrowed brow, it will be your hand caressing them. Every time I embrace them, you will be there to inhale their scent. My unfailing presence in their lives will be your joy and pride in them. Karen and I will be their anchor through the uncertain periods of their lives. They will know you through us even if they will be denied your physical presence."

My mother would never realize how much she had already touched the lives of my very young children. She would not be there, on that fateful morning, to see my daughter crying inconsolably on the carpet outside her bedroom when I received the devastating telephone call from my sister that Mahmee had just died. She would not be able to see the vacant look in my children's eyes as my wife and I would try to bravely forge ahead with the daily routines of life during the initial weeks after her death. She would not see my mummified reactions and aching need to cling to my wife and children as my depleted heart lay shattered in my chest. Yet it was my wife and children as well as my mother's hopes and dreams that enabled me to slowly reconstruct the rhythms of my life with the additional inspirations of my mother's wishes.

My mother also spoke nostalgically about her frequent visits to my brother's house over the years. She missed the ability and stamina to drive the multiple hours deep into upstate New York to my brother's mountainous haven on a lake. The many outings, dinners, and quiet evening conversations in the countryside over the years still felt inadequate. She wanted more time and a much greater vehicle to express her affections.

"Dai dai ah, don't forget about *Ghor ghor* [elder brother]. He doesn't say much because he holds so much inside. He jokes quite a bit and usually enjoys being outrageous for effect. As you know, this is all his brave face. He cares very, very deeply but is hesitant to show it. Family is everything to him. He has no children of his own, so your children will be like his children. Everyone sees only his zest for avocational activities like skiing, cooking [which he is quite outstanding], fishing, windsurfing, and spectacular vacationing. All these activities do nothing to reveal his sensitive and caring heart. Love him for me and continue to give him the familial nourishment that he needs. He always thought that I never fully understood him because of my critical attitude. I believe that in his heart of hearts, he realizes that I truly know him and his innermost self. Be sure to remind him that I have never abandoned him and have always loved him dearly. I may have been clumsy, but my heart's connection with him never changed from when he was a baby until now, with my death hovering over me. He is my eldest son. He will always be my heart's son. That type of love can never fail. Even when I am gone, that love will allow me to be with him in his heart and mind. You will also help to keep me alive for him. Be gentle, though, for life has been hard for him and he, in turn, has been very hard on himself emotionally. He should continue to take comfort from me through you. Watch out for him. His disappointments may make him forget that buried deep inside of himself lies the memories of a still bright-eyed little boy with sparkling intelligence and happy, carefree love while nestled in my arms. That lovable little boy is my *ah Jack.*

"Also remember *ah Dee dee* (elder sister), Dai dai. *Ah moy* [a term of endearment for my sister] may be married into another family, but she will always be your elder sister. Look after her and help her if she is ever in need. Love her as I would love her. Remind her that I will always be with her in her heart as well. She had always been the shy and hesitant one, but she possesses strength and talent that she should not be afraid to use. There is so little time to convey so many feelings that I have for my children and particularly my only daughter. You, Dai dai, have to help me maintain a presence in her life when I am gone. Guidance and wisdom are your strong suites but help her to understand the depth of my affections for her."

Once again, I said "OK, Mahmee." By this time, I felt like a confidante designated to carry out the last wishes of a dying person. My own emotions were in turmoil, trying to affect a task-oriented and diligent demeanor while simultaneously dealing with the chaotic sorrow of my own feelings.

My mother knew that we would all grieve for her. She was, however, more concerned for the spiritual well-being of everyone else, so she often repeated her desires for me to follow through during our late-morning "teas." I believe she wanted me to feel in her place when she could no longer be here to feel. She wanted me to weep for every member of her beloved family. She wanted me to cry for my father. She wanted me to cry for my brother. She wanted me to cry for my sister. But who will cry for me? I would gradually understand that I would have to cry for me, and I would indeed cry for years to come.

My mother was so much a part of the integrity of my moral and emotional fabric that her two-year ordeal with illness and finally death tore an enormous gap in my soul. That vacuum in my heart seemed irreparable. Everyday life was thereafter permanently changed. Her hopes and dreams, however, continued to live in me. My memories remained alive with the thousands of conversations with her over decades. The spirit and content of those conversations continue to enrich the life and legacy of my own family.

Spring, 1989

My mother's final visit to my home in Wisconsin occurred in the spring of 1989. Despite my daily conversations with her by telephone, I was still shocked by her physical appearance when I greeted her and my father at the airport. She was quite jaundiced and hunched over, as if carrying a large weight even though she held nothing in her hands. Her movements were slow and deliberate. I could tell that it was a struggle for her to maintain her attention and some semblance of alertness to her surroundings. She shuffled her feet with tedious dragging motions while refusing my offer of a wheelchair to negotiate the moderately long walk to my parked car. The squint of her eyes and deep furrows of her brows reinforced my perception of the depth of her struggles. I insisted that she sit while I went to retrieve her luggage. She complied while my father maintained his customary standing position ingrained from decades of restaurant work. During the forty-minute drive from the airport to my house, my mother would intermittently doze off. Even the short peace that accompanies sleep for most people was denied to my mother as she napped with a tortured facial expression. Her short and slightly labored breathing expressed through trembling pursed lips accentuated the difference between her illness induced near-metabolic coma from the normal restful slumber of nature's regular circadian rhythms. My father sat stoically in the car, but I could not start to imagine his emotional inner turmoil while helplessly watching the diseased deterioration of his life's companion. He had repeatedly instructed me to carry on with life as usual in my mother's presence. He was concerned that the very discussion of my mother's illness with her would only reinforce her daily fixation on it and aggravate her sadness and psychological burden. My father relied on my professionalism on this matter, but he knew not what he was asking of me. Complying with his wishes ran counter to my very core instincts that urged me to hug and console my mother. The opportunity to weep with her during this last remaining coherent time of her life before the desperate struggles of the very end would have been cathartic for me and comforting for my mother. My father's request strained my heart to bursting every time I glanced at my mother's eyes, which pleaded for a last heart-to-heart communion. The conflict and concussion of this dilemma would repeatedly strain my rapidly thinning emotional reserves over the course of my mother's stay with me and ultimately extracted a terrible price from me in later years. That price would exceed my innate capacities and eventually cause a tearing injury that would reach my very core.

My parents came to visit because of my young son's birthday. It was a joyous time for them especially since it celebrated the birth of their only male grandchild. I was glad that my children were preoccupied with the abundance of gifts and festive activities arranged by my wife. I did not want their innocence and happiness to be dampened by the somber atmosphere that filled my heart. Even my mother put on a brave face by smiling through all the picture taking, unwrapping of gifts, singing of songs, and blowing of candles. The joy she felt was genuine, and it at least offered some respite from the foggy interference of her illness. My mother even discovered the energy to participate in an outing to the local zoo. She did, however, acquiesce to the use of a wheelchair as it was patently unrealistic to expect to walk the type of distances that formed the routes through the exhibits. My children not only enjoyed the zoo and its animals, but they also delighted in taking turns riding in the wheelchair on my mother's lap. The joy of the experience was obviously reflected on my mahmee's face. Her smile was unforgettable, and even the glow of her eyes was momentarily revived. She seemed deeply contented and fulfilled to be here with us in her final hours. I continued to hope for divine intervention to provide some untapped opportunity that can prolong her happiness if even for a few more days.

During the remainder of my mother's stay, she was dominated by an overwhelming sense of fatigue. This caused her to spend much of her days lying and sleeping on the family-room couch. I would spend my free time just sitting in the room with her to absorb her resting presence even though she was unaware of me. My children and daily work offered some distraction for me so that I did not and could not constantly dwell on my mother's state of illness. The pall of her condition, however, assailed my mind and senses when I looked upon her while impaling my heart when I was alone and away from her side. It was difficult for me to avoid noting the swelling that was developing around her ankles due to the progressive failure of her liver. Her skin had assumed the orange tinge that is so typical of patients nearing hepatic coma. The shocking jaundice of the onetime whiteness of her eyes proved most difficult for me to adjust to. My mahmee would frequently look at me with those heavily discolored eyes mixed with a deep sadness, which pleaded for help and some way to prolong her time with me. She also verbalized this plea, which her eyes spoke so loudly and desperately. It was a plea that continuously agonized me without pause because I was powerless to help her. I, the son who fulfilled her hopes and dreams. I, the son who, for years, had shared and listened to the detailed depths of her emotions. I, the son who was specifically trained to heal and had done so for numerous strangers, both rich and poor. In the end, this son would be totally unable to help his own mother in the hour of her greatest need. The sympathy from my heart, my eyes, and my touch were all that I could offer. I tried to transmit my love and pain whenever I sat next to my mahmee on the couch and grasped her weak, jaundiced hand to stroke like she had affectionately performed for me my entire life. It was during one of these transient sessions, when I was holding her hand, that she asked me the most difficult question of my life.

"Dai dai ah, am I dying now?"

Summer, 1989

The progression of my mother's illness accelerated rapidly after she left my son's birthday celebration at my house. I was already appalled by the differences in my mother's health between Christmastime of 1988 and May of 1989. She was still able to easily participate in normal activities such as travel, meals, and standing for periods at a time at Christmas, but her ability and stamina to engage in those same routine activities were severely curtailed just five months later. My mother would frequently recover from transient periods of fatigue over the past two years, but those debilitating periods gradually grew longer and longer. In the spring of 1989, those dark periods finally merged and dominated virtually every hour of every day. The sight of my mother shuffling with the aid of my father toward the check-in counter at the airport after I had dropped them off in May would haunt me forever. I was later shocked to learn that her condition would quickly turn even more drastically for the worse very soon after her return to Staten Island.

When I was young, I could never have predicted that hospitals would become very familiar to me. In my young mind's eye, they were generally intimidating places where nothing good ever happened to me. Mind-numbing fear and arcane rituals permeated the atmosphere, and pain was a foregone conclusion of my visits there. All of my adult life, however, has been spent working and virtually living in hospitals. In other words, I am very comfortable in the hospital environment, the very type of place that filled my heart with dread as a youngster. The summer of 1989 reproduced the fear of my childhood despite an adult's overfamiliarity of hospitals. This was the summer that my mother was finally hospitalized until her death. It may not be entirely accurate to say that my feelings that summer were exactly the same as those from my childhood. I would better characterize my emotional state as a severe sense of numbness. Every time I entered the hospital through the front doors, my mind felt numb. My movements grew more mechanical the closer I approached my mahmee's room. I realized that my mannerism and speech must have appeared blatantly wooden to the other visitors in the room, but they were probably too polite to draw attention to it. When I reached my mother's bedside, the numbness would progress to include a buzzing undertone, which muffled my hearing. This caused a personal isolation that accentuated the crushing sensation around my heart. My only saving graces, which formed a lifeline for me through this terrible time period, were the calm soothing voice and presence of my wife as well as the gentle, loving touches of my small children's hands.

My children also provided some sensitive and memorable interludes during my tortured emotional storms in my mother's hospital room. I believe both of my children understood, at some level, the gravity of the situation, but my oldest child might have had a clearer grasp because of her more developed maturity. She would stand by my mother's bed and reach out to touch my mahmee's jaundiced, placid hand. Periodically, my mother would experience transient episodes of relative lucidity amid the fog of her semicoma. During those blessed respites, she would recognize my daughter and her loving, gentle touch. Even during this most extreme hour of desperation, my mother would voice concern for my daughter and offer her some of the untouched hospital food on the tray next to her bed. On one occasion, my daughter crawled up onto the bed to lie beside my mother after she had relapsed back into a confused semicomatose state. My daughter naturally expressed in a physical way what was laid bare in her heart. Her eloquent child's gesture spoke volumes, which I could not even begin to verbally articulate.

My mother's hospital room was frequently occupied by a steady stream of visitors. These people were a combination of relatives and friends, whose lives were touched by my mother. All came to not only express their sorrow but also their gratitude for my mother. I truly appreciated everyone's efforts to pay homage to my mother, but I also found the regularly irregular interruptions to be a bit distracting. It was a distraction not because of the polite attention that I felt obligated to give but because I was emotionally preoccupied by the crushing turmoil in my heart mixed with the heavy background numbness of my mind.

While people stood around the room conversing in respectfully low monotones, I was often lost within my own numb thoughts, glancing at my mother's sad but strained semiconscious face and asking myself a lifetime of rhetorical questions. How can I ever repay my mother for a lifetime of love? How can I repay someone who gave to me without ever asking for or implying any desire for compensation? How can I repay someone who knew my most ruthless and contemptible characteristics but still maintained the faith to expect the most honorable behavior from me? How do I repay the warmth and comfort of her embrace that soothed a lifetime of disappointments and anger? How can I repay her expectations to be more than what I am when she was fully aware of my severe limitations and multiple layers of incompetence? How can I ever repay my mother for giving me the most valuable gifts, gifts that cannot be bought, gifts that cannot be seen, gifts that spring from an unending source, the intangible gifts that can only be felt in one's heart? How can I ever repay her for those early-morning smiles that nourished me for the duration of an entire school day? How can I repay her tolerance and humorous acceptance of my continually sullen and sulking countenance during my sullen and sulking early teenage years? How can I repay my mahmee's determined devotion to me when I consistently ignored her to attend to my own selfish career development? How does a person repay another person who creates the very foundation that defines who he is? How does a son ever repay his mother?

Regret can be a dominant emotion during the end of a person's life, but that also frequently applies to the people who love the dying individual. In the classic guilty fashion of a Confucian sense of filial piety, I wondered why I wasn't a better son. Why did I never, once in my life, just take my mother's gentle hand in my own, look directly at her soft eyes, and simply say, "Thank you, Mahmee"? Why did I ever pause in expressing my affections for my mother especially since it was always so evident that she lived for her children's love? How could I have been so lacking in insight that I allowed a sense of professionalism to interfere with my lavishing the love in my heart on my mahmee? What have I ever done for my mother in her life other than provide her with an unending source of demands and unappreciative behavior? Why couldn't I have done more for my mother? Why did I always have excuses? How could I face myself when I did not even have an excuse? Did not my mahmee deserve better from her children? Why do I address these issues in my mind now when it is too late to do anything about it?

During the course of my mother's hospitalization, there was the expected flurry of dreaded activities that typically surround a person's death. The grown children spent many evenings making "decisions." My father constantly put on a brave face by busying himself with logistical details such as the funeral arrangements and dinners for mourners. What do we do with Dad? Who will look after him? How many times can we visit? What would Mama have wished for? There was also the stream of advice from well-wishers ranging from close older relatives giving guiding instructions to the "children," to sympathetic acquaintances who just want to find some opportunity to help in any way possible. During one of these "busy work" sessions conducted in a quiet murmur in my mother's hospital room, I took a moment to glance at my now nearly constantly comatose mother. I noticed that she was experiencing a rare lucid period and was looking at everyone with a very sad expression. No one else noticed, so the conversations continued as if my mother was not even in the room. I excused myself from the small gathering at the foot of the bed and walked up to my mother. She looked up at me with lidded eyes but did not say anything, so I bent down and placed my face close to hers and pressed my cheek to her cheek.

I softly whispered, "Don't be afraid, Mahmee ah." These would be the very last words that I would ever speak to my mother.

She answered, "I am not afraid." Those were her very last words to me.

Mulberry Street, 1989

The beginning of Mulberry Street in Manhattan is home for a cluster of funeral parlors. Being in the heart of New York's Chinatown, these Chinese-run establishments cater to a near completely Chinese clientele. Though my parents had not lived in Chinatown for several decades, many of their friends and relatives did, so the choice of one of these funeral parlors to service my deceased mother was an easy decision for my father.

The ceremony was so typically Chinese. The walls were completely covered by a multitude of flower wreaths. Each wreath was accompanied by a ribbon of Chinese characters indicating the names of the people who had given the flowers to honor my mother. Having disappointed my mother by quitting Chinese school (which usually ran for two hours every day after regular "American" school) in second grade, the writing on the ribbons was completely indecipherable to me. A large contingent of mourners throughout the day formed a nearly nonstop line to pay homage at my mother's casket. Incense burned, and an unending loop of Chinese funeral music played softly in the background. It was difficult for me to look at my mother because the mortician performed his duties quite inadequately in my judgment. My mother bore only a superficial resemblance to herself in life. The heavily applied makeup created a caricature rather than a person. None of this really mattered to me, however, as I wandered emotionally and was spiritually lost. There was a large hole in my chest, and I needed to remind myself to breathe. My impressions were only generic with no specific visual details because my sight was continuously blurred by the nonstop welling of tears in my eyes. I needed to maintain an oh-so-tight hold on my wife's hand in order to save myself. The innocent and affectionate touch of my young children's hands within my own coarse fingers was an unexpected soothing balm providing a small comforting oasis in the void that filled my heart.

Parents die every day, leaving their children, of all ages, to feel like orphans all over the world. Why does this rationalization fail to diminish my pain and longing for my mother? Is this because this is happening to me and not some theoretical someone else? Perhaps. I'd prefer to think that my pain is especially acute because this particular tragic death involves this uncommonly holy woman. This specific stroke from death's blade cut egregiously deep within me because of the special relationship between this particular mother and my particular unworthy heart. I found myself spending long moments staring at the photo of my mother near the casket and wanting just five more minutes with her to say goodbye and give my thanks to her. These five minutes will elude me for the rest of my life. This regret will be my burden to carry. This I will shoulder every day because I fully acknowledge and accept my responsibility for it. What I could not have anticipated was how I would be moved to tears years later when I would feel the loving assistance from the hands of my wife and children, greatly reducing my burden when my heart began to crack and buckle from the years of carrying this weight. I lost my mother, but my family would let me know that I was not alone. Their love would sustain me. How can such a significantly flawed individual be considered deserving of these blessings throughout his life? A tiny pinch of self-reflection is all that is required for this particular individual to be humbled.

The finality of my mother's death was punctuated in my mind at the crematorium. I have very little recollection of the limousine ride from Manhattan to Queens, but the main gathering room at the crematorium remains a vivid memory. The muted wood paneling of the room eerily reflected my somber mood. I don't believe I even took a single breath as my mother's casket was slowly transported into the open portal of the far wall. The closure of the portal walls signified a definitive ending, which allowed me to finally exhale. The final disappearance of the casket and physical closure of the portal doors, however, did not allow for a neat and tidy simultaneous psychological closure. That process would take years for me. I could already see the totally crushed look on my father's face. Through the deep sorrow that was drowning every corner of my being, I remember a small cogent thought that slowly crawled to my heart as I stared at the closed portal doors. I felt a simultaneous, almost completely discordant, sense of honor and privilege for having been granted the great opportunity to have been a son to my extraordinary mother. I also vowed to never violate the integrity of the great intangible gifts that my mother gave to me during our time shared during life. I was surprised by the clarity and vision that developed in my mind's eye during the wake and funeral. My mother's lifetime of messages to me became so clear that I didn't understand how I let obfuscation, rationalization, and misplaced priorities distort my perceptions. This apparent contradiction of an enlightening event during a tragic occasion also felt quite natural and true to me. In time, I was looking forward to going home with my wife and children. Part of me, however, felt a great deal of sympathy for the mourning still to come for my father, brother, and sister.

Second Life

I believe my father would have agreed with my assessment that the year after my mother's death was the toughest year of his life. My father's depression made the passing of each day seem like an eternity. Everyday life had lost its flavor, and work was beginning to seem like the burden that it is to most people on the planet. Every night, my father would lie down and sleep on the makeshift basement bed that was my mother's. There were no real strong motivations to get up every morning. The continued visits by Regina provided the sporadic rays of sunshine in my father's life. Her good company, along with the good food that she would bring, could brighten anybody's day. The remainder of the time, however, merely passed as an unknown waiting period until my father could join my mother in death.

Life, however, can be so full of surprises even when the plot and ending seem entirely predictable. In my father's case, this valuable surprise came in the form of a person, Tingke. When my father's cousin, who took care of him in China, was ill, she was cared for at her home in California by a remarkable person named Cora. Cora's patience and genuine affection endeared her to my father's cousin, who spoke effusively to him about Cora. Cora had a sister, Tingke, who lived in New York, but she needed affordable housing and was trying to explore different options. The reputation of Cora and the call of another human being in need provided the motivation that was lacking in my father's life. He offered Tingke housing with him in Staten Island. After all, he was in a relatively large house with two separate floors of living space, by himself, and he could also use the company. He also never brought up the topic of compensation.

Tingke proved to be a life saver. My father found her honesty, integrity, compassion, humility, and complete lack of duplicity to be refreshing and so in tune with his own life's values. Tingke allowed my father to gain another daughter, whom he could love, support, guide, and share. Through her, my father regained a sense of purpose in life. Beauty, happiness, and music returned to the house. Life was reborn for him when his soul was near death. The bounty multiplied exponentially over the next decade as my father shared Tingke's joy at each new stage of her life including the beginning her own family. My father was able to participate in Tingke's wedding to her husband (Frank), who, of course, had to pass the scrutiny of my father's judgment and gain his approval. My father was also able to impress upon Tingke and Frank the practical and personal benefits of living with him in his house on Staten Island. The later birth of Tingke's son offered my father a sense of love and fulfillment that he had not experienced in a long, long time. He had the chance to re-experience the joys of being a father and grandfather. This was something that even he could never have dared hope for or even guessed at. Fortune continued to shine upon my father with great abundance, and he was most appreciative.

In the beginning, my father's relatives viewed Tingke with some degree of suspicion. She was frequently but surreptitiously referred to as that "Shanghai girl" by my relatives. It, superficially, seemed to be an unusual arrangement with my father, and more than one person used terms such as "impropriety" and "inappropriateness". I guess people refused to believe that genuine altruism, sincerity, and trust could actually exist in a real person, at least not in New

York City. Over time, however, everyone was eventually as taken with Tingke as my father. They all appreciated her kindheartedness, complete selflessness, and loyalty to my father. Tingke not only came to be accepted but was viewed as a magical tonic, which relieved the great tragedy of my father's life. I was able to see that she and her whole family loved my father as much as I did. They cared for him, waited on him, and respected him in a way, which was highly unusual for people who are not directly related by blood. The love and affection that they held for each other, however, seemed to exceed even the connections of genetic bonds. My father was alive again, and he reveled in his rejuvenated role as patriarch of a dynamic and growing household.

Through Tingke, my father also gained a whole new host of friends. All of Tingke's friends and relatives were also quite taken by my father. In the end, everyone referred to my father as "Uncle Mark." This greatly pleased him. My father enjoyed the company and sincere friendships. This was a new population of people for him to help and serve. I was always pleased to hear my father's excited voice discuss his new friends over the telephone. I was even more amused by the fact that most of these new friends, like Tingke and her family, spoke Shanghainese while my father's Chinese was limited to Cantonese and Toisanese. The language mismatch, however, never seemed to hamper communication between my father and his new friends. The inevitable development of mutual goodwill and generosity was evident even to me, who lived a thousand miles away.

My father's relationship with Tingke also had additional travel benefits for my father. Tingke would take my father to places that he had never before visited. This would include the Grand Canyon among other sites in the United States. Through Tingke, my father would have the opportunity to wander through the grand Chinese metropolis of Shanghai. He would be able to see firsthand the history and splendor of Beijing. He would even, finally, be able to walk along the Great Wall.

Tingke would also be the means by which my father would meet Nancy. Nancy was a writer who worked for a major Chinese publisher with bases in Shanghai and Hong Kong. Nancy maintained a residence on a quaint small island off the coast of Hong Kong. Her easy manner and open demeanor allowed for the quick development of a friendship with "Uncle Mark." My father had an open invitation for vacation at Nancy's residence on the island, and he took advantage of it on an annual basis at the very least. My father would frequently describe the island, where no motorized vehicles are allowed, as idyllic and highly reminiscent of his childhood in the beautiful Toisan countryside, except it has a spectacular view of the ocean. He would wake up every day to converse with the other elderly people who lived on the island. When he became hungry, he would merely stroll down to the beach where the fishermen had docked their boats, pick out a freshly caught flopping fish, and then bring it to a local restaurant where the fish was rapidly cleaned and cooked exactly to my father's specifications. The fresh air, friendly people, peaceful atmosphere, spectacular scenery, and perfectly spiced fish cooked to perfection represented heaven on earth to him. My father would frequently mention to me how he could easily be amenable to spending his remaining days on that island. He was always thankful to Nancy for the opportunity to have this experience at this late stage in his life.

My father's association with Nancy would have another unusual benefit. Nancy, as a writer, was interested in the details of my father's life. She was writing a piece about the lives of Chinese people who left the country to live abroad especially during the time period before the Communist revolution. My father became a perfect source of inspiration for her, and they spent many hours immersed in conversation. This would ultimately result in an impressive article about my father's life featured in a national Chinese publication. When the article was given to me in translated form, I was both amused and surprised. I realized that magazines are in the business of selling themselves to the advertisers and the reading public, but I always felt that hyperbole should have at least some connection to the truth, no matter how faint the tread. The mixture of fact and fantasy, however, would only be appreciated by someone like me and probably no one else. So I guess there would be no realistic fear of the magazine having to face issues of accountability concerning this article. I would be willing to wager, however, that Nancy would be surprised to learn that the true facts about my father's life are even more spectacular and unbelievable than the fiction.

My father had survived war, gunshot wound, poverty, politics, severe gouty arthritis, crushing restaurant work, decades of smoking and hard drinking, chronic pulmonary disease, cirrhosis of the liver, financial duplicity, rapid accumulation of a financial fortune, betrayal of relatives, opportunistic predators, dealings with organized crime, total financial ruin, life-threatening carotid artery disease, bladder cancer, and death of the dearest person in his life. He lived to be granted a rare second chance to relive life, and he gratefully took full advantage of this gift from God for thirteen years after my mother's death. He lived those final years with grace, constant good humor, unwavering virtue, careful attention to his health, strong determination to positively affect the lives of everyone around him, and great love for his second family. Finally, at the age of eighty, he was challenged with the one final obstacle that he could not overcome. Esophageal cancer would claim his life within six months of diagnosis. The last few months would inflict such severe suffering on him that it would far exceed even my father's considerable physical and mental stamina. My father expressed gratitude for his wildly blessed life, but the magnitude of his suffering during this final malicious disease would have him asking to die in order to end the torture.

Hospital, 2002

For the second time in my adult life, I found myself feeling overwhelming dread and sorrow in a hospital setting. I tried to adopt a brave and compassionate face, but it did nothing to abate the enormous emotional pummeling that a son feels when he gets to watch his other parent die after having already witnessed the heart-crushing death of his first parent. I was impressed by my sibling's seemingly dispassionate but still empathetic demeanor, particularly on the part of my brother. They seemed to have adapted well, but during this trying time period, this skill was totally beyond my physical capabilities or psychological will. I would not have been surprised, however, if they actually felt as emotionally devastated as I was (if not more so), but they simply possessed a greater ability to function in relatively normal fashion in spite of their heavy hearts.

I had been keeping company with my father every day and partly into the night for several days. It was painful for me to watch my father suffer, but it was also amusing to see that he maintained his alertness and usual mental edge by keeping track of the daily habits of all the doctors and nurses. He could recite their schedules and anticipate not only their words but also where they would most likely park in the lot outside his window. It was so typical of my father to maintain a vague semblance of optimism or seemingly irrelevant distraction in the face of extreme suffering with no hope for recovery. I would break my near-constant vigil at my father's side only to sleep and sparingly partake in the delicious Shanghainese feasts that Tingke would routinely prepare every evening. Eating and sleeping, however, did not come easily to me and I forced myself to at least minimally engage in those activities because my wooden rational mind insisted on their necessity. How could I feel any hunger, let alone think of its satisfaction, when I had just witnessed my father's nonstop second to second struggle to stay alive? He was being fed through a poorly executed "G-tube" (gastostomy tube—where a hole is made between his stomach and his anterior abdominal wall), which constantly scorched him from the reflux of his highly acidic stomach secretions onto his skin. He was no longer able to swallow anything, so his mouth was constantly dry. How could I taste any food when my father could not taste anything but his own dried crusty oral secretions? How could I sleep when my father had not slept in weeks and will not be able to sleep until the moment when he will never awaken? When each living moment is consumed by a desperate struggle for breath amid a nonstop stream of choking mucous, my father is not even granted the simply luxury of a moment of sleep. He could not sleep even though he was groggy, totally fatigued, and nearly delirious from the inability to sleep. A person might tolerate this for a short time period of several days, as I have personally experienced during my training as a physician, but it was beyond belief for me to witness my father endure this state for weeks with no relief in sight. I watched my father significantly deteriorate with each passing day with his body weight now even less than his most emaciated form during the worst moments of his World War II experience. His strength deteriorated proportionately, and he was no longer even able to perform the simple tasks of wiping his own brown mucous as it slowly drooled from his lips. I helped him with his acts of basic urination and defecation. It broke my heart to watch him endure the unendurable during his bowel movements when his legs turned purple and his upper body collapsed on the bed while he screamed through a trembling voice, "Ah yah, ah yah, death, the pain is beyond comprehension. Ah yah, I am torn and broken. No more, no more, no more!" To add insult to body-destroying injury, I calmly and tenderly wiped his buttocks clean after these terrible episodes. It was a soothing and a loving moment for me as I was able to do something for my father in his time of greatest need. It was, however, a totally humiliating moment for my father who had always been very proud of his personal hygiene and self-sufficiency. He never imagined ever needing assistance from anyone else to wipe clean his own fecal stains from his anus let alone having his youngest son do this for him. He felt ashamed and defeated.

The final time that I accompanied my father to his radiation treatment in the hospital, he was frantically attempting to gasp oxygen from his oxygen mask, constantly bobbing his head as he faded in and out of consciousness and totally swaddled in multiple layers of blankets. Even though it was the summer, he trembled nonstop under all the blankets. He simply could not keep warm, and he had no relief. After his treatment, I greeted my father with a smile, which quickly changed to concern and sadness. My father had emerged from the treatment room, profusely apologizing to the technologists. They told my father to not give it a second thought as it was quite a routine, if not completely expected every day for them. They insisted that my father had caused them no trouble at all. When I asked my father what had happened, he said, in a hushed, horrified tone between his gasps for breath, that he had been incontinent on the table during the treatment. He was nearly crying when he continued to tell me that this had never before happened to him in his entire life. The tumor in his chest was destroying every last morsel of his defenses including any facsimile of dignity or self-esteem. His disease had stripped him utterly naked and then proceeded to really stomp on him.

My father's embarrassment did not reflect my own sentiments. I grew up being recognized as "Mark's son" everywhere in New York City. Contrary to conventional wisdom, I did not feel any loss of my sense of individuality. In fact, being Mark's son was a desired part of my identity that I embraced with pride. I also realized that being Mark's son would place me under scrutiny by everyone, but I did not feel that to be a burden. It was a challenge that I welcomed as an opportunity to excel and justify the badge of honor that came with the name. I did not subvert my own identity to conform to familial expectations but rather sought to supplement or add to my father's legacy with new ideas and achievements that were my own unique contributions. My father's embarrassment during this time of utter despair, therefore, bore no relationship to what I was feeling in my heart. As I was aiding my tortured father to endure another round of basic bedside toiletry, which he could no longer complete with any competency on his own, I felt only pride and tenderness for this man who is a better person than I could ever hope to be. His debilitation and complete collapse at this near-death stage of his life did nothing to diminish my opinion of him. It had quite the unusual opposite effect of highlighting his lifetime of strength and honor in my mind. Even when he emphatically insisted on his capitulation to his disease and clearly indicated a desire to end it all in the presence of my brother, my sister, and me, I felt honored to be in his company and to carry on his name

Mulberry Street, 2002

Over the course of thirteen years, the mortician at the funeral home on Mulberry Street showed no improvement in his skills. My father's body appeared just as garish as my mother's did. My father lay in a casket in virtually the exact same spot as my mother's casket thirteen years ago. The funeral parlor was again completely lined with flowers as it was during my mother's funeral. I was also touched by the presence of a large wreath from my department in Wisconsin as a sign of both empathy and respect. A long procession of darkly dressed people paid homage to my father, but the volume of pilgrims, though large, was not nearly as large as it could have been. I had insisted on the funeral being held as soon as possible after my father's death. I know that my father would have wanted to expedite the process and minimize the mourning. This left very little time for notification of the considerable number of people who would have wanted to know and come. Even given the limited opportunities for people to attend, the funeral was still filled with a substantial number of well-wishers.

Once again, I felt numb to the whole experience. I greeted and thanked many people in a mechanical fashion even though I tried hard not to betray the emotional shock that incapacitated me. My wife's kind hands still provided a critical lifeline for me, but I no longer had the loving small touches of my children to feel in my other hand. What my children now provided was better in many ways than at the last funeral. They were tall, striking, and independent young adults who comported themselves in a reserved though open, respectful yet engaging, and utterly mature fashion. More than one relative approached me to mention how impressed they were about the appearance and behavior of my children. They would additionally whisper that my mother would have been extremely proud of my two children had she lived. In their eyes, my children were uncommon in their sense of propriety, sincerity, and conspicuous absence of self-absorption. My children provided me with a sense of hope and optimism for what is right and good in the world during a moment when so much was going wrong within my inner world.

I was able to occasionally glance at my brother and sister to try to gauge their status. I was, unfortunately, unable to provide them with much of any emotional support as it required all of my resources (and then some) just to hold it all together within myself. They seemed strong and quite stable though I would not have been surprised if they were inwardly suffering as much as I was. Their capabilities, in every respect, had always exceeded me since childhood, but I still have some regret in not making the opportunity to have helped them during this difficult period. This was, after all, a very tragic event that would leave each of us with an equally deep, permanent personal scar.

Another person whose grief matched my own was my wife. She had always been there to comfort me, but I neglected to comfort her during this difficult period of mourning. I had lost my second parent but Karen had, in effect, lost her third parent. Karen's gracious and loving father died a few years before my mother. Both of my parents treated Karen as if she were their biological daughter, and she, in turn, loved them as a true daughter. My wife's loss, therefore, was in some ways greater than my own because she had now lost her father for the second time. Still, she never faltered in her ability to comfort me, and she never even hinted at adding to my own emotional burden by drawing attention to her own grief. My mother was right about my wife. She is the rare gem whose beauty and value are defined by the quality of her person rather than the visibility of her actions. My mother added that those very qualities are opaque to the blind eye through which the shallow-minded person views the world but become strikingly brilliant to those who can see the world with their heart.

The funeral passed by in a blur for me. I found it difficult to perform the normal cataloguing of daily events when my heart was in such turmoil. I greatly appreciated the practical experience and guidance from my aunt, who was the wife of my father's younger brother. She helped my brother and me to negotiate the many details of the day that needed attending to. Two events, however, distinguished themselves in my memories of those dark days. One was the meal at the end of the funeral. That meal was very important to my father because he had originally intended to survive just long enough to hold this meal a month later in August with all the members and extended members of the family. Eating and especially eating well was very important to my father ever since I could remember. Nothing was more joyous to him than sharing superb food with good company and family. This postfuneral meal, therefore, was held in the very restaurant with the very menu that my father had himself specifically planned out for that August celebration, which he would never live to see. It was a grand multicourse meal experienced in the style that my father would have loved and insisted on. It was a fitting tribute to my father. The second event that stood out in my mind that day was also a fitting tribute to my father. It occurred at the crematorium before the gathering at the restaurant. The short speech by the funeral director was utterly forgettable, but the sight of the American flag draped on my father's coffin was a singularly touching moment for me. The slow folding of that flag and its presentation to my brother will be etched permanently in my mind and heart. That flag was so perfectly symbolic of everything that defined my father and his life. It represented everything that he believed in and was so proud of. It was so appropriate for my father's death to be honored by the use of that flag to envelop his coffin. It was also so very appropriate that that very same flag be handed over to my brother for honor and safekeeping. My brother's acceptance of that flag signified the official closure to the extraordinary lives of my extraordinary parents. My brother, my sister, and I stood there, overwhelmed by feelings that were difficult to fathom, let alone describe.

Epilogue

This book was meant to be a short memorial to my remarkable parents. It was impossible (and also not my intent) to include all the details or fascinating sidebars of their lives. To have included them would have evolved the story into a daunting tome or at least a trilogy. I felt that the details, though colorful and also inspiring, were less important than the very essence that defined their short time alive. I hope I have managed to distill and describe part of that essence in some fashion through my limited use of the written language. If I have succeeded, at least in some small measure, then I will have created the seed for the cultivation of the legacy that my parents have started. I hope that my children, their children, and their children's children will understand their connection to an extraordinary past and then to use that connection to derive more strength and inspiration to build upon that legacy. I also hope that these words will offer some comfort for them when they are in need, and I am no longer available. These words are my voice, and a quiet conversation with me will always be right here on these pages.

I wrote this book as a memorial, but I also wished to use it as a vehicle to express my own hopes and dreams for my children and their children. What I wish for them is no more and no less than what my own parents wanted for me. Of course, there is the baseline wish for satisfaction of fundamental needs that ensure physical survival, but I want more than just survival for my children. Much more. What I want for them, however, are the most valuable and, therefore, least tangible of gifts. These are the great gifts that are only derived from within yourself and cannot be bought for or stolen from you. My gifts to you can be felt but cannot be touched. They may be seen but not with your eyes. They are revealed in the small seemingly insignificant moments of quiet refection and self-examination that transform you and the breath of your everyday life without ever changing how you look in the mirror. The quality of your life and the excellence of your person will only be determined by yourself and the character of what lies inside you. My hope is that you will be able to draw inspiration from my parents just as I had been fortunate to have been lavished a lifetime of inspiration from them.

Parents feel so much for their children, and I am no different. How, however, do I adequately express what is in my heart? This book is one small attempt though limited by its inadequacies. It is, also, neither complete nor a blueprint. It is, instead, merely a starting point. My wish is for you to feel my good-night kiss on your forehead every evening and the touch of my hand on your face when you wake up in the morning, long after I have been reduced to a faint memory in a faded picture. When you feel the peace of the darkening sky streaked by radiant hues of blue and pink that are painted by the setting sun below the horizon, I will be sitting beside you. When you are true to yourself, I will be in your heart. When you find the serenity of inner harmony amidst the cacophony of everyday struggles, I will be smiling. When you develop sufficient strength to wish to feel humility rather than to humble, I will say well done. How do I express my deep hope for you to cultivate the type of intelligence that prefers to solve rather than dazzle and deceive? When life pushes you past the edge and your struggle becomes desperate, I will be holding your hand. When you only need to see a little further to understand your heart, you will be standing on my shoulders. When you make a conscious choice for honor, integrity, and decency, I will salute you. When you choose the truth and turn away from arguments of convenience, my hand will be supporting you from behind. When you allow compassion to take root inside of you, my hand will be the touch that you feel on your chest. When your heart sustains the most hurtful bruises from life's disappointments and regrets, my chest and arms will embrace you. When you periodically lose your way and can no longer see a familiar reference point, I will lead you back to yourself.

Why would I do all this? Because I have been granted the great honor of receiving your love and the even greater privilege of loving you. I want you to embrace life and allow all that is good in life to wash over you. Understand the past, but don't dwell on it or grieve for it. Use it, instead, to forge ahead to a future that is unique to you and to remember that you are not alone.